PRAISE FOR

Ties That Tether

"A beautiful, heartfelt story about the power of love, identity, and family. *Ties That Tether* is a delightful debut that romance lovers won't want to miss!"

—Chanel Cleeton, *New York Times* bestselling author of
The Last Train to Key West

"Lovingly written and heartfelt. *Ties That Tether* is a beautiful exploration of culture, family, and romance. Azere's journey to find her own voice should resonate with anyone who's ever felt trapped between conflicting worlds and expectations."

—Helen Hoang, *USA Today* bestselling author of *The Bride Test*

"*Ties That Tether* takes the reader on a rich, emotional journey. A big, bold story about finding ourselves amidst the struggles of family loyalty, honoring one's culture, and the endless facets of love. Loved every glorious moment of this book!"

—Jennifer Probst, *New York Times* bestselling author of
Love on Beach Avenue

"If you like snarky, clever stories, Azere's narration is *chef's kiss.*"
—*The Washington Post*

"[An] intriguing examination into the dynamics of family relationships and what it means to have pride in one's culture and heritage. It also holds some unexpected twists and turns that will keep readers engaged until the end."

—The Associated Press

"Igharo's impressive debut tackles interracial relationships, ambition, and family with evenhanded clarity and just a hint of melancholy. (And some very hot love scenes.)" —BookPage

"Happily ever after is hard-won and satisfying in this #ownvoices romance." —Shelf Awareness

"Igharo's debut beautifully depicts the tension between self-determination and the desire to live up to family expectations. . . . Clever and heartwarming storytelling. Readers will be rooting for Azere from the very first page."

—*Library Journal* (starred review)

"An unexpected and heartfelt romance about true love and the sacrifices we make for it."

—Sonya Lalli, author of *The Matchmaker's List*

"*Ties That Tether* was a roller-coaster ride from page one and holy cow did I love it. Jane Igharo chronicles Azere's journey in such a beautiful, wrenching, and relatable way. I laughed and teared up and cheered and yelled. Best of all, Jane Igharo delivers a happily ever after that made me smile until my cheeks hurt." —Sarah Smith, author of *Simmer Down*

"A Nigerian immigrant herself, Igharo tackles issues like immigration, cultural identity, and interracial dating in a compelling way. While a love story at heart, this book is so much more than that. It's a must-read for your summer vacation." —Betches

THE

sweetest
remedy

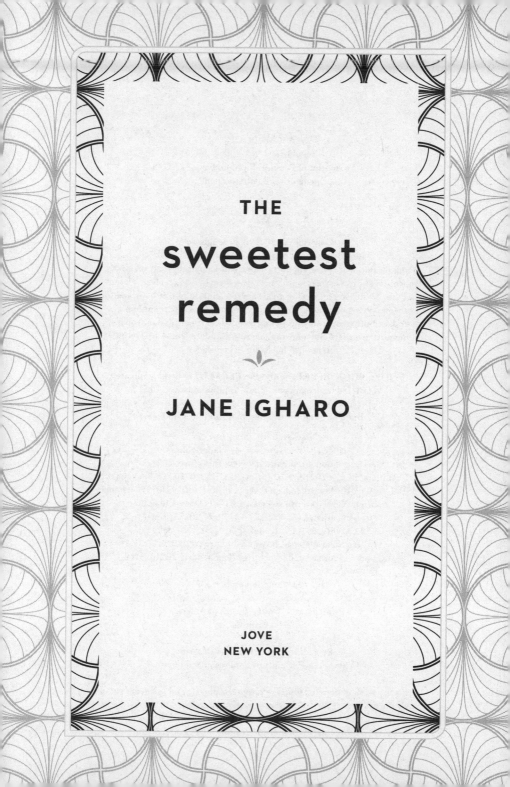

JANE IGHARO

JOVE
NEW YORK

A JOVE BOOK
Published by Berkley
An imprint of Penguin Random House LLC
penguinrandomhouse.com

Library of Congress Cataloging-in-Publication Data

Names: Igharo, Jane, author.
Title: The sweetest remedy / Jane Igharo.
Description: First edition. | New York: Jove, 2021.
Identifiers: LCCN 2021025767 (print) | LCCN 2021025768 (ebook) |
ISBN 9780593101964 (trade paperback) | ISBN 9780593101971 (ebook)
Subjects: GSAFD: Love stories. | LCGFT: Domestic fiction.
Classification: LCC PR9199.4.I37 S94 2021 (print) |
LCC PR9199.4.I37 (ebook) | DDC 813/.6—dc23
LC record available at https://lccn.loc.gov/2021025767
LC ebook record available at https://lccn.loc.gov/2021025768

First Edition: September 2021

Printed in the United States of America
1st Printing

Book design by Kristin del Rosario
Title page art: Fan pattern © tabosan/Shutterstock

To Nigerians everywhere—at home and in the diaspora.
I am in awe of your talent, resilience, and innovation.
I dey hail una.

THE
sweetest
remedy

ONE

HANNAH
san francisco

Hannah stepped into the bustling room and knew she had made a mistake.

A huge mistake.

She should have stayed home. Instead, she was at a fancy cocktail party packed with some of San Francisco's finest.

Her best friend, Flo, was already sipping a drink and chatting with a bald-headed gentleman—probably some Silicon Valley tycoon she wanted to snag as a client for her real estate firm. This was the only reason Flo came to these sorts of events, and usually, she dragged Hannah along on the promise they would have a good time. But now, Hannah was alone and watching a man maneuver around a waiter and approach her with a haughty, overstated gait that seemed like a desperate plea for attention.

"Hey. I'm Blaine." He flipped his blond hair from his sun-tanned face and grinned with the confidence of a man well aware of his Ryan Gosling–esque appearance. "And you have to be the most beautiful woman I have ever seen."

The most beautiful woman. Hannah suppressed a snort. Did

men ever tire of doing that—spitting lies and cheap lines at women as if they were items and the currency for purchasing them was deceit? *Get your woman here*, she imagined an enthused merchant at a bazaar saying, *two shining lies for one pretty woman*. Hannah presumed her father had done the same to her mother— spun the sweetest lies and the slickest pickup lines—right before he knocked her up and took off.

"I'm sure you get this a lot," Blaine went on, his gaze shifting over Hannah. "But you look so exotic. What are you? I mean race." He brought his wineglass to his lips—sipped, swallowed, and smirked. "What are you mixed with?"

Hannah hated that question but concealed her annoyance and offered a routine response. "I'm part black and part white."

"Yeah. But what's your ethnicity?"

As Blaine proved, some people were never satisfied with Hannah's routine response.

What's your ethnicity? Hannah hated that question more because although she had the answer, she didn't really have the answer. She could tell people about her American mother. That part was simple. But what could she tell them about her Nigerian father, who she'd met only once? What could she say about his Yoruba culture she knew nothing about? *What's your ethnicity?* That question also indirectly asked her another. *Who are you?* And similarly, Hannah had the answer, but she didn't really have the answer.

She sighed. She should have just stayed home to work on her article before the deadline on Monday. Better yet, she should have volunteered at the youth center like she did a couple of times a week. Rather, she was attending a cocktail party in a luxurious penthouse that, through its floor-to-ceiling windows, had a spectacular 180-degree view of the San Francisco Bay Area. The interior—with its pale settee that curved into a sphere and its textured wall coverings that made the space seem some-what alive—combined simplistic sophistication with a dramatic flair. It was a setting Hannah did not fit into.

She glanced at her ensemble of a white T-shirt and a leather pencil skirt and sighed. Her outfit could not compare to the de-signer cocktail dresses that clung to the slim figures of every woman in the room. And her red Nine West stilettoes, which were rubbing against her sore toes and surely cleaving a layer of skin, could not compare to the Christian Louboutin pumps with their signature red soles reflecting on the polished floor. Han-nah had felt chic when Flo picked her up. Now, she felt inferior amid all the glamour.

"Okay. Maybe I can figure it out," Blaine said, shifting his narrowed eyes over her features as if attempting to associate them with a specific ethnic group.

His gaze stilled on her hair—a billow of ginger-blond coils that hovered above her shoulders. Her hair often muddled people, made them reconsider what they had concluded. For others, it was her nose with its short bridge and wide base. For some, it was her lips—the plumpness too proportionate and unexagger-ated to have been the result of injections or a cosmetic lip kit. These features—hair, nose, lips—were set against a fair complex-ion with a warm, golden undertone. It was a combination that often prompted questions. And sometimes, if Hannah was so unlucky, prompted the guessing game.

"Okay. I've got it," Blaine said. "You're Russian and Ethio-pian."

Hannah snatched a glass off a platter a waiter held. She needed a drink. "You know what?" she said calmly. "You're really starting to get on my nerves, so I think I'm just gonna go."

"Wait. What?" Blaine's eyes widened with surprise. "I thought we were having fun—getting to know each other."

Did he really believe his intrusive questions were fun? Or that she enjoyed his guessing her ethnicity with the excitement of a game-show contestant? Some people really were clueless.

Hannah downed her drink, dropped the empty martini glass on a tray a waiter was parading, and walked past Blaine. She navigated through the cluster of poised people and headed toward the open balcony doors.

On the terrace, the mid-June breeze with its mild warmth and briny flavor cooled her cheeks that were hot due to her irritation. *The nerve of that guy.* She pressed two fingers to her pulsing temple as she surveyed the space. There were a group of people at the far end of the terrace, engaged in conversation. She slipped her aching feet out of the Nine West stilettos and wiggled her toes against the cool, smooth cement. Releasing a pent-up breath, she leaned into the iron railing and took in the view—the lit Golden Gate Bridge stretched over dark waters.

"Hey."

Hannah spun around, her attention on the tall, lean man wearing a pale blue blazer over a white button-down. There was a pocket square peeking out in a puff of navy blue and burgundy. He didn't wear a tie like most of the men inside, and yet he still exuded sophistication. His expression was serious, his lips pressed in a hard line.

"Um . . . hi," Hannah greeted.

"Hi. I saw what happened inside with that man," he said. He had an accent. Actually, it seemed like multiple accents—perhaps two distinct ones that morphed into something novel. An African one and an English one. It was interesting. In a sense, regal. And attractive. He ran a hand over the trimmed beard that neatly enclosed his lips. "He was . . . um . . ." He couldn't find the right word.

Hannah, however, had many. "Rude. Insensitive. Unaware. Obnoxious. Intrusive." She held up five fingers and wiggled them. "Take your pick."

He pondered briefly, tapping his chin. "Is all of the above an option?"

"Hmm." She held up a sixth finger. "Looks like it is."

"Then all of the above. I think that sums it up best."

"Yeah." Hannah nodded. "Me too." She laughed, maybe even giggled, and it was light and sweet and unexpected. Where the hell had that come from? Only minutes ago, her cheeks were burning hot with irritation. They weren't anymore.

She dropped her hands and watched him gaze at the view beyond the terrace. She noted how moonlight touched his deep brown skin and cast a silvery shimmer over the gentle slants of his cheekbones. He was handsome but in a way that wasn't immediately obvious, especially under the current dim lighting. She had to pay attention, take notice of the subtlety in his features. Like the natural squint of his eyes and the ease in which his bones structured his face—not with sharp, hard angles but with soft ones.

"What a view, right?" he said.

"Yeah. It's pretty amazing." She forced her gaze away from him. "It totally makes up for Flo ditching me . . . I guess."

He turned to her. "Who's Flo?"

"My best friend. She brought me as her plus one, then bailed the moment we walked through the door."

"Why would she do that?"

"She's working the room, on the lookout for new clients. She's a Realtor, and even though she said she was coming for pleasure not business, I didn't really buy it. The girl loves her job and is damn good at it." Hannah shrugged. "I can't fault her for it." She regarded him, an eyebrow slightly raised. "What about you? Business or pleasure?"

"Unfortunately, business."

"On the hunt for potential home buyers?"

"Not exactly. The host owns a start-up I would like to purchase. We had a two-hour meeting this morning, and just when I thought we had a deal, he invited me here. Along with the three others interested in buying the company." He chuckled then frowned, quietly considering something. "I'm starting to think this might be some kind of *Hunger Games* situation."

"Hmm." Hannah looked through the open doors and examined the well-dressed guests. One woman wore an elaborate headband, heavy with pearls and multicolored jewels. Another wore a short, fuchsia dress with too many layers of ruffles. When she looked at him again, she nodded. "Yeah. Everyone in there can definitely pass as citizens of the Capitol."

He glanced inside to deliberate, and when he turned to Hannah and their eyes connected, they laughed out loud. The sound surprised Hannah just as the giggle had surprised her earlier, but she embraced it completely. As their laughter died down, they looked at each other, a glint in their eyes.

"I'm Lawrence." He extended a hand to her.

"Hannah." She took his hand, and her heart broke out of its routine rhythm, banging briskly and shortening her breaths.

They fixated on each other, smiling. And then, abruptly, a phone rang. The repetitive chime disrupted the moment.

Lawrence released Hannah's hand and reached into his pocket. His brows furrowed as he looked at the screen, at the caller ID. "Would you please excuse me while I take this?"

"Yeah," Hannah said. "Of course. Go ahead."

He stepped a few feet from her and brought the phone to his

ear. He listened, and then he spoke, his whisper still discernible.

"Oh my God." He pressed his eyes closed and shook his head. "Okay." Now he nodded. "Okay. I'm on my way, Tiwa. Okay? I'm on my way." After ending the call and releasing a deep sigh, he returned to Hannah. "I'm sorry, but I—"

"No need to apologize." It was obvious he had just received bad news.

His shoulders sloped, and his eyes glistened with tears he fought back by blinking rapidly.

"It's okay." She gave him a sympathetic smile. "Go." She didn't want him to, but he definitely had to. "I hope everything works out."

"Thank you. Goodbye." He turned and hastened away.

As Hannah watched him leave, she tried to disregard the connection she'd felt. It didn't matter. He was gone now. And that was that.

"There you are!" Flo shouted, stepping onto the terrace. She approached her best friend with rushed steps that made her silk dress flap behind her. "Jeez. I've been searching this entire place for you."

"Well, I've been out here." She didn't want Flo to detect her disappointment, so she paid attention to her voice, ensuring it had a believable measure of liveliness. "I was just getting some air and talking to . . ." What was the point of telling Flo about him? "Some of the other guests."

"Oh. Great. Happy you had some company. I'm . . . um . . ." Flo frowned, her attention on Hannah's bare feet. "Um . . . why aren't you wearing any shoes?"

Hannah looked down, her eyes widening. She'd forgotten about her lack of shoes. Had Lawrence noticed that? Maybe not. He hadn't mentioned it. She brushed off her embarrassment and laughed. "My feet were killing me. I needed a break."

"Right. Anyway, sorry about basically abandoning you." Flo's alabaster complexion, already flushed from the suddenly cool air, lost more of its natural hue. "But I'm all yours for the rest of the night. We can stay or get outta here—it's up to you. Anything you wanna do."

"Really?" Hannah eyeballed Flo skeptically. "Anything I wanna do—no complaining?"

"Yep. No complaining."

The confirmation was all she needed to hear. "Let's go back to my place. Order a pizza and watch a movie."

"Come on," Flo groaned. "It's a Friday night."

"You said no complaining. Remember? You wanted me to pick, and I have."

"Yeah. But I just thought you'd make the right decision—do the right thing, you know?"

Hannah chuckled. "This is the right thing." At least it was for her. It had already been an eventful night. She just wanted to go home. "I'm in the mood for anything with Michael B. Jordan."

"Hmm." Flo smirked and fiddled with the pearl pendant on her necklace. "Okay. All right. Looks like there's a light at the end of this tunnel after all. Let's find something where he's shirtless like seventy percent of the time."

Their eyes went wide and together, they said, "*Creed*," before bursting into loud laughter.

"Hold on a minute." Hannah cleared her throat and dug a hand into her purse. "My phone's going off." She pulled out the device that was both vibrating and chiming. "It's my mom." After reading the text messages, she frowned.

"Is everything okay?" Flo asked, stroking an auburn tress behind her ear.

"I don't know." Hannah gawked at her phone, unblinking. "She wants me to come by the house."

"Why?"

"She has something to tell me. It's about my father."

TWO

⚜

HANNAH

The scent of Hawaiian Breeze nauseated Hannah.

The artificial fumes the three-wick candle released usually soothed her. Now, as she sat on the burgundy couch with her mother, the tropical aroma triggered a sickening sensation in her gut. She put the cap over the container, and the flames went out.

"Mom," she said, her voice soft. "What's going on?"

Hannah's mother said nothing. Her blue inflamed eyes wandered around the living room as if she had lost her nerve and was trying to find it within the rustic interior of the town house.

Two minutes passed. The air was clearer, no longer heavy from the candle's fumes. Hints of lasagna wafted. It was past eleven on a Friday night. Hannah wished they could go into the kitchen and bond over a good meal like they used to when she lived at home. But then she looked at her mother, whose eyes still wouldn't meet hers.

"Mom." Hannah breathed deep and mustered the courage to voice the question she'd asked herself since receiving the text messages. "Is he dead?"

Her mother ruffled her strawberry-blond hair that was usually in a slick ponytail. She looked at Hannah, turned away, then nodded. "Yeah. I got the call a few hours ago. His lawyer reached out. He told me he died yesterday. Honey, he was sick. Prostate cancer."

"Oh." Hannah wanted to act casual and unbothered by the news, and she succeeded for approximately five seconds. But then her lips puckered and quivered, and she released a rough, broken sound that shocked even her.

She was crying for a father she had met only once in all her twenty-eight years, a father who never wanted her. But as tears fell, Hannah understood that she wasn't mourning his death at all but a fantasy—the idea of all they could have been, if only he had just shown up.

"I'm so sorry," her mother said, holding her. "I'm so, so sorry."

"It's fine." Hannah stopped crying, patted her cheeks dry, and composed herself. "I'm fine." She stood promptly and grabbed her purse off the couch. "I'm gonna go. I have this article to write for work, so . . . yeah. I . . . I gotta get it done."

"Honey, this is a lot to take in. Maybe you should stay—sleep over tonight."

"What? No. I'm fine. Good night, Mom. Love you." She shuffled along the cramped space between the couch and the whitewash coffee table, then marched to the front door.

"Hannah, wait. There's more."

"More?" She turned around, exhausted. "What is it?" *What more could there possibly be?*

"Why don't you sit down. Please."

Hesitantly, Hannah retook her position on the couch.

"According to the lawyer who called, your father's funeral is in Nigeria in two weeks." She fidgeted with the cord on her silk robe. "And you've been invited."

"Invited." Hannah cocked her head. "What do you mean? I don't understand. What exactly am I being invited to do?"

"It was your father's wish that all his children, including you, attend his funeral and the reading of his last will and testament. In Nigeria."

For a minute, Hannah said nothing. She fixated on the landscape painting on the white wall and then gradually came to understand her mother's words and all it implied. "No. I'm not going to Nigeria." It was the only rational response.

"Sweetheart, I understand how hard this is for you, but—"

"I am not going." She enunciated each word as if her mother was suddenly hard of hearing.

"I know this is asking a lot, but it was his final wish."

"I don't care, Mom!" A sob scratched her throat, made her voice tiny and raspy. "He got you pregnant and just took off—went back to his family in Nigeria."

Hannah knew how it all happened. When she was a child, she would recall the details as if her mother and father were characters in a tragic love story.

Once upon a time, there was a young woman called Lauren Bailey. Lauren was a waitress in a hotel restaurant, working her way through graduate school. One day, Lauren met Wale, an older gentleman who visited the hotel frequently from a faraway land called Nigeria. They started seeing each other. They fell in love. They were happy for a few months. But one day, Lauren told Wale she was pregnant, and Wale returned to Nigeria to a wife he'd kept a secret and never came back. The end.

"He didn't want me." And that was at the core of the story. "He left because he didn't want me. And just because he sent you a hefty check every month doesn't change anything. Honestly, I wish you hadn't even taken his money."

"His money is the reason you could get braces," her mother

said, a sharpness in her tone. "It's the reason you could take ballet classes and piano lessons and go on that high school gradua-
tion trip to Europe. His money is the reason you're not stuck
with a load of student loans. So yes, he wasn't the best father,
but at least he did something."

"Something," Hannah said, "but not enough. He didn't do
enough. And honestly, I don't owe him anything."

Tension overpowered the scent of Hawaiian Breeze and lasagna. It made the air dense, heavy, hard to inhale. They sat in
silence for several minutes. Then Hannah's mother sighed.

"You're right," she said. "You owe him nothing. But . . ." She
paused. "But you should go. Not for him but for yourself. He has
four other children. Honey, you have siblings."

Hannah was aware of her father's other children. In high
school, she googled him often—desperate for any detail about
him. On his Wikipedia page, she'd learned he was an oil tycoon
with other businesses in real estate, shipping, and finance. There
was a picture of his children on the same page—three girls and
one boy. She studied that picture repeatedly, imaging herself in
it, wondering how much she would stand out, how much she
wouldn't fit in. It had been years since she looked him up or
studied that picture of her siblings. They were strangers, and
she had accepted that that was all they would ever be to her.

"He wanted you to meet them, Hannah. He wanted you to
meet your siblings."

"He had years to make that happen, so why did he wait until
now?"

Her mother contemplated in silence, then shrugged. "I don't
know. But I know you've always been curious about him and
them and even his culture." She huffed. "I hate that I couldn't
help you understand where he's from."

But she had tried. When Hannah was a child, her mother

would research Yoruba history and culture. Then she would present her findings in diagrams and collages. However, despite her attempt to educate, young Hannah detected a lack of certainty and authenticity in the lessons that made her reluctant to learn.

"I know this isn't how you imagined getting to know your father and his family. So, if you don't want to go, I'll understand. Really. I will." She held Hannah's hand tenderly as if it was made of glass. "But will you just think about it?"

When Hannah was younger, she wouldn't have thought twice about it. Back then, she was like a child at the windowsill, waiting for her daddy to come home. She imagined him showing up one day, claiming he'd made the biggest mistake of his life by abandoning her and her mother. She imagined a reunion and waited for it—hoped for it.

At nineteen, she realized the reunion would never happen. Even then, she had to deal with the shame of wanting someone who did not want her. That had been the hardest part, being absolutely sure that her father did not and would never want her. She eventually learned to accept his permeant absence, to make peace with it, and move on.

And although she hated to admit it, Hannah knew her father's absence had created holes in her, holes where portions of her identity should have been. But she didn't dwell on that. Instead, she filled those holes with other things—an excellent job as senior writer at a top women's publication, a loyal best friend she had known since college, and a mother she loved more than anything in the world. Hannah had taught herself to be content.

She needed nothing else.

THREE

LAWRENCE
san francisco

Lawrence sat beside Tiwa on the couch in her suite at the Fairmont. With her long legs huddled to her chest, she gazed out the window, her somber brown eyes on the cluster of concrete towers that made up San Francisco's financial district.

"I can't believe it," she said, "my father is dead." She rushed the words as if eager to get them out of her mouth, to speak them once and never again. "I thought he had more time. The doctors said he did."

"I know." There was a sudden tightness in Lawrence's throat as his heart pounded. "Tiwa, I . . ." Unable to find the words to express himself, he grew mute. For a moment, it seemed like time had snatched him and hauled him into the past, to the day his mother died.

He was ten at the time, leaping over puddles as he walked home from school with his book bag slung over one shoulder. There was a smear of mud on his white-and-green-plaid uniform from when he had fallen earlier in the schoolyard. A young woman hawked on the littered Lagos street, one hand supporting the bowl of pure water on her head, the other wiping the sweat that drenched her fatigued face. All around, cars honked, people hollered, engines revved up and died as they slowed in the infamous Lagos traffic. An *okada* zipped past him; there was a woman on it, clenching the driver tightly, the child on her back clenching her even tighter. As Lawrence came closer to the worn, rusty gate that surrounded the tin-roof bungalow, he smelled his mother's *efo riro* soup. His mouth watered, but he soon noticed a smell stronger than stockfish and spices—smoke.

He ran frantically; his feet plunged into pools of rainwater that stained his white socks brown. There was a crowd in the small compound, wailing neighbors who didn't notice him squeeze between their bodies and into the shabby house where he lived with his mother. The front door led to a small space that was both the living room and the kitchen. The acrid air burned his eyes and scratched his throat. Between the breaks of white fog that veiled the room, Lawrence saw his mother beside the blackened kerosene stove. She was motionless on the cracked, chipped tiles—her eyes wide-open yet unstaring, the wooden spoon she had used to stir the soup still in her hand.

The news of Chief Jolade's death took Lawrence back to the frightened boy who became an orphan at ten. Tears pricked his eyes. He wanted to mourn the man who had been like a father to him, the man who had taken him in after his mother's death, but then he looked at Tiwa's expressionless face and knew this wasn't his loss alone.

"Tiwa." He draped a blanket over her bare shoulders that quivered. "I'm so sorry. I'll make arrangements for us to go home."

"No." She shook her head. "Dad wanted us to come to San Francisco and close the deal. How did it go tonight? Did you hear anything?"

She had planned on attending the party with him but hadn't

been up for it, too preoccupied with thoughts of her sick father before eventually getting the news of his death.

"You called. I had to leave the party."

"Then we'll—"

"Let it go, Tiwa." He knew it wasn't about business for her. It was about doing one last thing for her father. "It's okay," he assured her. "They'll be other opportunities. Right now, we have to go home."

She nodded slowly, unsure but accepting. "Yeah. Okay."

He blew out a breath, relieved she hadn't argued—something she was infamous for. "Tiwa, I understand how you must feel right now. I understand how devastating this all is. If you want to talk, I'm here."

They had been best friends since they were children— basically siblings. He knew she wasn't an expressive person. He knew she wouldn't accept his offer, but he still had to make it.

"And what would you like me to say?" She turned to him sharply; her short, slick bob whipped her face as she moved. "My father is dead. Talking won't bring him back. Nothing will." Her lips shuddered, and her eyes filled with tears. For just a moment, it seemed like her hard exterior had cracked and all the softness she kept locked away was leaking out. It seemed that way for only a second, and then her lips straightened to a firm line and strength resurfaced in her dark eyes. She stood and tossed the blanket aside. "I'm going to try reaching Segun and the twins." She marched to her bedroom, her phone in her shaking hand.

The door thudded closed, leaving Lawrence alone in the living room. His face dropped into his hands. Tears he could no longer hold back fell. That horrid childhood memory cropped up, the details clearer than ever—the scent of *efo riro* soup entwined with smoke, the crowd of neighbors who had either gathered to grieve or gape, his mother lying still, the wooden spoon in her hand flecked with the residue of the leafy soup.

More tears fell. His heart pounded. His skin dampened with sweat.

He would go back to Nigeria. Back to the house he grew up in, to a family that was not his by blood but one he loved just the same. And for the second time in his life, he would have to say goodbye to someone he loved.

FOUR

SEGUN
new york

The club on the Lower East Side of the city was packed and lively, as it was every Friday night. The crowd cheered and booed artists as they saw fit. Wisps of smoke drifted in the dim space above bobbing heads and elevated hands. The air was musty and reeked of weed and cheap liquor. Sweat flecked Segun's forehead. In just a few minutes, it would be his turn. It was his first real performance, and the crowd had been savage all night, but he had the right soundtrack, dope-ass lyrics, and a shitload of swag—a winning combination.

He ran a hand over the cornrows that lined his scalp. The shaved detailing on his sideburns was neat and bold and drew attention to the diamond studs in his ears. There was no doubt about it. He looked damn good. As he adjusted the gold chains around his neck and admired his Air Jordan sneakers, he thought of the years he had spent in Nigeria under the microscope of his father. Back then—when his father wasn't tormenting him with long lectures on how to become a successful businessman—Segun would watch American movies like *Hustle & Flow* and *Straight Outta Compton*. He would mimic the accents, slang, and gestures of the male actors. Often, he would spend hours listening to Kendrick Lamar, Nas, and Tupac, studying hip-hop culture and using it as a blueprint to create his own music. He was mesmerized by African Americans. Looking at the energetic crowd and the artist swaggering onstage, Segun found himself still in awe of them. They were black but a different type of black, a kind of black he desperately wanted to be—one utterly different from his father.

For a moment, he wondered what his father would say if he saw him now, standing backstage at a club with a new appearance, pursuing a career as a rapper. He conjured the voice and the would-be words in his mind.

Segun, I sent you to America for an education. Now look at yourself. Only ten months in the country, and you have turned into a wayward child, pursuing a career as a babbling fool. You are nineteen years old and you are absolutely senseless.

Segun pushed the monologue out of his head. He couldn't think about how disappointed his father would be. Tonight, he had to stay focused. Tonight, he was going to kill it onstage—do the damn thing like it had never been done before. He would pave his own way, separate from his father's name and legacy.

As he began a mental rehearsal, his phone vibrated; he pulled it out of his skinny jeans and looked at the screen. It was a call from Nigeria. He recognized the number; it belonged to his father's lawyer, the man he had always called uncle even though they weren't relatives. African Americans didn't have to do that shit. If you weren't blood, you were called by your first name. Segun thought he would give it a try.

"Dayo," he said with the phone to his ear. "'Sup, man?"

In Nigeria, if Segun had referred to his elder in this manner, he would have gotten a backhand slap on his face. A slap so firm, so sound, he would have felt the effects of it in his toes.

"*Ehn?*" Dayo paused as if taking a moment to glance at the phone to determine he had dialed the correct number. "Segun, is that you speaking?"

"Yeah. It's me. Now, you gon' answer my question or what? 'Cause I ain't got time for all this."

The line went silent. Perhaps Dayo needed a moment to come to terms with what he had heard. A few seconds passed, and he cleared his throat and said: "Segun, your mother has been trying to reach you for hours to no avail, so she asked that I contact you."

"Hell yeah. She been blowin' up my phone all day. What she want, man?"

"Segun, she wanted to give you some news."

"Yo, please tell me she ain't planning on coming down here again. She treatin' me like I'm some kid or something. That ain't right, man. And I ain't 'bout—"

"*Oga Americanah*, will you shut up your dirty mouth?" Dayo snapped, his patience at its end. "I called to tell you that your father has passed."

Segun laughed. "What? Fuck is you talking about, man?"

"Your father, Chief Jolade, is dead."

The music stopped. The rapper onstage received cheers from the hyped-up crowd. The MC appeared and introduced the next artist. "Lil Sege."

It was time for Segun's entrance. It was time for his introduction to the world of hip-hop, a world he had long idolized. The MC motioned for him to step onstage, but Segun remained fixed. The rowdy, restless crowd started booing. The stage manager urged him to go on. Segun did not respond. His mind went blank. He began to babble, combining words that created incoherent sentences. His tongue loosened and lost hold of his forged American accent and dialect. *Yo* became *ehn* and *man* became *oga* until he was speaking pidgin English and then his native language, Yoruba.

Then he completely let go of his alter ego and shouted "Jesus!" and threw his hand on his head in a manner that was distinctly Nigerian.

"Segun," Dayo said gently, "it is time to come home."

FIVE

SHOLA
london

At dawn, the sun's sharp rays steadily split through the dim sky. The air, still damp and earthy from last night's rainfall, poured through the open veranda doors, filling the two-story Knightsbridge apartment with dewy freshness.

Shola sat inert on the velvet chesterfield sofa with her hands on her knees and one leg tucked behind the other—just as her strict boarding school teachers had continuously taught her. A balmy, sluggish breeze slipped through her hair; the cowries on each lock of twist rattled—one tapping her temple and another her eyelid. She allowed the slight inconvenience and tolerated others like the pang in her stomach and the itch on her neck.

Shola did not move. She could not move. For hours, she'd been frozen—a fixture in the glitzy apartment with its silver and gray palette and mirrored wall. The only action she managed to perform was to text her twin sister, telling her to come home.

Now, she held back tears, waiting for Dami to walk through the front door, so she could utter unbelievably heartrending words.

Dad's dead.

It was a Saturday, and Shola had planned to go to the Arts Club for brunch and then to Harrods. There were a few accessories she wanted to pick up for an upcoming photo shoot. Of course, her plans had changed. She sighed and glanced at the watch on her wrist—the Rolex Lady-Datejust in Everose gold. A few weeks ago, after she had won the Cosmopolitan Influencer Award, her father had sent her the watch with an engraved message on the case back—*Always Proud. Love, Dad.*

The last time Shola spoke to him, he had suggested the whole family spend part of the summer in their home in Dubai. She was looking forward to the holiday, looking forward to seeing her whole family. It suddenly occurred to her that her family would never be whole again. The truth was a punch in the gut that made her breath hitch. Tears filled her eyes just as the front door swung open and Dami waltzed into the apartment with all the carefree disposition of a child.

"Hey," she said, pulling off her metallic chrome Dr. Martens.

"Hi." Shola quickly regained her poise and tapped her chest, a silent plea for her heart to settle down. "How was it? How did you do?"

"Killed it. As usual." Beats headphones, embellished in red and white Swarovski crystals, hung around Dami's neck. She had six pairs in different colors—all a gift from their father for every city she had deejayed in. "I'm at Tramp tonight. Try not to miss this one. I always do better when you're there. Please come."

"Yeah. Sure." Shola looked through the open veranda doors where the sun beamed too brightly and the world carried on while hers stilled.

"I thought you were spending the night at Ben's. You practically live with him these days."

"Yeah." Shola turned to her sister. "Change of plans." The news of their father's death had altered her Friday night plans with her boyfriend as well as her Saturday morning plans. Undoubtedly, it would alter the rest of her life. "Thanks for coming home."

"Well, I was gonna stay over at Marlo's but then you texted. So here I am—present but absolutely knackered." She flopped on the sofa and crossed her legs—not in the manner their boarding school teachers would approve of. Her short dress crumpled up and revealed her pink underwear. "Now, why did you text me before the crack of dawn, asking me to come home? And this better be good." She picked up her phone, fixed a dent in her Afro, and posed with pursed lips.

As Shola watched her sister, she remembered when their parents enrolled them in a London boarding school. They were sixteen and identical—one easily mistaken for the other. They wore the same clothes and always wove their hair into two French braids. They were twenty-four now and had changed so much. Shola wore a variation of twists and braids, and Dami's hair was big and curly and usually set in an Afro. Dami's style was artsy and Shola's, Afrocentric. They had even found their own creative career paths—one with music and the other with fashion. Their father had been so proud of them, and now he was gone.

"What's wrong with you?" Dami asked, eyeing her sister. "You don't look so great. Everything okay?"

Shola blinked and refocused on the news she had to deliver. "I have something to tell you."

"Okay. Go ahead." Dami tossed her phone on the gray ottoman, shaking the metal tray that held a small pot of hydrangeas and three crystal candlesticks. "What's up?"

"It's about Daddy." Shola paused and searched for the right words, the right phrasing. She came up with nothing. There was no way to sugarcoat the news. "He's dead. Dad's dead."

"What?" Dami's brows bumped together in a scowl. She watched her sister skeptically as if searching for proof she was telling a distasteful joke. "What the hell are you talking about?"

"Mommy called me. She said he'd been sick for a while. He had cancer. Everyone knew—Lawrence, Tiwa, everyone, but Segun and us. He didn't want us to worry. He didn't want us to know he was sick." Shola released a shaky breath. "Now he's gone."

"No." Dami sprung to her feet. "You're lying. He's not. He can't be . . . be dead." Tears came down her cheeks, leaving a streak through the layer of shimmering bronzer.

"I know." Shola stood and took her sister's hands. "I can't believe it either. But he's gone. Dad's gone."

In sync, the twins wailed. They fell into each other's arms and then onto the couch, crying and mumbling encouragement as they consoled each other.

"I can't believe this is happening," Dami said, clinging to her sister. "Did you talk to Segun and Tiwa and Lawrence? Are they okay? Are they going home?"

"Yes. I spoke to them. They're going home. We're all going home."

Shola and Dami had not been to Nigeria in two years. Though Shola had found a way to carry home with her—in the hairstyles she wore, the thin twists and box braids and cornrows that clung to her scalp and swung against her back. And even in her clothes—an array of styles created with African textile.

Sometimes, she found it was the least she could do to keep home close—maintain this outward appearance, an often exaggerated idea of what it meant to be Nigerian or African in general. But in London, this appearance served a purpose. It told people she was proud of her culture, of who she was. And Shola was proud because her father had taught her to be.

SIX

❦

HANNAH
san francisco

On Monday, Hannah made the biggest decision of her life.

In response, her mother called a man named Dayo, who immediately emailed Hannah instructions to get a visa and two days after that, emailed her a business-class plane ticket. Destination: Lagos, Nigeria.

On Thursday, a day before her departure, Hannah pushed a fork through bits of kale and tried to ignore the anxiety that had given her a sleepless night and an unproductive morning in the office. Despite her attempt, the nerves were impossible to disregard. She tossed the fork on the plate and huffed.

"Not hungry?" Flo said, pulling round sunglasses from the crown of her head and over her narrowed eyes. "You've hardly eaten a thing."

"I don't have much of an appetite today." A fly buzzed above Hannah's head. She swatted it and protected her drink with one hand over the rim. The salad, she didn't bother to guard. She had given up on it, her growling stomach be damned.

"Maybe we should have gotten a table inside." Flo dipped

sweet potato fries into a glop of ketchup. "It's so damn hot to-day."

And the massive umbrella wedged in the middle of the round table did very little to ease their discomfort. The humid air moved sluggishly, transporting a nauseating concoction of ciga-rettes, fried food, body odor, and old trash. Hannah surveyed the outdoor space—people conversing, cutlery clicking, servers gliding through the cluster of the lunch crowd. Their waitress was nowhere in sight.

"Hannah, what's going on?" Flo sipped her Pepsi; her small lips left an imprint of red on the white straw. "You seem tense. Is it about Nigeria?"

"Yeah." Hannah gave up on tracking down their waitress and looked at Flo's tinted Ray-Ban glasses. "I'm supposed to be leav-ing tomorrow, but . . ."

"But what? Are you having second thoughts?"

"Yes. Absolutely. I don't even want to go, but my mom wouldn't give it a rest."

All weekend, Hannah received numerous pestering phone calls and text messages from her mother, each persuading her to go on the trip. It had driven her insane and eventually driven her to say yes.

"She's convinced going will be good for me or something." Her shoulders slumped. "I don't know."

"Well, maybe it will be. Just think about it." Flo leaned into the table, her chest pressed against the rounded edge. "You have a whole 'nother family on the other side of the world. That's kind of amazing."

"I don't need another family. I have my mom."

For years, it had been just the two of them. Her mother, or-phaned at sixteen, had only one living relative—her grandmother.

Though, she had died when Hannah was six. With no one else, only the two of them, they'd created their own family. It was small, but it was everything a family should be. Hannah's childhood had been filled with love, warmth, and stability. Her mother had always been there—at every school event, every dance rehearsal and tennis match. But she wasn't just there physically. Even as a young single mother juggling a full-time job as a middle school teacher, she had been present emotionally. Hannah grew up in a happy home, with a mother whose disposition was calm, tender, and sweet. They laughed a lot—in the kitchen as they failed at new recipes, on the couch as they watched cheesy romantic movies, and on the long rides they occasionally took through the countryside. There were so many memories of holidays and birthdays and vacations—so many good memories. Even with only one parent, Hannah had never lacked the essentials. She'd always had everything she needed. Even now.

"My mom's enough," she said gently. "She's all the family I need."

"Yeah. Of course." Flo smiled. "I know. And I'm not saying push your mom aside and make room for your siblings. I'm just saying it's a cool opportunity to get to know them. This might be a good thing."

"A good thing?" Hannah scoffed. "I don't even know what I'm getting myself into."

She would be walking into the unknown alone. And though her mother had offered to come along, Hannah believed it was best she stayed in San Francisco—far away from her father's possibly resentful and unforgiving wife, who might consider her the other woman.

"Honestly, I don't know what to expect. What if his family

doesn't like me? What if they think I'm some sort of impostor because—let's face it—I don't exactly fit in?"

"And what if they love you? What if you totally fit in because you're family? What if this turns out to be the best decision you ever made?"

Hannah considered the possibilities and uncertainties of the "what if" scenarios and shrugged. "But what about the Youth Hope Center? Their annual fundraiser is happening in a few weeks, and I'm supposed to help prep."

She'd assisted in organizing the event since volunteering at the center five years ago. The fundraiser was usually a fun night for the kids, who dressed up and met some of the donors who enabled the center to have summer camp and computers and after-school activities like rock climbing and swimming. The event was important, and Hannah thought it would serve as the perfect excuse to cancel her trip.

"Maybe I should just stay. In case someone at the center needs me."

"You'll be gone for only a week. There'll be enough time to prep for the fundraiser when you get back. Stop looking for a way out."

"Ugh. Fine."

"Besides," Flo said, "keep in mind that if you need backup while you're down there, just call me and I'll be there."

"Really?" Hannah laughed. "You'd leave your job, your clients and come to Nigeria?"

"Absolutely. With my fists ready to give a smackdown to anyone who messes with you. Don't underestimate me. Remember in college when I punched Brian Thomas for getting too touchy with you?"

Hannah would never forget the day Flo's small fist came in

perfect contact with the cocky frat boy's nose. There had been blood and tears and neither had come from Flo.

There was no doubt about it. If Hannah needed reinforcement in Nigeria, her best friend would be there, offering both moral support and combative defense.

It made her feel slightly better.

SEVEN

HANNAH

Rather than folding clothes into her suitcase, Hannah drove from her home in Potrero Hill to the Youth Hope Center in the Mission District. It was a little past six in the evening, and at this time, the neighborhood had a distinct charm. The restaurants she drove past were bustling; customers overflowed from the inside onto the patios. If Hannah rolled down her window and got a hit of the various aromas wafting in the air, she would be tempted to stop and grab chicken tacos from one of her favorite spots, La Taqueria.

With no detours, she drove directly to the center and parked her red Mazda in front of the large beige building. A vibrant mural covered one wall—the word *HOPE* the focus of the stunning piece. Hannah relaxed into the leather seat and studied the images painted inside each block of letter. She squinted, making out the details of a cable car in *H*. *O* contained a skull in honor of the Mexican holiday Day of the Dead. Hannah loved the colorful patterns and flowers on the pale skull. Just as her stare settled on *P*, she flinched, alarmed by a *rat-a-tat* against her car window.

Mariana, a sixteen-year-old girl who frequented the center, stood on the other side of the glass, waving while using her other hand to secure the bag strap on her shoulder.

Hannah turned off the engine and stepped out of the car. "Hey. How's it going?" she asked.

"Okay." Mariana pulled a brown tress from her tanned face and watched Hannah. "How about you? You were just sitting there, staring into space. Were you daydreaming or hallucinating?"

"Neither." She chuckled lightly. "I was just admiring the mural."

"Why? It's not like you haven't seen it before."

"That doesn't mean I can't take a moment to appreciate it now and then. You should try it sometime."

"Nah. I'm good." Mariana flapped her eyes as if both bored and tired. "Anyway, what are you doing here? Thought you didn't volunteer on Thursdays."

Hannah didn't. But she couldn't stand another minute in her apartment, packing with the knowledge she would get on a plane to Nigeria the next day. She needed to avoid that reality for a while.

"I had some free time. Figured I'd just drop by." She stuffed her car keys into her pocket, and they walked from the curb to the entrance.

The weather was warm, cooler than it had been during lunch with Flo. Every bicycle stand had a bicycle chained to it. With people walking in and out of the center, the large wooden doors didn't stay closed for long. It was clearly one of those busy evenings.

"So, I read your article," Mariana said as they entered the building.

"Oh yeah?" Hannah turned to her after waving at a group of kids leaving the center. "Which one?"

"The one you wrote last week, about the importance of female communities." She broke eye contact and shrugged. "I liked it. It was good."

"Thanks. I appreciate that." And Hannah did because she'd learned years ago, when she started volunteering, that a teenager's approval is rare. She pressed her lips in a firm smile and tried to act nonchalant so Mariana wouldn't revoke the approval.

They continued down the hallway, the doors on each side opened. The rooms they passed hummed with conversation and laughter and even music. Hannah loved the sound. It confirmed the center was supporting the kids in the community and the kids were receptive.

"Do you think you'll host another writing workshop?" Mariana asked. "The last one was pretty cool."

Another approval. Hannah fought the urge to pump her fist in the air. "Yeah. Sure."

"Really? That would be amazing. And you know what? You could also include a prize for the person who shows the most promise. They could get a summer internship."

"A summer internship where?"

"You know. *Teddy Girl.* Where you work. I mean, you already got the hookup and everything, so . . ."

Hannah stopped walking, folded her arms, and turned to Mariana—her posture serious even with the smirk on her face. "Is the workshop some ruse to get yourself an internship?"

"Um . . ." She looked from Hannah to the floor and then up again. "Okay. Fine," she conceded, rolling her eyes. "I want an internship at *Teddy Girl.* That would be freakin' amazing. But I wanna earn it. That's why I suggested the workshop." She smiled—sweet, innocent, hopeful. "So? What d'you think?"

Mariana's initiative was impressive, and so was her willingness to earn the internship. It was admirable. "It's a good idea," Hannah told her. "I love it. I'll speak with Caroline to see if we can set up another workshop, and then I'll make arrangements at work."

"Seriously?" Mariana bounced on her toes, grinning and yelping. "Yes! Thank you!"

"But if this happens, know that I'll give you no special treatment. When I choose someone for the internship, I'll base it strictly on merit. I might pick you, and I might not. Nothing's certain."

The possibility didn't faze Mariana at all. A smug smile appeared on her pink lips. "Oh, I'm not worried. I've got this. You'll see." She turned and walked down the hall, her bag swinging in response to her quick strut.

"See what?" The center's program coordinator, Caroline, stepped out of a room. She stood beside Hannah and watched Mariana's departure. "What's she talking about?"

"Another writing workshop."

"Oh. You know, that would actually be nice." She pulled a pen from her messy top bun; it was one of three pens wedged into the knot of silver and black curls. After scribbling in a notebook, she turned to Hannah with an arched brow. "Hey, what are you doing here? You're not usually here on Thursdays."

"I was free. Thought I'd stop by to see if you guys need a hand with anything."

"That's so thoughtful, but shouldn't you be at home, getting ready for your trip? I thought you were leaving tomorrow." Caroline assessed Hannah, her gray eyes filled with the sort of warmth and tenderness that could tempt anyone to reveal their darkest secrets and biggest fears.

Hannah had no secrets, but she had a major fear—going to Nigeria. Though she didn't want to discuss that or even think about it. That was why she had driven to the center.

"I was done packing and had some free time, so I dropped by. Anything around here for me to do?"

She didn't have a specific task at the center. Usually, she did whatever needed to be done—from administrative work to manual labor. Just last week, she spent the evening in one of the recreation rooms, filling the cracks with drywall. A month ago, she'd used a makeshift net to teach some of the kids how to play tennis. And last year she'd led a writing workshop. She'd enjoyed doing that most, sharing her passion for writing with the kids, some who seemed just as passionate.

"Well." Caroline hooked her arm around Hannah's and led her toward the gymnasium, where sneakers squeaked against the floor as a group of boys played basketball. "There's always something to do around here."

WHEN HANNAH GOT HOME THAT NIGHT, SHE LOOKED AT the half-packed suitcase on her bedroom floor. The room was dark, but the glow of streetlights slipped through the blinds and reflected on the suitcase, highlighting all the empty spaces her clothes and shoes could fill. She tousled her curls and groaned.

In just a few hours, she would be on a flight to Nigeria. With no distractions, she faced this fact and her apprehensions alone. If she fixated on her fears for too long, she would change her mind. In need of words to drown out her thoughts, she connected her phone to speakers and pressed Play.

An orotund voice filled the apartment, narrating one of Hannah's favorite books, *Wild Seed* by Octavia E. Butler. She listened to the story attentively and began folding clothes into the suitcase, gradually filling it with everything she would need for her seven-day stay. But there was one thing missing—one thing she needed but did not have.

She thought of the word on the mural. *HOPE.* She wished it was something tangible, something she could pocket and take along with her. That would make the trip easier—hope that, even though she was in a foreign country with people, a family she did not know, everything would be okay.

But Hannah didn't have hope to fuel positive thoughts, only the fears resounding in her head, overpowering the audiobook, and making her heart palpitate.

EIGHT

HANNAH
lagos, nigeria

The hot air was dense, especially with the accompanying smell of exhaust fumes and dry soil. Hannah stepped out of Murtala Muhammed International Airport, and the heaviness of the air settled in her lungs and on her skin. She was in Nigeria, a completely different world, and she was alone.

This was a mistake. The thought had occurred to her several times during the luxurious business-class flight. Now, in a country where she knew absolutely no one, her fear resurfaced. She tried to dismiss it while walking on the concrete pathway that led to an opening with parked cars. Arriving travelers rushed past her and into the arms of their loved ones. It was one happy reunion after another.

Already, Hannah missed her mom. She missed San Francisco and the safety of her world. She didn't want to admit it, but she feared that being in Nigeria, in her father's home, would make her a little less content with her life. She feared the child she used to be, the one who dreamed up reconciliations and happy endings, was still somewhere inside her, eager to be a part of her father's world.

Unwilling to fully confront that fear, she shook the thought away and searched for her ride. She had communicated with Dayo before leaving San Francisco, and in his last email, he had given simple instructions.

When your plane lands, step out of the airport and someone will be there to pick you up.

He'd also included a number in the email, but she would use it as a last resort. Until then, she would wait.

Two minutes went by. The duffel bag she carried was heavy on her shoulder; the leather straps pinched her skin that was already flushed and moist from the heat.

In any normal situation, two minutes would have been nothing to fret about. This situation, however, was anything but normal.

Another minute passed. Hannah dug her teeth into her lip just as she spotted a middle-aged man step out of a black SUV. He was dressed formally and stood in front of the car—one hand in his pocket and the other holding up a sign with her full name. Hannah exhaled and approached him.

"Hi," she said. "I'm Hannah."

"Ah. Wonderful. Nice to meet you, ma. I am Solomon, the family's driver. Mr. Dayo sent me." He lowered the sign, tucked it in his armpit, and opened the rear door. "He is waiting for you at the house. I will put your bags away, and we can be on our way."

"Sure." She slid the duffel bag off her sore shoulder and extended it to him. "Thank you."

In the car, the air conditioner freshened her damp skin and soothed her slightly. As Solomon drove away from the airport, she looked through the window.

Lagos, Hannah found, was a vibrant city with a distinct aura of urgency. Through the tinted car window, there was heavy traffic. Drivers communicated their frustration, not only by honking their horns but also by flailing their arms through the window and raising their gruff voices.

The streets teemed with cars, yellow buses, motorcycles, rickshaws, and determined hawkers who hollered catchy tunes to entice customers. They sold ripe bananas, polo shirts with distorted Gucci logos on them, chilled water in small plastic bags, and so much more. Swiftly, they maneuvered between slow-moving vehicles, showcased their merchandise to drivers and passengers, and sang their brassy tune that blended with the piercing boom of horns and the exasperated bellows of drivers.

As the Mercedes moved farther, the streets became less congested. The number of hawkers lessened until there were none at all. On a wider, smoother pavement, the car accelerated.

Lagos was like any other metropolis with high-rise buildings and highways. But soon, they crossed a massive bridge and a suburb of mansions replaced the urban scenery.

Solomon provided a passcode at a security gate before entering a street with massive, extravagant homes. It was a different world, separate from the chaos of honking horns, screeching drivers, and tenacious hawkers who had a desperation in their eyes and a haste in their movements. There was a clear line—marked by the crossing of a bridge and then a guarded gate, a clear distinction of class. Hannah felt a pinch of guilt as she acknowledged this divide, as she noted her position on the other side of the line, in a Mercedes with a chauffeur.

The car pulled up to a steel gate that slid open and gave way to a straight, wide path lined with coconut trees and cycads. The plants, which added a tropical touch to the immense estate, stopped short of a magnificent pillared building with tall arched windows. There were several balconies on the second floor, each enclosed with curved iron railings.

As the car drew close to what Hannah could only consider a palace, she noticed intricate gold molding on the pillars fixed at the sides of the front door. The glittering color was the perfect accent against the beige building; it added an imperial flair to the neoclassical-style mansion.

Hannah gaped and tried to reconcile where she was with where she had come from—the people on the street who had been vying for the attention of passengers and hustling under the smothering heat. People lived like that, and people lived like this, in a secluded paradise.

The car stopped, and she stepped out. Her feet landed on the interlocked stones paving the estate's grounds.

"Madam, I will tell Mr. Dayo you are here," Solomon said before marching into the house.

"Yeah. Sure," Hannah murmured absentmindedly, tilting her head back to view the entirety of the house. It was spectacular even with the sun gradually setting, its beam on the building receding.

"Hannah. You're here. Welcome."

She stopped admiring the house and turned to the front door, to the man in a black three-piece suit. He stood erect, hands behind his back, dignified. He had that hot older-guy thing going on, sort of like Idris Elba. His features were handsome, and the specks of white in his neat beard stubble and shaved hair were just the right amount. Hannah had an idea who he might be.

"Dayo?"

"That's me." He stepped forward, smiling warmly as he shook her hand. "It's wonderful to finally meet you."

"Yes. You too."

"How was your flight?" He released her hand. "I hope it was pleasant."

"It was. Thanks."

"And how are you doing? I imagine a lot must be going through your mind right now."

"You don't know the half of it." She pushed her fingers into her hair and tousled the tight curls. What would happen once she stepped inside? She couldn't imagine anyone being pleased about her arrival. This was a very bizarre situation. She bit her lip, tasted blood, and released it. "Can you give me an idea of what to expect? How do you think they'll react? Are they even okay with me being here?"

"Well." He cleared his throat. "Here's the situation. I didn't exactly disclose the fact that you are coming. Or that you exist."

"What?" Hannah said, an edge in her tone. "You've told them nothing about me?"

"I thought it would be best to wait for you to arrive and then tell them everything at once."

"Really? You thought that would be best?"

"Yes. But I'm now realizing I might have made a mistake. I probably should have told them everything days ago—given them an opportunity to absorb the news before you arrived." He rubbed his tense forehead. "I'm just a little out of my depth here. Your father passed, leaving me to handle this situation. I'm trying to keep everything under control—avoid chaos, especially since emotions are already high. But perhaps I could have done better. I apologize."

Hannah sighed and nodded. It was an unusual situation. She imagined there was no set way to go about it. "It's fine," she told him, her tone calm.

"Thank you." He exhaled. "So? Shall we go inside?"

"Um . . ." She took one hesitant step forward, then halted.

"No need to be nervous, Hannah. This was your father's home. And he wanted you here. It was his wish."

She nodded and followed Dayo through the door. Her sharp nails pierced her sweaty palm, and her heart thumped.

In the lengthy foyer, Hannah dawdled behind and examined a portrait of her father. She had a picture of them together—of her sitting on his lap while they both smiled at the camera. Her mother had taken the Polaroid photo when Hannah was eight, the one time she had met her father. He looked different in the portrait—older, fuller, not as handsome.

At the end of the foyer, double doors led to a grand space with a two-way staircase. The area was cream-colored with arched windows and gold crown molding. Three crystal chandeliers dangled from the high ceiling, emitting a warm glow over the artistic marble floor. Hannah's breath caught in her throat as she gawked, utterly and shamelessly amazed.

"This way," Dayo said, directing her to the left. "The living room is just this way. The family is waiting. Are you ready?"

She imagined the dazed, angst-ridden expression on her face conveyed she was not ready, but she nodded and said, "Yes."

NINE

LAWRENCE
lagos, nigeria

Sitting in the living room with the whole family, Lawrence looked around and tried to determine what had changed about the space. It looked different somehow. Perhaps the maids had rearranged some of the furniture. He wasn't sure.

Taking a new angle, he cocked his head and narrowed his eyes. And then slowly, it dawned on him. The room was the same; the decor had not changed. The only difference was the absence of Chief Jolade.

In the evenings, after dinner, he would lounge in this room—a cup of tea or a strong drink in his hand, depending on the kind of day he'd had. His wife would sit beside him, and Lawrence and Tiwa would sit across from them. For hours, they would discuss business or politics, debating passionately and then laughing when more lighthearted topics came up. With the twins and Segun abroad, they had spent many evenings like that. But they would never have those moments again, and this room would never be the same.

"So what do you think this is about?" Tiwa asked Lawrence,

shuffling closer to him. "Why do you think Uncle Dayo called a family meeting?"

Lawrence shrugged. "I have no idea. I'm sure it's nothing."

"It's probably about the will," Segun suggested, reclining on the couch. "Maybe he wants to read it."

"No," Tiwa said. "I don't think that's it. He sounded very serious."

"Well, the will is very serious," Segun said. "I wanna know what I got."

Tiwa glared at her younger brother. "Segun, please. If you have nothing reasonable to say, then just don't open your mouth."

"Whatever." He sank deeper into the blue cushions, where his mother also sat, poised and regal—her grief guarded by an exterior of calm and elegance.

She had never been a talkative person, but an observer, a silent contemplator. However, Lawrence noticed that since her husband's death, she'd had even less to say. Her stare was often far off, her eyes fixed on an object without really looking at it. Whenever she caught Lawrence watching her, she would force a smile to convince him she was okay. But she wasn't. None of them were.

"Well, whatever Uncle Dayo wants to tell us, can he just be quick?" Shola muttered. "I want to go to my room."

"Me too," Dami added.

"Patience." Iya Agba, who sat between the twins, took their hands. "I'm sure he will be here soon. Eh? Just relax."

They did. Shola rested her head on her grandmother's shoulder, while Dami rested hers on her grandmother's lap. The action seemed to cut their age in half. They looked so young suddenly, so helpless and weary and hopeless. Lawrence was certain they all felt the same way, even those who hid it well.

"Are you sure you don't know what's going on?" Tiwa asked Lawrence again.

He groaned and met her gaze. "No. I don't know anything, T."

Looking in her eyes was the only way to convince her. Everyone knew he couldn't lie while keeping eye contact with Tiwa. It had been that way since they were children. He would look into her steely eyes and be propelled to talk. It was like she had an invisible hook she threw down his throat to fish for truths.

"Who did that to you?" she'd asked him when they were ten.

His mother had just died, and he was living with the Jolades. He had transferred to Tiwa's school, and it hadn't been an easy transition. He didn't speak much. It was as if his mother's passing had shrunk his vocabulary. His classmates thought he was strange, and one day, on the schoolyard, one beat him up for it. When teachers and Chief Jolade asked about his bruised cheek and swollen lip, he'd said, "No one." The only person able to get the truth out of him had been Tiwa.

She'd asked one question, demanded it with a fierceness most grown women don't have. And Lawrence told her everything. He'd expected her to tell her parents. Instead, the next day, she approached the boy who had beaten him up. He was a year older than her and a few inches taller too. But Tiwa slapped him hard across his face, then drove her knee into his groin. As he dropped to the ground and moaned, she glowered down at him and said, "If you touch Lawrence again, if you try it, you will see what I'll do to you."

That was his best friend. She could stand up to just about anyone and get the truth out of him if she wanted to. This time however, he had no truths to reveal.

"Okay." She sighed and crossed her legs. "I guess we'll just wait for Dayo."

It seemed like the only option, so they did. They waited.

And a minute went by.

And then two.

And then three.

And then the closed living room doors opened.

Lawrence sat up straight. He narrowed his gaze. He blinked sharply to clear any haze from his vision. He considered a reasonable explanation for what he was seeing: he was imagining things. People did that when they were sleep-deprived, and he hadn't slept much since he returned from San Francisco.

San Francisco. His time there had been brief—cut short by the news of Chief's death but made memorable because he had met her.

"Hannah?" He stood and approached her.

"Lawrence." Her lips were caught between gasping and laughing; they somehow managed to do both. "What are you . . ." She huffed, disheveling her curls. "What are you doing here?"

"I was wondering the same about you." He was confused, but he was smiling.

They stood face-to-face just as they had that night on the balcony. He remembered it well, even the little details like her bare feet and purple toenails. He remembered how witty and easygoing she was. They had laughed, and then he'd held her hand—the warmth of her palm meeting the cool of his. In that moment, he had felt excited and uncertain, charged with anticipation. And then with one phone call, everything changed.

"Is this why you called a family meeting?" Tiwa asked, her tone snappy. "To introduce us to Lawrence's girlfriend?"

"She isn't his girlfriend," Dayo said. "Well . . . um . . . I don't think she is."

"We've met before," Lawrence explained. "Briefly. Last week in San Francisco."

"Oh." Dayo nodded. "I see."

"Okay." Tiwa tapped her foot. "Well, if she isn't his girlfriend, who in the world is she?"

Yes. That was a question Lawrence had not yet considered. Who was she?

TEN

HANNAH

All eyes were on Hannah. She felt less like a person and more like a walking question mark. Uneasy, she averted her gaze from the inquiring faces and examined the massive cream-colored and gold-specked room that had similarities with what Hannah now referred to as the great hall. Curtains draped the edge of the tall windows; the embroidered material was a soft blue, matching the three camelback sofas hosting six people who still had eyes on Hannah.

"Everyone." Dayo cleared his throat. "Before I get into the thick of things and explain why I asked you here, allow me to do a quick introduction." He took a deep breath. "This is Hannah. Hannah, this is Sade." He pointed to a striking fair-skinned woman in a coral caftan; the loose material draped her slim physique and cascaded over the chair and onto the Persian rug. "She's Chief Jolade's wife."

Hannah forced a smile, an attempt at lightening the mood. Sade attempted nothing. She appraised Hannah, an eyebrow arched and her lips straight. The callous stare definitely had the power to shrink someone—to make them feel small, like less than what they were.

"This is Chief Jolade's oldest child. Tiwa."

Hannah knew that face. She had seen it before, while examining the picture of her siblings on the computer. Tiwa's features were still the same, but her face had matured; it was leaner and more elegant, especially with the sleek, straight bob that curved and met her pointy chin.

"These are the twins," Dayo said, turning to the second sofa. He pointed at the twin with long twists. "This is Shola." Then he pointed at the twin with an Afro. "And Damilola." He looked at the elderly woman seated between them, her cheeks full and round much like her body. "This is Grandma Kemi, or as we call her, Iya Agba. She is Sade's mother."

The elderly woman was the only person who smiled. It was a big, warm smile; it lifted her droopy cheeks, and the loose skin around her eyes gathered. Hannah returned the gesture then followed Dayo's gaze.

"The gentleman with the bored expression on his face is Chief Jolade's son, Segun."

"'Sup," Segun said, shifting his eyes between Hannah and his phone.

Tiwa, Shola, Damilola, and Segun, all with the same deep brown complexion as their father. Hannah was standing in front of her siblings, in front of the faces she used to study. It was strange and unbelievable, and Lawrence was present too, making the strange even stranger. She looked at him and smiled slightly—caught between happiness and confusion. How did he fit into all of this? Who was he? A relative? That didn't sit well with her.

"Enough with introductions," Sade snapped. Her voice—

heavy with a Nigerian accent—was cold, sharp, beautiful, like a shard of ice. "I would like to know who this woman is and what she is doing in my home."

"Well." Dayo pulled out a handkerchief from his pocket and patted his moist forehead. "Before I begin, I would like to apologize for how this whole situation is unfolding. I—"

"Just tell us what is going on," Sade demanded.

"Right. Of course." Dayo inhaled and exhaled, undoubtedly gathering courage. He really was out of his depth. "As you all know, when Chief was younger, he spent a lot of time abroad, building his father's multiple businesses."

Everyone nodded.

"Well, during his time in America, he started a relationship with a woman, a white woman who conceived. She had a baby girl." He looked at Hannah. "This is her. This is Chief's daughter."

Beside Hannah, Lawrence tensed. He opened his mouth, then closed it when nothing came out. It seemed like he and everyone in the room didn't have the words to express their astonishment. However, their faces—their wide eyes and slack mouths—conveyed the emotion perfectly.

"Is this a joke?" Tiwa asked. "Is this some sort of joke?"

"No," Dayo answered. "Your father told me everything before he passed away. He wanted Hannah to attend the funeral and meet all of you. She'll be staying here. In the house."

Tiwa laughed, a forced, mirthless laugh. "I'm waiting," she said. "I'm waiting for the punch line."

It didn't come.

She stopped chuckling, the truth finally sinking in. Her expression hardened. She glared at Dayo. "You knew about her all this time, and you kept it from me . . . from us?"

"Tiwa." He spoke her name tenderly, uttered each syllable

with a degree of care. With his doleful eyes on her, there seemed
to be a silent exchange between the two of them. "Your father
asked that I should. I was honoring his wishes."

She clenched her jaw. Obviously, she had a lot more to say
but held her words back.

"Hannah, I'm sure you are exhausted," Dayo said. "Lawrence, will you please see her to a guest room? I have a few more
things to discuss with the rest of the family."

Hannah was exhausted—not just from her long flight but
from the current situation. She needed to step away and process
everything. She needed to give them a moment to process everything. It had been naive not to consider how her arrival would
affect them. She saw it now though, how confused and shocked
and crestfallen every one of them was. And maybe their reaction
had more to do with the fact that they had been lied to
for years. It must have been heartbreaking. Hannah couldn't
imagine it.

"Good night," she said to no one in particular, and followed
Lawrence out of the room.

ELEVEN

HANNAH

The grand stairs led to a drawn-out corridor. As Hannah walked alongside Lawrence, still recovering from the scene in the living room, she focused on the simple act of inhaling and exhaling. She concentrated wholly on the subtle, seamless way air moved in and out of her body. She concentrated on the small gears within her that functioned collaboratively to make something so complex, so very simple.

Breathe in, breathe out.

Gradually, the knots in her stomach loosened.

Lawrence stopped at a door and pushed it open. "Your room." He motioned for her to enter.

She did not.

"Would you like me to go in first? To check for monsters?"

"Ha. Funny." She smacked his arm playfully and entered the room, her steps slow as she inspected the space that was larger than her apartment.

Back home, her place was a riot of colors and patterns, nothing uniting to form a specific or intended decor. Here, the decor was intentional—shabby chic. The colors were minimal and tasteful. White curtains draped the tall windows, filtering the waning natural light. The walls were lavender, and the French-style bedframe and its matching dressing table and wardrobe were a shimmering silver that complemented the crystal light fixture on the ceiling.

"The en suite is straight through there." Lawrence pointed at the door beside the walk-in closet.

Hannah's attention was elsewhere—at the scenery through the closed glass door. Stunning mansions and a body of water extended far off, dusk casting an ocher blaze on both. The view within the estate consisted of a rectangular pool with a vanishing edge and a tennis court.

"There's a tennis court." She stated the obvious with unabashed enthusiasm. She relished that emotion, made the most of it, as she had felt many things since deciding to come to Nigeria, and excitement had not been one of them. "I used to play in high school. I was on the team and everything."

"Well, I guess you and Tiwa have something in common," Lawrence said, stepping beside her.

"She likes tennis?"

"Loves it. She plays often. Maybe you can join her sometime."

"I don't know about that." She turned away from the view and looked at Lawrence, who, to her surprise, was studying her. "She didn't look particularly pleased to see me. Understandably."

"Yeah. Tonight was unexpected. To say the least." He squinted and considered her deeply. "The news shocked everyone, including myself."

Hannah shuffled to the snow-white chaise longue at the foot of the bed and sat. "I've been wondering," she said. "How do you fit into all this?" Finally, she would get the answer. "Are you a family relative?"

"Um . . . well." He sat beside her, leaving a small gap between them. "My mother used to work for the Jolades. She was their maid for years. They were always kind to her and me. Sometimes, when school was on break, she would bring me to work with her. I used to play with Tiwa." He took in a deep breath, then let it go slowly. "When I was ten, my mother died. It was sudden—a brain aneurysm."

"Lawrence." She started to extend her hand to his but then withdrew it, suddenly uncertain. "I'm so sorry."

"Thanks." He looked at her hand, the one that had been so close to touching him. "Anyway," he continued, "my father died a little after I was born. My mother was the only family I had. It was always just the two of us." His lips curled up in a half smile that gradually straightened. "When she died, I had no one left. I would have ended up in an orphanage or on the streets. Chief Jolade took me in. He loved me, cared for me, gave me the same opportunities he gave his children."

He took Lawrence in, cared for him, loved him—loved someone else's child but not his own. Hannah shook her head. She hated the thought. At least she'd had her mother. Lawrence had been an orphan. Her father had done a good thing. He wasn't the heartless bastard her resentment often portrayed him as. Though Hannah couldn't help but wonder, not about her father but about herself. *What's wrong with me? Why couldn't he love me? Why wasn't I good enough?* She hadn't asked herself these questions in years. Being in Nigeria was doing something to her, unearthing old insecurities.

"The Jolades embraced me like I was one of them." He stared off as if recalling the memories that supported his statement. "They're good people, Hannah. And once they get over this shock, you'll see it."

She nodded. "Thanks for sharing that with me—for telling me about your mom."

"You're welcome." His eyes, which had been narrowed as if adjusting to the sight of her, returned to their usual size. "It's crazy, don't you think?"

"What is?" she asked.

"The fact that you're here."

"Yeah. It is." Hannah couldn't control the wide grin that stretched across her face. She was still stunned. The world, even in its vastness, shrunk to allow this coincidence. Seeing him had been a surprise. A pleasant one.

She had been on edge for days—since agreeing to come to Nigeria. With the travel arrangements made on her behalf and then the journey to another country, it had seemed like Hannah was falling. She was uncertain of where she would land . . . where she would crash. Though, when she saw Lawrence, a familiar face, it briefly seemed like she had landed in a soft place—cushioned, safe, embraced by a comfort she had felt at a swanky cocktail party in San Francisco.

"That night at the party," she said, "when you got a call—"

"I received the news that Chief passed. That's why I had to leave."

"Minutes after you left, I got the same news. My mom told me. Then she told me he wanted me to attend the funeral. We didn't even have a relationship, but here I am." She sighed and looked around the room. "I have to admit. This isn't what I expected."

"What isn't what you expected?"

She looked at him, contemplating how to explain herself without sounding ignorant and offensive. "I know my father was successful, but I didn't expect this . . . this place, this house. It isn't really the image that pops into my head when I think of Nigeria." She bit her lip. "I'm sorry if I sound like a complete idiot. I don't mean to offend you."

"It's fine." He chuckled lightly, clearly unbothered. "I get it. There are extremely poor people in this country. But there is also a middle class. And those who are well-off.

"Though, unfortunately, one group is larger than the others. And that's the image of Nigeria people are accustomed to. They have no idea places like Banana Island also exist in Nigeria."

"Is that where we are? Banana Island?"

He nodded. "Some of the country's wealthiest people live here."

"Like my father and his family."

"Yes. This is the Jolade family home. The twins live in London, and Segun currently goes to university in New York, but whenever they're in the country, they stay here. And Tiwa lives here."

"And what about you?"

"I moved out a few years ago—got my own place not too far from here, somewhere on the island. Though, I've been staying here since I returned from San Francisco—since Chief passed. I think it's best we all stay together right now."

Lawrence—who was the true epitome of tall, dark, and handsome—was also thoughtful. Hannah's heart skipped, somersaulted—did everything but move steadily. Her eyes burrowed into his with constrained focus as they tried not to shift to his lips or his fit physique that was apparent in the T-shirt he wore. When a thought occurred to her, she found something else to focus on.

"Chief," she said. "You and Dayo call him Chief. What's that about?"

"Your father held a chieftaincy title, meaning he was a leader here in Lagos—not in a political sense but more in a traditional sense, regulating traditional laws."

"Oh. I see. Interesting."

"You know," Lawrence said, considering Hannah's face, "you look like her a little. Like Tiwa."

"I . . . um . . ." She didn't know what to make of the comment. Should she accept it, dispute it, say thank you? She pressed her lips together and said nothing.

"It makes sense. You two are sisters."

Sisters. Right. Hannah had a sister—three in fact, and a brother. They were no longer frozen, unaging faces in a computer. They were real. They were downstairs. She had not fully absorbed these facts. She did so now. Sitting on a velvet chaise longue with a man she was undeniably attracted to, in a magnificent house that belonged to her father, in a country she had vaguely claimed as hers for years, she thought of her brother and sisters and felt something break open inside her.

The door she had closed off for years—the family she thought she could do without, the father she convinced herself she did not need, the culture she swore meant nothing to her— cracked open just a little. She didn't mean for it to happen. It just did. Seeing them made it happen. Being in this house made it happen. There were pieces of her father here— fragments of who he was at her fingertips, just waiting to be assembled, so she could finally get a complete picture of him. She shook her head, convincing herself that she didn't want to know him—she didn't need to know him. She wanted to shut that door completely and dismiss her curiosity, but it felt as if the child she used to be, the one who dreamed up reconciliations and happy endings, was on the other side, pushing the door open.

"It's always just been me and Mom," she told Lawrence.

"You have no siblings back home?"

Hannah shook her head. "My mom never got married or anything, so it's always been just us."

"Then you two must be very close."

"We are."

"Yeah." He nodded and smiled. "I was with mine too."

"I'm sorry, Lawrence."

"Don't be. It happened a long time ago."

"It doesn't matter." She touched him this time, allowed her hand to fall on his. "I'm still sorry." She squeezed his hand just as he squeezed hers, and then his finger reached out and tucked a lock of curl behind her ear. Hannah inhaled sharply, her heartbeat quickening.

"You must be exhausted." He drew his hands back and stood reluctantly, as if acting against his will. "I should let you rest. I'll ask Solomon to bring your bags up. And I'll send Mary to help with whatever you might need."

"Um. Okay." Hannah's voice, heavy with disappointment, was small. "I know who Solomon is, but who's Mary?"

"A maid."

"Oh." She wanted to refuse the service but didn't want to appear rude. "Okay. Thank you."

"No problem. Good night." He walked to the door, and just as he turned the knob, Hannah spoke.

"I'm happy you're here," she said. "I'm happy we met again."

"Yeah." He nodded, his lips angled in a smile. "So am I. Good night."

Solomon arrived shortly after Lawrence left. He placed Hannah's luggage by the closet while watching her with kind but inquiring eyes. Mary arrived next, curtsying before presenting a phone.

"*Oga* Dayo told me to give this to you," she explained. "He said it is yours as long as you are here, so you can make calls to America if you need to."

"Oh." It was thoughtful, since making calls on her cell would have cost a fortune. "Thank you." She took the iPhone and watched the maid who stood erect, awaiting instructions. Hannah gave none, and Mary eventually left the room.

Alone, Hannah dialed her mother's number. It was 9:16 p.m. in Lagos. San Francisco was eight hours behind, so it was 1:16 p.m. there. Her mother answered the phone after just one ring.

"Hannah, honey?" Her tone was tight, nervous, uncertain, yet hopeful. "Is that you?"

"Yeah, Mom. It's me."

She released a long breath. "Thank God. You made it. Are you safe? Are you okay? How was the flight? How are they treating you?"

"Fine." It was such a relief to hear a familiar voice, her mother's especially. "Everything's fine, Mom. Actually, things are a little tense right now."

"Tense! What do you mean? Do you want me to come get you?"

Hannah laughed. *Do you want me to come get you?* As if she were a child who wasn't having fun at summer camp rather than an adult on another continent. "No, Mom. No need for a rescue. I'm good."

She told her mother about everything—the country, the house, the family. Her mother listened attentively and offered words of reassurance, the only thing she could do while thousands of miles away. When the conversation ended, Hannah felt more at ease and called Flo to fill her in.

"Lawrence and I are not related. Thank God."

"Hannah, please tell me you're gonna hook up with him."

"Flo!"

"What? You deserve to have some fun. The last guy you dated was Marc, and he was . . ." She grunted. "Marc is the cautionary tale you'll one day tell your future daughter. He was a lying ass."

To be more specific, he was a lying cheater. He had cheated on Hannah twice. The first time, she'd forgiven him. The second time, she would have forgiven him again. But Flo had talked her out of it—convinced Hannah she deserved better. That relationship had lasted ten months and ended a year ago. Hannah was over it. She just hadn't dated since.

"From what you've told me, Lawrence is really hot and seems like a nice guy. So, don't hesitate to straddle him when the opportunity presents itself."

Hannah snorted with laughter. "Sure, Flo. I'll make sure to do that. Thanks for the advice."

"Anytime."

Hannah ended the call and looked around the large room. She thought of taking a shower, but sighted her handbag on the bed and looked through it. Inside, there was a half-eaten bag of mint Milano cookies, a copy of *Beloved* she was almost through rereading, and at the very bottom, a Polaroid picture. Bringing it along had been a last-minute decision—a hasty and thoughtless grab, stash, and dash.

She looked at her father, young and handsome, a broad smile on his face. She looked at herself—eight years old, a teddy bear in her arm, and a proud grin on her face. That was the first time she'd met him, but she'd leaned against him so comfortably, as if he'd always been there—at every birthday and Christmas and dance rehearsal. As if he had been the kind of father to make Sunday morning waffles and throw her over his shoulders. He hadn't been that kind of father, but eight-year-old Hannah had hoped he would be. It wasn't just happiness on her small, young face. It was optimism—optimism that had eventually wasted away. Well, Hannah wanted to believe that it had.

But it was still there, inside her, pushing a closed door open.

TWELVE

SHOLA

Like the rest of the family, Shola was quiet, incapable of expressing the swarm of thoughts crowding her mind. She hadn't worked through the first batch of madness when Dayo cleared his throat.

"There's more I need to discuss with you all," he said, sitting beside Tiwa. "But first, I would like to read your father's instructions." He reached for the leather briefcase atop the coffee table, opened it, and brought out a single sheet of paper.

"Instructions?" Segun asked, a lazy expression making his red puffy eyes droop.

Shola wondered whether her brother was high or had just been crying intensely. Then she concluded, based on his appearance and behavior, that it was a combination of the two. He was the only person in the room who hadn't seemed shocked, angry, or betrayed by the recent news. He was unnaturally relaxed, considering the situation.

"You know what?" Segun said, his tone mellow. "I ain't up for all this." He stood promptly, then swayed, unsteady on his feet. "Imma head out."

"Sit down, Segun. Now." Dayo spoke sternly. His grip on the slowly crumpling paper showed he was losing his patience. "If you cannot show respect for anyone here, the least you can do is show respect for your late father. Now, sit down and be quiet before I beat some manners into you."

Segun obeyed quickly, like a child whose fear of chastisement was greater than his desire for rebellion.

Again, the room was silent.

Dayo cleared his throat and huffed. "Chief knew he was sick."

"Yeah. And he told everyone but Dami, Segun, and me." Shola's chin trembled, and her grandmother's arm came around her. "He didn't tell us."

"You all were abroad, living your lives," Dayo said. "Your father didn't want to interrupt that. He didn't want you all—the youngest in the family—to worry."

"That wasn't his call. We had a right to know."

"Yes. You did. Shola, your father wasn't a perfect man. He made mistakes. The biggest one was not being a part of Hannah's life. He sincerely regretted not knowing her and not allowing all of you to know her."

His regret changed nothing. It didn't console Shola in the least. He had lied about so much. The damage had been done.

"As some of you already know, he was planning a family trip to Dubai. He thought he had more time with you all. He planned on inviting Hannah so everyone could meet her before he passed." Dayo sighed and pressed a finger against his temple. "This was not the scenario he envisioned, but he planned for it. He left instructions."

"What kind of instructions?" Dami asked.

"Well, he asked me to ensure Hannah came to Nigeria for the funeral. He wanted her to stay here, in the house, so that everyone could get to know her and she could get to know you all."

"Well, I'm not interested in getting to know her." Tiwa sprung to her feet. "So I guess I'll be staying in a hotel."

"No one's going anywhere," Dayo asserted. "You're all staying in this house until after the funeral."

"Says who?" Tiwa's brow arched, a challenge.

"Your father. It's part of his instructions. Everyone stays in the house until after the funeral, when the will is read."

"But what if we don't stay in the house?" Shola asked. "What then?"

"Well, there are conditions. According to Chief's instructions, if you all don't stay under the same roof and get to know Hannah, there won't be a reading of the will."

"Ah!" Segun was now alert, as if his high had cleared just enough for him to realize the gravity of the situation. "Uncle Dayo, what are you talking about?" For a moment, shock caused his tongue to slip out of rhythm with his false American accent. When he blinked sharply, he assumed the intonation again. "What you talkin' 'bout? What you mean there ain't gon' be a reading of the will?"

"There will be no reading of the will because there won't be assets to distribute. The properties and the companies will be sold, and the money will be donated to various charities. All of you will be left with nothing."

"No," Tiwa objected before anyone could process. "That can't be true."

"Here." Dayo extended the paper to her. "It's the codicil. It contains your father's instructions, detailing everything I just explained."

Tiwa snatched the paper and ran her eyes across the words.

She looked up after reading, fuming as she handed it to their mother. "So he's basically forcing us to spend time with her."

That was exactly what it seemed like.

"Don't think of it that way," Dayo said. "Like it or not, she's family. Your sister."

"So, let me get this straight," Segun began, "all we gotta do is live with this girl until the funeral and then we get our inheritance?"

"Technically, yes." Dayo rolled his eyes. "But your father's intention was to have everyone connect with Hannah."

"Well, yeah," Segun said. "We can do that, right?"

"Well, I certainly can't," Shola said. It didn't matter what their father had threatened to take from them, Shola wanted absolutely nothing to do with Hannah.

"I can't do it either. I won't," Tiwa affirmed. "We don't know that girl. She isn't a part of this family, and we owe her absolutely nothing. What in the world was Daddy thinking—that a threat would instantly have us fawning over her?" She snorted. "I'm really starting to wonder if he knew us at all."

"Okay," Iya Agba said, standing. She rolled her shoulders and retied her wrapper, tightening the multi-patterned cloth around her waist. "That is enough. Everyone is very emotional right now, so you should all get some rest. Tomorrow will be better."

"I don't see how, when she's still going to be here," Tiwa said.

"It will be better because we would have had some time to absorb this news. And hopefully, we will give Hannah a better welcome. I'm going to speak with Chef Andy—tell him to make a big breakfast for the whole family. It has been a long time since we have done that. It will be nice."

"So that's it? A big fancy breakfast? You're just going to let her into our lives, make her feel at home in our home? What about—"

Iya Agba held up her hand, silencing Tiwa. "Listen. I am an old woman. I do not have the energy or the time to be making trouble with one small girl, who I don't even know and who has done nothing to me. As for the rest of you, I know this situation is difficult. But like it or not, that girl is your family. Your father wanted her here. We must respect his wishes." She dropped her hand, and the tension left her face. "He might not have been a perfect man, but he was a good man. Remember that. And remember that he meant everything to us." She looked at her daughter, who had said little since Dayo revealed the news, and sighed, sympathetic yet still resolute. "Every one of you will be at breakfast tomorrow. With a much better attitude. Good night." She left the room in an unhurried stride, and a moment of silence passed.

"Well," their mother finally said, rising. "This day has offered far more than I bargained for." She assessed her children, her soft gaze meeting all of them—from the oldest to the youngest. She stopped at Segun and held his cheek. "Stop smoking that nonsense. Hmm? And try to get some rest."

When he nodded, she looked at the rest of them.

"Mom," Shola said. "Are you—"

"I'm fine." She held a strained smile in place for a few seconds, and when it began to turn downward, she spun around and walked out of the living room.

Tiwa said nothing. She only glared at Dayo, shook her head, and then strode off.

"Well." Segun adjusted the baseball cap on his head. "Since everyone's leaving, can I head out now, Dayo?" After noting the infuriated look on the lawyer's face, Segun took a step back. "I mean, Uncle. Uncle Dayo. Um . . . I'm gonna go now." His exit was quick and clumsy, lacking all the swag he probably intended it to have.

Shola and Dami sat side by side and watched Dayo pack up his briefcase.

"Ladies, I know all this is a lot. But just try to take it easy, eh?" He stood, prepared to leave. "I'll drop by frequently to check on you all and to see how things are going. But if you need anything, anything at all, just let me know. Okay?"

They nodded, and he left like everyone else.

"Are you okay?" Dami asked.

Shola turned to her twin, certain the answer was clear on her face.

"I know." Dami blew out a loud breath and sagged deeper into the chair. "This is insane. I can't believe—"

"Daddy lied to us for years?"

"I was going to say, I can't believe we have another sister." It started slowly—the grin that spread across Dami's face as she repeated the words *another sister*. "It's insane. But it's kind of amazing. Don't you think?"

Shola shook her head. "I don't get it. Aren't you upset—angry at Daddy? He lied to us for years. Not to mention he cheated on Mom."

"Yeah. I know. It's all so messed up. These past few days have been hell, and then Uncle Dayo comes and throws this at us. I'm still light-headed from the shock." She sighed and took her sister's hands. "But I'm also tired, Shola. I'm so tired of being sad and angry. I'm tired of this dark cloud hovering over this whole family. I just want to try to look at the bright side. And maybe she's it."

"Seriously? Are you delusional?"

"She smiles just like Dad. Didn't you notice?"

"No. I didn't."

But Shola had. When Hannah had walked into the living room and sighted Lawrence, she had smiled; the shape of her lips and the limit of its extension were so familiar. As Shola watched her, she had thought to herself, *This girl smiles like my dad. Strange.*

None of them had their father's smile, so that part of him seemed lost forever. But then a stranger had walked into their home, wearing it. And Shola had been caught between jealousy and gratitude. She still was.

"I noticed," she admitted to her sister.

"Don't you think this is like . . . sort of a miracle? We lost Dad, but we—"

"Don't." Shola pulled her hands from Dami's grip. "Don't blow this up into some sentimental bullshit. This is not God compensating us for our loss. This is Dad finally owning up to his lies. Except he isn't here to deal with it." Her voice, although it wavered, increased in volume. "There's a damn stranger in our home, and we're just supposed to be chummy with her?"

"Well, I don't mind being chummy with her. I happen to like her."

"Like her? You don't even know her."

"Well, she's my sister, so it's an automatic like for me."

Shola rolled her eyes, annoyed and slightly envious. Sometimes, she wished she could be more like her sister. Dami processed things quickly. She didn't let things fester. You could offend her and within five minutes, she would no longer be angry. She felt things gravely but worked through them quickly. While Shola would probably go through all the five stages of grief, Dami would likely skip a step or two. Their father had been like that. That's who Dami and even Segun had gotten it from. Shola and Tiwa were more like their mother. They processed things slowly and reconciled them in their own time.

That's what Shola needed. Time. So she could see this situation as anything other than utterly disastrous.

THIRTEEN

TIWA

Unconsciously, Tiwa's mind reeled back to the first time her father gave her advice, a bit of wisdom he had gained on his arduous journey to build an empire.

She was nine at the time, playing with dolls on the carpeted floor of his home office. He had ended a business call by slamming the phone on the receiver and cursing. When he sighted Tiwa just beneath him, he sighed and motioned for her to sit on his lap. She abandoned her dolls without a second thought and settled into her favorite spot.

"Ọmọ mi," he had said, gently bouncing her on his knee. "In business and in life, always expect the unexpected and suspect the least suspicious. Remember that."

Those words impacted Tiwa. They made her overly vigilant, enhanced her already cynical personality, and made her trust very few people. Though minutes ago, she learned that her father and Dayo—two people she trusted immensely—had deceived her. It was hard to believe.

She leaned into the iron railing on the balcony. For once, the far-off view of the island did not relax her. Nothing could. There was a stranger in her home—a woman she had no intention of claiming as a sister. The fact that her father had devised some sick idea of a family reunion enraged Tiwa. The fact that Dayo had known about Hannah and had hidden it, infuriated her. She tried to stay calm, but suppressing her emotions was like trying to swallow sand.

She turned away from the view beyond the balcony and looked into her bedroom. She examined the slender maid hunched over, diligently setting a Chinese porcelain tea set onto the velvet ottoman. She considered taking her frustration out on the young girl but decided there would be very little relief and satisfaction in it. Tiwa didn't need a scapegoat. She needed someone deserving of her rage. When the wooden door creaked open and Dayo entered the room, it was as if some force—equally intent on retaliation—had fulfilled Tiwa's petition.

"Mary," Dayo said to the maid whose stare only ever shifted between her duties and her shoes. "Please excuse us."

"Of course, sir." She didn't raise her eyes, but she smiled. "Ma, can I get you anything else?"

"No. You may leave."

She scurried away, her shoes squeaking against the floor as she hastened down the corridor.

"Tiwa," Dayo said, "I'm sure you have words for me."

She eyeballed him, her flinty stare moving from the top of his head to his polished black loafers. "Many, actually."

"First, let me explain." He closed the door and joined her on the balcony. "Your father—"

"You lied to me." It was that simple. "You lied. Do you know how it felt to have that information sprung on me like that? Meanwhile, you've known about her for who knows how long, and you've kept it from me." She paused. "I trusted you."

"Don't make this about you, Tiwa. For once, don't make

everything about you and your constant need to be in control."

She leaned away, a hand to her chest as she tried to understand how the tables had turned. Why was she being reprimanded when he had been deceptive? How had this come about? She needed to control the conversation again—to reestablish who had acted disloyal in the scenario. It certainly wasn't her.

"You lied to me."

"Your father was my client. He told me many things, all of which I had to keep confidential. And apart from that, he was my friend. He confided in me."

"Great." She crossed her arms. "It's good to know where your loyalties lie."

"You're taking this too personal."

"How else am I supposed to take it? Eh? Please. Tell me."

"Tiwa." He stepped forward and closed the space between them. The cool breeze ruffled her hair that was usually neat, each strand sleek and precisely placed to form the bob that framed her angular face. His finger brushed her forehead, pulling away a few displaced strands. "Baby." His thumb stroked her bottom lip in a tantalizing manner that made her pant slow and deep. "You have to understand where I'm coming from. I was in a very difficult position."

"But . . ." Within seconds, Tiwa's good sense dwindled. She struggled to retain control, to recall the root of her initial anger. "I'm really upset with you." Her body language did not support that statement. She leaned into him, her lips slightly pursed. "I trusted you."

"I know, baby. And I'm sorry."

"Are you apologizing because you know you were wrong?"

"I'm apologizing because I upset the woman I love."

It wasn't the apology she had hoped for, but it was enough to defuse her anger and give way to an overwhelming emotion.

Desire.

It swelled inside her—larger than life, incapable of being ignored or suppressed. She gave in to it, wrapped her arms around his neck, and joined their lips. Two quick pecks and her mouth opened, allowing his tongue to caress hers. His motion was slow then fast, gentle then vigorous—an alternating combination he had mastered. As their hands pulled at each other's clothes, heat exploded in Tiwa's stomach. Warm flutters traveled to her chest and her head. She felt airy, weightless, unable to think clearly.

He did this to her often—made her delirious with a single touch, a single kiss. Sometimes, it was a simple look—the squint of his dark eyes, the slight arch of his right brow, and a smile so subtle, the gesture was only apparent to her.

"Hey," Dayo said, pulling back. "We should probably take this inside." He led her into the room; it was white except for the decorative pillows on the bed that added an accent of red.

"Shit." Tiwa turned around and looked at the balcony. "Someone could have seen us." The possibility unnerved her. She bit her lip. "What were we thinking? We have to be more careful."

Dayo watched her, his eyes narrowed. "Hmm." He sighed, tucked in his white shirt, and straightened his jacket and tie. "No need to worry. I'm sure no one saw us."

"Wait." She looked him over—as poised and put together as he had been when he walked in. "Are you leaving? I thought you—"

"You thought I would stay, make love to you, and then sneak out before the sun comes up or before your family sees me?"

That was exactly what she thought, but she didn't voice it. "I don't understand. Are you angry at me?"

"No. I am not angry. I am just tired." He rubbed his forehead. "I'm tired of lying and sneaking around like a child. I'm tired of being your secret boyfriend. I am forty-four years old. I am too old for all this nonsense."

She shrugged; her raised shoulders hit the gold hoops that dangled from her ears. "What do you suggest I do?"

"Tell your family about us. It's time, Tiwa. When your father was alive, I wanted to tell him, but you were adamant about keeping our relationship a secret because—"

"Because you were his friend, and I was his daughter. Do you think he would have been okay with that?"

She knew for a fact that he wouldn't have been. He'd said so himself.

Tiwa remembered the day her father sat in the living room while she watched an episode of *Friends*. He did that often— appeared just as she put on an American TV show. Of course he never watched quietly. He always had something to say. His favorite phrase was, "Americans take things too lightly." The teenagers on *Riverdale* couldn't share a kiss without him repeating this phrase, followed by extensive criticism.

"How can all these small-small children just be kissing and having boyfriends and girlfriends in secondary school? Secondary school! This is nonsense, *na*. What Nigerian child can try this? What Nigerian parent would even allow it?"

"Daddy, I can just leave if you want me to," she would say, annoyed.

"No *o*. Stay. Enjoy your show." He would be silent for a few minutes and then start up again. "So they are even kissing in school, and the teachers have not brought out a cane to flog them? In my day, if—"

"Daddy!"

"Okay. Okay. Sorry. I won't talk."

He wasn't a fan of teen dramas. He only enjoyed *Friends*. Usually, he would laugh with Tiwa. Though, on the day her favorite episode aired, he had not laughed. Tiwa remembered the details clearly. It was the episode when Monica told her parents she was dating their friend Richard, a man twenty-one years older than her.

"Do you see what I mean?" Tiwa's father had said, slapping his hands together. "Americans take things too lightly. Can you just imagine one of my friends dating my daughter and even having the audacity to look me in the eye and tell me?" He'd laughed a dry, humorless laugh. "I would just kill him. As God is my witness, I would kill him. End of story. A child that you watched grow up, a child that should be calling you uncle is now calling you baby. What's the meaning of that? That's absolute nonsense, *na*."

Tiwa had been twenty-five when her father made that threat, and twenty-nine when she started dating Dayo.

Their relationship started five months ago, during a business trip to Abuja. Without her father, things had been less formal. Dayo had asked Tiwa not to call him uncle, as she always had because of their fifteen-year age difference. For the first time in her life, she called him by his name. She remembered the way her lips moved against the two syllables—gentle, cautious, unsure.

Later in the evening, as they ate dinner, she was no longer cautious with her pronunciation or her movements. She extended her arm across the table, touching his hand while laughing at his jokes. She remembered suddenly being nervous about her appearance. She touched her hair and checked her reflection in the silverware repeatedly, until he told her she was the most beautiful woman in the room.

They had shared many moments during the three-day trip,

each one gradually altering their relationship. On their last night, when Tiwa couldn't sleep, she had knocked on his hotel door, intending to ask for a sleeping pill. He answered the door shirtless, only wearing pajama pants. She tried to avert her gaze from his firm chest and lean stomach. She failed. For a few seconds, it was silent. They ogled each other, their desire hindered by logic. Though, in the end, they disregarded logic. They fell into each other's arms, kissing and then making love.

When Tiwa woke in the middle of the night, her naked body against Dayo's, she remembered her favorite episode of *Friends* and her father's reaction to it. She knew his threat was exaggerated. He wouldn't kill his friend for dating her, but he certainly would be furious. Tiwa wanted to protect her relationship from all that drama, so she had kept it a secret and convinced Dayo to do the same. In the beginning, it had been fun and exciting. They snuck around, shared subtle, suggestive glances, and stole kisses when no one was in the room. Now, Dayo was tired of it all.

"It's time your family knows about us," he said. "We could tell them together."

She looked at the four-poster bed where she wished they were lying, holding each other. That's what she needed, not this conversation. "My family is going through a lot right now. I can't possibly spring this on them."

"I know, and I'm not asking you to do it right now but . . ." He paused and shook his head. "Tiwa, do you even love me? I say it all the time. I tell you how much I love you, and you've never said it to me. Not once. Do you love me?"

She didn't have the answer to that question. She cared about him. Very much. But love? She wasn't sure. And this wasn't the best time to work through her emotions. She was already dealing with so much.

"This isn't a good time to talk about all this."

"I only asked you a simple question—yes or no."

She said nothing. She didn't know what to say.

"Well." Dayo nodded slowly, his expression downcast. "I suppose your silence speaks volumes. Good night." He grasped the doorknob, and she moved swiftly and held his arm.

"Wait." Her grip on him shook, the fear of losing him more evident than she would have liked. "Please. Just wait. Let's talk about this. Just stay the night, so we can talk."

"Tiwa." He turned to her, his gaze soft. "I have never met a woman like you. You're stubborn, outspoken, and audacious. You're everything I am not, and I love that. When I think about my future, you're in it. Not as my secret girlfriend. As my wife."

Wife. Did he just say that? Her heart pounded, while her knees quivered behind the lengthy fabric of her dress. Where was all this coming from? They'd spoken about marriage only once. She'd playfully asked if he planned to remain a bachelor for the rest of his life, and he had answered, "No. I plan on getting married." That had been it—their entire conversation on marriage. And now, he was basically proposing to her. And she was confused. Or was she happy? Or was she scared? Her emotions weren't entirely clear.

"Tiwa, I want a life with you. But if I am being foolishly optimistic about our chances, I need you to let me know. Has this all been just fun and games for you, or is there actually a future for us?"

Again, she didn't know what to say. It was all just too much. She needed time to think and work through her feelings, but he didn't give her that. He turned the knob and walked out.

"Dayo, please," she whispered as he stormed down the hallway. "Let's talk about this."

To her surprise, he stopped and turned.

She exhaled, thankful. "Come back inside." Preferably quickly. Before someone sighted their lovers' quarrel.

"I'm not coming in."

Tiwa gasped, shocked he had rejected her.

"I just need you to do one thing for me," he said.

"What?" The meekness and desperation in her tone had disappeared. "What do you want?"

"Be nice to Hannah. She didn't ask for all this. Don't direct your anger at her."

It took Tiwa a moment to understand Dayo's words—the name he had mentioned, the concern laced around that name, the request itself. How could he think of Hannah when their relationship was basically falling apart? No longer able to stand the sight of him, she slammed the bedroom door, cursing.

Alone, she sank into the Egyptian cotton bedsheets and pressed her eyes closed. The cool breeze coming through the open balcony doors made the white curtains flap, swelling then deflating slowly. The fresh air didn't relax Tiwa. Nothing could.

Everything seemed to be crumbling. Her father should be here, dealing with the mess he had created. *He should be here. He should be here.* As the thought circled through Tiwa's mind, her anger faded, replaced with a heavy sadness that shortened her breaths and made her shake.

She buried her face in a pillow, where her cries were muffled, and allowed herself to fall apart.

FOURTEEN

HANNAH

At a little past nine in the morning, the sun shone brilliantly through the tall windows in the great hall. It was Sunday, and as Hannah left her room and climbed down the stairs, she hoped everyone had gotten over the initial shock of her arrival. It was false hope, but she clung to it.

On the landing, she exhaled. Unsure of where to go or what to do, she fidgeted with the short hem of her sunflower-yellow halter dress, looking from left to right, expecting the worst but desperately praying for the best.

"Hey! Hannah!"

The abrupt shout came from behind. Hannah noted, with surprise, the cheerful tone that accompanied her name. She turned and faced Damilola, who strode toward her beaming.

It was a beautiful smile, and it seemed sincere, but Hannah didn't know what to expect from the person who, just hours ago, had been stunned at news of her existence. "Hi. Hey. Good morning." Nervous, she couldn't settle on one greeting. "How are you?"

"Okay." Damilola lowered her eyes, her glee replaced with

shame. "Listen. I want to apologize about last night." She looked up, and her lashes fluttered quickly. "We weren't very welcoming."

An apology. Hannah had not expected that. She didn't think it was necessary. "This whole situation is . . . unique, to say the least," she said. "You all were shocked. I get it. There's really nothing to apologize for, Damilola."

Damilola. It was a beautiful name and likely Yoruba. Hannah had pronounced each syllable just as Dayo had during his introductions, but her pronunciation lacked something—something significant, a rhythm her tongue could not catch.

"Call me Dami. Everyone does."

"Sure." It was a simpler option, but Hannah was more than willing to learn the correct pronunciation.

"Breakfast should be ready in a few minutes. Sit beside me at the table." She hooked her arm into Hannah's and moved toward the dining room.

Initially, the contact shocked Hannah, but Dami's bubbly nature quickly calmed her. "I like your accent by the way."

It was a combination of a Nigerian and English accent, the same one Shola, Tiwa, and Lawrence had. Though, the dosage varied in them all. With Tiwa and Lawrence, the Nigerian intonation was stronger. With the twins, the English intonation was stronger. In them all, the unique combination was sophisticated.

"Thanks," Dami said. "I went to boarding school in England when I was sixteen. Same with Shola, Tiwa, and Lawrence."

"What about your brother? Didn't he go?"

"You mean our brother?" Dami grinned at Hannah and arched a brow meaningfully.

"Right." *Our brother.* It would take some getting used to.

"Daddy never trusted Segun enough to send him off to another country at that age. Besides, Segun was more interested in going to America."

"Oh. Why Amer—"

The double doors in the great hall swung open suddenly and interrupted Hannah's question. Lawrence came through shirtless. His brown skin glistened; sweat slid along the hard lines that defined his chest and abdomen.

"Hey. Good morning," he said, smiling at Hannah. The natural squint of his eyes added an intensity to his stare.

"Um . . ." Hannah couldn't help her reaction; her mouth dropped, and her eyes went wide. She cleared her throat and gave way to one word. "Hi."

"How was your night?"

She cleared her throat again and gave way to another word. "Good." It was all she could produce, and thankfully, it was just as effective as a multi-word sentence.

"My night was good too, Lawrence. Thanks for asking," Dami teased. "Hannah and I were heading to the dining room for breakfast."

"Right. Breakfast. I just got in from a run. I'll shower and join you guys."

Once he disappeared up the stairs, Dami turned to Hannah, who was still in a trance. "So, would you like me to pick up your jaw from the floor and reattach it, or would you rather do that yourself?"

The words snapped Hannah out of her stupor. She doubled over, chuckling. "I'm sorry. I couldn't help it."

"Well, neither could he. He was ogling you like he'd lost control of his eyeballs. And you weren't even half naked." Dami giggled. "I wonder what would've happened if I hadn't been here."

Hannah flushed and wondered the same as they entered the

dining room. They sat side by side at the mahogany table that could seat twelve. Breakfast was already spread out—slices of bread on a silver platter, a colorful assortment of fruits, a stack of pancakes, and a few things Hannah did not recognize. Rather than staring quizzically at the spread, she surveyed the room, which, like the rest of the house, had gold trimmings along the ivory walls and the high ceiling. It was lavish, regal, and elaborate, not the kind of setting Hannah was familiar with.

She felt the urge to look elsewhere—at something simpler. Her eyes roamed before landing on the French doors; there was a garden just beyond them. Though, it was nothing like the scanty tomato and herb garden her mother nursed back home. This garden was expansive and lush with colorful flowers unknown to Hannah. A skilled and likely expensive landscaper had probably designed the formation of each plant, each stone that created a pathway, and the massive tiered water fountain. Suddenly, Hannah felt an overwhelming sense of inferiority.

"Good morning!"

The lively voice caught Hannah's attention; she looked to the dining room entrance, where Sade's mother stood.

"Good morning, Iya Agba," Dami said.

"Hello, sweetheart." The elderly woman walked to the table and stroked her granddaughter's cheek tenderly before turning to Hannah. She smiled at her. "How are you doing, dear?"

"I'm fine, Kemi. Thank you."

"My dear, in Nigeria, we do not call our elders by their names. It is considered disrespectful," she explained, still smiling.

"Oh." Hannah frowned. "I didn't know. I'm sorry for offending you."

"No problem. Just call me Grandma or Iya Agba. Iya Agba means grandmother in Yoruba. And call Sade Auntie. Do not go and call her by her name o. Call her Auntie. Understand?"

"Yes."

"Yes, Iya Agba," she urged. "Go ahead. Try it." Her eyes were warm and inviting.

"Yes, Iya Agba." Hannah liked the pronunciation. She liked the fact that it was a Yoruba word—the first she'd learned.

"Eh-heh." Satisfaction expanded Iya Agba's lips farther. "Good girl. You are learning small-small."

The amiable exchange didn't surprise Hannah. Apart from Lawrence, Iya Agba had been the only one to welcome her with a smile the day before. She had a comforting nature. It put Hannah at ease.

"My dear, I am sure last night was a little chaotic for you," she said, taking a seat across from Dami, who inspected her glitter-coated fingernails nonchalantly. "You must understand that we were in shock." Her accent was fully Nigerian. She stressed each word, abbreviating none in her speech. "But although we are hurt and frustrated, we cannot take that out on you. You have done nothing wrong." She touched her tall head wrap as if ensuring it emulated the Eiffel Tower rather than the Leaning Tower of Pisa. "The only person we should be angry with is your father. He should have told us about you. But what can we do now? Eh?" She slapped her hands together and shrugged. "Like I told everyone last night, he was not a perfect man, but he was a good man. I loved him very much—as if he was my son."

"What about his parents?" Hannah didn't intend to ask, but she couldn't resist. It was difficult not to feed a curiosity that had been starved for years. "Are they still alive?" Did she have grandparents?

"Unfortunately, no. They died many years ago."

"Oh." To Hannah's surprise, she felt a pinch of disappointment.

"Anyway, my dear," Iya Agba continued, "I did not say it last night, but welcome. Welcome to your father's house. He was a good man." She stared off—a faint smile on her thin lips. Moisture gathered in her grieved eyes but didn't fall. "He was a very good man." She looked at Hannah again. "Welcome home, dear."

Home. Hannah had never considered the word before, but she did now as if it had suddenly gained another dimension. In her head, she turned the word on all its sides, examining it. *Home.* It had always had a simple meaning—her cozy apartment or her mother's house, the place she had grown up in. But could it mean something else now?

"I'm starving," Segun announced, entering the dining room with a shoulder-bobbing swagger that seemed forced. "What's for breakfast?"

"Tell me there's *akara*," Shola said, trailing behind Segun. "I haven't had those in forever."

Tiwa entered the room next, her mother beside her. The two women shared the same expression Hannah could only describe as bored and bothered. Sade, again in a chiffon caftan that swept the floor, sat at the head of the table; her daughter sat beside her. Neither glanced at Hannah.

It was intimidating but also disappointing. Hannah had begun to relax a little with Dami and Iya Agba, but now she felt on edge again—unwelcome.

"Where is Lawrence?" Iya Agba asked.

"He went for a run earlier. He's just taking a quick shower," Dami answered.

"Okay. Well, he can join us when he is ready. Everyone, bow your heads while I pray over the food."

The last time Hannah prayed before eating a meal was when she was twelve, when her mother was still determined to raise a good Christian girl. But as Hannah grew older, both she and her mother became lukewarm Christians who only attended church on certain holidays. She kept her head bowed however and listened to the prayer. Though, the sound of footsteps entering the room distracted her.

The chair beside her squawked as it got pulled from the table. Hannah opened her eyes and watched Lawrence sit down. He wore more clothes now than he had earlier, and still, she couldn't take her eyes off him. But she forced them closed eventually, before he caught her gawking.

The prayer ended with a resounding amen from everyone around the table.

"Hannah." Iya Agba picked up a porcelain teapot and poured hot water into a cup with calm elegance. "I asked the chef to prepare something you might be more familiar with." She pointed at the stack of pancakes topped with fruits.

"Thank you. That was very thoughtful, but I'd rather have what everyone else is having."

Tiwa snorted. It was the first thing she had done to acknowledge Hannah's presence since entering the room. It was childish, and Hannah chose to ignore it.

"Those look good," she said, pointing at the platter of golden-brown puffs that resembled beignets. "What are they?"

"*Akara*," Dami replied. "They're made of beans. Try it." She scooped one onto Hannah's plate. "Go ahead. You'll love it."

After slicing through the round, fluffy puff with a knife, Hannah ate one half. "Mmm," she said, chewing and savoring the piquant flavors that came undone in her mouth. "Delicious."

Iya Agba grabbed the serving spoon from her granddaughter and piled more *akara* onto Hannah's plate. "My dear, eat very well. Your body has been deprived of Nigerian food long enough."

Hannah laughed and ate ravenously, as if the *akara* provided some essential vitamin her body lacked. When Lawrence drizzled milk onto a yellow custard, her throat ached with a new craving.

"It's called *pap*," he said. "Here." He handed her a spoon and pushed the small bowl of custard to her. "Try some. It goes well with *akara*."

She scooped a portion and swallowed. It was sweet and creamy. Following Lawrence's suggestion, she switched back to the savory *akara* and suppressed a moan as the two flavors combined in her mouth.

"Hey." Lawrence smiled. "You've got a little something . . ." He gently brought a napkin to the corner of her lips. "Here."

"Thank you."

She liked him, her attraction beyond physical. She considered his brown eyes, searching for evidence he felt what she did. She needed a sign and thought she had detected one just as somebody shrieked.

"Great!" Tiwa rose to her feet and frowned at her phone. "Just great! As if I'm not dealing with enough."

"Tiwa, what is it?" Sade asked, her tone flat. "Why in God's name are you screaming?"

"The blogs. They know about her." She glared at Hannah. "They ran the story—'Chief Jolade's Long-Lost Half-Caste Daughter Comes Home.'"

"What? Half-caste?" The term took Hannah aback. "That's really offensive."

"Not in Nigeria," Dami whispered in Hannah's ear. "Most people don't say biracial or mixed race. They just say half-caste. Don't take it personally."

She tried not to, especially since she was trying to understand why her arrival in Nigeria was at all newsworthy.

"How the hell did they find out about this?" Tiwa went on. "Who told them? Who?"

"Tiwalade, calm down," Iya Agba said. "You know how these people are—they pry and get information one way or another."

"Well, I'm going to find out exactly how they got this piece of information." She stormed off without another word.

"Well, this has been fun." Segun stood and flipped his hood over his cornrows. "But I got places to be. Deuces."

"Be home by seven," Iya Agba said. "Your auntie is coming here. We have to pick the color of the aṣọ ẹbí for the funeral."

"'Ight." He walked out of the room, still with that forced swagger.

"Iya," Sade said. "Let's discuss funeral arrangements."

"Of course." Iya Agba stood and followed her daughter to the door. She waved goodbye to those still at the table before leaving.

"Well, I'm going to freshen up," Dami announced, standing. "Hannah and I are going shopping."

"What? We are?"

"Yeah. I think we deserve some retail therapy. Shola, would you like to join us?"

"No." Shola rolled her eyes. "I would not."

"Suit yourself." Dami pranced away, unbothered by her twin's attitude.

"You see," Lawrence said to Hannah. "Things are looking up."

"Yeah. They are." She smiled and leaned into him slightly. "What are you up to this morning?"

"I'm actually heading out now. I have to handle some things at the office."

"Oh. What is it you do?"

"Tiwa and I run Chief's tech company. Unfortunately, it often requires working on a Sunday." He sighed. "Well, I should go. Have fun with Dami. I'll catch up with you later." He stood and walked through the door, meeting Hannah's gaze before turning into the passageway.

With Hannah's attention on Lawrence, it took her a few seconds to realize she was not alone. Shola was still at the table, sitting with her arms crossed.

Unnerved, Hannah shifted in her seat. "Um . . . are you sure you don't want to come shopping? You're completely welcome to."

Shola pushed her chair back and rose, a striking figure in a crop top made from African textile. "I don't need an invitation from you to hang out with my sister." She scowled at Hannah and marched out of the dining room, the layers of multicolored beads around her slender waist moving along with her hasty stride.

FIFTEEN

HANNAH

Usually, when Hannah went shopping, she wore comfortable shoes. Preferably sneakers. They were sensible. They allowed her to stand for hours and move swiftly. Every Black Friday experience had proven that with shopping, sneakers were the way to go.

Dami, however, was oblivious to this fact. Her baby-pink peep-toes were gorgeous, but not ideal for standing in long cashier lines or racing to an item before another approaching customer or outrunning an aggressive pack of bargain shoppers.

Hannah looked at her beige ballet flats and pressed her toes into the cushiony gel insoles. They weren't sneakers, but they'd work just the same.

Solomon pulled the Bentley into a parking spot in front of a charcoal-colored gate. On the concrete wall connected to the gate, one word stood out—*ALÁRA*.

"Madams." Solomon glanced at the back seat. "We have arrived."

"Ugh! Finally." Dami blew out a prolonged breath as if she had done more than lounge in the back seat during the twenty-minute ride. "Hannah, you're going to love this place. Trust me." Her smile was so wide, it was a wonder her tiny, round face contained the extent of it.

"Have a good time," Solomon said, holding the door open.

"Thanks, Solo." Dami stepped out. Her heels hit the ground with a *clank*.

"Thank you for the ride." Hannah smiled, trying to display as much gratitude as possible.

"No problem, ma." He nodded, and his chauffeur hat tipped forward with every head bob. He must have been in his fifties. The folds that hooded his eyes and the whites that flecked his shaggy brows and mustache supported that claim.

"Come on, Hannah!" Dami was already a few feet ahead. "Let's go!" She giggled and twirled with every step, and the lightweight material of her dress rose in a circle above her knees.

"Okay! Coming!" With excitement suddenly pulsating inside her, Hannah realized Dami's youthful exuberance was contagious.

She hurried after her through the gate and stopped short of a peculiar cube-shaped building. It was orange and gray with geometric shapes—squares and scalene triangles—etched into it. A red decorative panel with a pattern of horizontal and vertical lines extended from the fourth floor to the second, overlapping the windows. The first floor was bare—simply glass, giving a clear view of the inside. Hannah had seen nothing like it—a modern structure that, with its vibrancy and heavy patterns, had an African aesthetic. It was exceptional.

"Dami, are you sure this is a boutique?" It could pass as a gallery or a museum, a treasure box for all things avant-garde.

"They definitely sell clothes in there, but I wouldn't exactly call it a boutique. ALÁRA is more than that. Come. You'll see."

She took Hannah's hand and pulled her toward the entrance and then through the door.

As Hannah had suspected, there was nothing ordinary about the interior. Like the outside, rectilinear patterns and geometric shapes designed the walls and ceiling. The space, painted in black and white, had an industrial quality and display platforms that came after each short flight of stairs. Furniture, carved wooden figurines, and clothed mannequins were artistically positioned on the ascending platforms. The exhibition-style retail space had up to ten customers who instantly turned when the woman at the front desk called out Dami's full name. They looked at Dami—recognition clicking in their eyes and then admiration and curiosity.

"Welcome back home," the young woman said, rushing away from the greeting desk. Her breasts jiggled as she pranced, bobbing rhythmically against the plunging neckline of her black blouse. She was voluptuous and tall, an imposing figure that enveloped Dami in a skintight embrace. "I heard about your father's death. I am so sorry. I'm praying for your family."

"Thanks, Mariam." Dami squeezed the woman affectionately.

"You're welcome, dear." She pulled back, and her eyes—dark, beady, and heavy with false lashes—fixated on Hannah. She cocked her head. "And who is this?"

"This," Dami said, beaming with pride, "is Hannah. We're sisters."

"Sisters." Mariam pursed her lips and nodded. "So the blogs were telling the truth."

"For once, yes. We met for the first time yesterday and are way overdue for some bonding. And as far as I'm concerned, shopping is the best way to bond."

"I couldn't agree more." Mariam gestured to the flight of stairs. "Feel free to go into your regular room. I'll have help waiting for you."

"Thanks, Mariam."

Hannah followed Dami's lead—up each short flight of stairs and then onto a display platform. Customers watched them as they climbed. Some lifted their phones; camera flashes went off. Hannah turned from the blinking lights. Dami appeared unfazed by what was happening.

It seemed like fame was attached to the Jolades. People noticed them in public. In fact, they were topics of discussion on blogs. What did that mean for Hannah? As the estranged daughter of Chief Jolade, would people subject her to the same intrusive treatment? Based on Tiwa's outburst at breakfast, it seemed like they already had. This didn't sit well with her.

When Hannah stepped onto the second floor, she entered a room that resembled a more traditional store layout with clothes on various racks. She joined the women rifling through the collection, eager to see what she might find.

"Hannah," Dami called out. "What are you doing?"

"Um . . ." She looked around in confusion. "Shopping."

"No. We don't shop there. This way."

We don't shop there. Strange, but Hannah didn't ask questions. She followed Dami to the third floor, where two girls stood beside closed double doors.

"Good afternoon, Ms. Jolade," they said in sync.

"Afternoon," Dami replied.

"I'm Mercy and this is Ini," one girl said. "We will assist you today."

They opened the doors, and Dami and Hannah walked through.

There was a fuchsia settee in the center of the copper-colored room and a two-piece coffee table atop a purple area rug. The space—a burst of vibrant colors—seemed more like a living room than anything else.

"Come on, Hannah." Dami sat and crossed her legs. "Sit."

"Yeah. Sure." She sat and looked around the room, searching for evidence they were on a shopping trip. The most customary indications—clothes, shoes, accessories, mannequins—weren't apparent.

"Can I get you ladies something to drink?" Ini asked.

"We'll have some champagne," Dami answered.

Hannah lifted a brow. *Champagne?* What kind of shopping trip was this? She glanced at Dami's heels and confirmed again that it was a shopping trip like none she'd ever experienced.

Ini left the room and returned shortly with two champagne glasses and a bottle of Moët. She popped the cork, poured the bubbling beverage, and handed a goblet to Dami and another to Hannah.

"To bonding," Dami said, raising her glass for a toast.

"Yeah. Bonding."

The goblets clinked together, and the ladies sipped—Dami leisurely and Hannah cautiously, as if she didn't quite trust the content in the glass. Who the hell sipped champagne on a shopping trip? Not her. She usually went for a Jamba Juice or a latte—something to keep her alert and energized.

"So, Hannah." Dami grinned. "We've already missed so much. I think it's time we really got to know each other."

"Sure."

Hannah couldn't deny she was curious. She'd come to Nigeria guarded, determined to hold on to her life in San Francisco, to the things she'd learned to be satisfied with. But she found that her guard was gradually falling, the need for more increasing as it had at breakfast when she asked about her grandparents. Her curiosity seemed involuntary; she couldn't control it and found herself slowly giving in to it.

"What do you do for a living?" she asked Dami.

"I'm a DJ. Shola's a fashion influencer."

Interesting. Such unconventional careers.

"Dad was very supportive of us pursuing our passions. He never pressured us into any of the family businesses. Well, he didn't have to, because Tiwa and Lawrence were willing to be a part of all that. They love all that serious, business stuff. That's why they left London and came back home after uni. Shola and I stayed and got our British citizenship. Different strokes, I guess." She shrugged and took a sip of champagne. "Anyway, enough about me. I'm dying to know more about you." She giggled as if they were teenage girls exchanging secrets. "What do you do for a living?"

"I'm a writer for an online publication called *Teddy Girl*."

"Oh. Another creative in the family. Love it!"

"Ms. Jolade," Ini said, stepping forward. "We've selected all our latest to show you both. Are you ready to see them?"

"Yes. Bring them in."

Ini and Mercy rolled in two racks of clothes; the mass of fabrics and colors swayed against one another as the girls moved forward. A third rack followed, displaying shoes and accessories that sparkled. Finally, the shopping could commence.

"This is Valentino." Ini pulled a black-and-white minidress with butterfly embroidery off the rack. "It only just arrived."

"And these Christian Louboutins will go perfectly with it." Mercy presented red pumps with intricate laser-cut details.

The salesgirls focused on Dami, awaiting her approval. While their lips remained smiling, the urge to please was clear in their eyes.

"Yes, to the dress. No, to the shoes. I already have a pair."

The girls scurried away, parting to create a yes and a no section. They presented another outfit to Dami, the same eagerness to please in their eyes. She made her decision all while sitting and sipping champagne.

Now Hannah understood why Dami had worn four-inch heels on a shopping trip. It was because her idea of shopping didn't involve bargain hunting or racing to a clearance item before another customer. For Dami—and perhaps for all the Jolades— shopping was a luxurious experience. Their wealth permitted it.

"Hannah, aren't you getting anything?" Dami asked. "I mean, I've seen your clothes and . . ." She bit her lip.

"And what? What's wrong with my clothes?" She looked down at her sunflower-yellow halter dress. "This is cute."

"Yeah. It totally is. But why don't we get you something exceptional?" She nudged her head toward the rack of clothes. "Come on. We're here to shop after all."

Hannah considered briefly, then nodded. "Okay. Let's shop."

Mercy and Ini showcased more items, and Hannah chose a few and tried them on, adorning herself in designer labels. She decided not to look at the price tags, certain she couldn't afford a thing. She was only having fun, entertaining Dami, who was voicing her opinions. Thankfully, there had been far more applauding and cheering than there had been booing.

"Come on!" Dami shouted at the closed fitting room door. "Come out! We don't have all day!"

"I'm coming." Hannah turned the knob and stepped out slowly, more gingerly than she had the last ten times—one foot out and then the other until she stood in front of Dami in a one-shoulder midi dress. The fabric, which clung to her body, had blue and yellow African prints. The salesgirls had paired the formfitting dress with gold strappy heels and a gold metal belt that pulled Hannah's waist inward and enhanced the curve of her hips.

With her thumbs twiddling, she waited for Dami's verdict— for a burst of boos or cheers. Though neither came. When Dami opened her mouth, she uttered only one word: "Wow."

Hannah smiled, grateful for the approval. She looked in the mirror that covered one wall and admired her reflection. She looked elegant. And despite her physical attributes, she looked like a Nigerian woman. It was a different version of herself— perhaps a version that would have existed had she known her father and lived in his world.

"You look incredible," Dami said, wide-eyed. "I'm kinda speechless right now. You have to get that dress. And of course, everything else you loved. It's on me."

"Thanks, but I can't let you do that." It was nice of her to offer, but it didn't feel right—accepting things, expensive things, from her when they had only just met. Besides, nothing else Hannah had worn mattered. She only wanted one thing. And if it wasn't too expensive, she could buy it herself. "How much is this?" she asked Ini.

"Three thousand, ma."

From the research on currency she had conducted before coming to Nigeria, Hannah considered the cost. Three thousand naira, as she recalled, was less than twenty dollars. "I'll take it! Do you have it in another color? Maybe I'll take two. It's only three thousand naira, so why not?"

"Um . . ." Ini frowned and looked from Hannah to Dami. "Ma," she said, fixing on Hannah again. "It's three thousand dollars."

Hannah felt it—the earth shift beneath the Jimmy Choos on her feet. Three thousand dollars for a dress. Her skin began to itch. She had developed a sudden allergy to the expensive fabric.

"I gotta take this off." She reached for the zipper at the side of the dress and turned toward the fitting room.

"Hannah, wait. What are you doing?"

"It's too expensive." She faced Dami and frowned. "I can't afford it."

"You're getting this dress, Hannah. And everything else you liked. I'll cover it. I already told you. It's on me."

"And I told you that you don't have to. It's too much money." Money that could be better spent elsewhere.

"Look." Dami stood and released a sharp breath. "You obviously love that dress, and you look spectacular in it. So let me do this for me. Please. Consider it a present. For every Christmas and birthday I've missed—all the ones Dad kept us from having together. Please. Just take it. I want you to."

Hannah studied Dami and knew that her offer to buy a three-thousand-dollar dress wasn't about splurging. The reason wasn't superficial at all. It was Dami's way of righting what had been done to Hannah—sort of like a gesture of consolation. And maybe for the Jolades, gestures were always grand.

"Okay." Hannah accepted the gift because rejecting it would have hurt Dami, and she couldn't imagine hurting someone so sweet. "Thank you."

"Of course." Dami smiled and turned to one of the salesgirls. "Ini, ring up my things and everything Hannah liked, including this outfit she's walking out of the store in."

"Yes, ma." Ini and her associate left the room, rolling the racks of clothes along with them and then shutting the doors.

"Wait a minute. What about my dress—the one I wore in?"

"Shh." Dami brought a finger to Hannah's lips. "Let's pretend that dress never happened."

They laughed, and their laughter filled the room—as beautiful and vibrant as the colors that decorated the space.

As their laughter died, Dami sat down and took on a more serious expression. "You know, Dad was planning a family holiday to Dubai, and he planned on inviting you. He wanted everyone to meet you before . . . you know."

"Really?" Hannah joined Dami on the couch. "He wanted to see me?" At the thought of what could have been, her lips stretched to a bittersweet smile. *What could have been but what wasn't.*

He'd had years to contact her, to introduce her to the rest of his family, to get to know her. But he had let all those years go to waste. She'd waited for him for so long, and he hadn't shown up. Recollecting her numerous disappointments made her throat tighten as she stifled a sob.

For years, she'd wondered why. *Why didn't he come? Why doesn't he want me? Why doesn't he love me? Why aren't I good enough?* She thought she'd stopped asking herself those questions. They were behind that closed door. But here she was—twenty-eight years old and still asking.

"Why did he wait so long?"

"I don't know." Dami watched her sympathetically. "I have no idea."

It occurred to Hannah that no matter how old she got or how much success she attained, no matter the depths of her mother's love or the extent of her best friend's loyalty, she would always have these questions, she would always wonder why.

"Hannah," Dami said. Her small voice was unsteady. "I don't know what kind of life you've lived without knowing Dad and us." Tears drenched her eyes, and her lips pinched together in a grimace. "I'm so sorry if things have been hard for you in any way. I'm so sorry if you've felt like Dad . . ." She huffed. "Like he didn't care. But you should know that I am so, so happy you're here. I'm pissed that he kept you from us. But I am so happy he fixed his mistake before he died—that he gave me a chance to know my sister."

She hadn't said, half sister. Just sister. *My sister*. Warmth gathered in Hannah's chest, wrapping around her heart, causing tears to sting her eyes. She would not cry. Because as she had often reminded herself, there is no crying in shopping—not even when there were no more samples at a sample sale.

She stared at Dami for a few seconds before doing the only thing that seemed rational—pulling her sister in for an embrace.

They held each other as something deeper than lighthearted pleasantries grew between them. They were bonding, consummating their sisterhood.

SIXTEEN

HANNAH

Hannah's mundane life had, since arriving in Nigeria, altered into something novel. The ordinary had become extraordinary. The three-thousand-dollar dress she wore out of the high-end boutique confirmed this. Her legs moved differently—graceful and sophisticated—having gained a new rhythm from the pair of Jimmy Choo sandals on her feet. As she made her way through the exit, customers watched her, admiring her like they hadn't when she was the girl in the yellow Target clearance dress.

Outside, the late-afternoon air was hot yet comfortable. The sun still shone in the cloudless sky, causing Hannah to squint while watching Ini and Mercy—each with shopping bags in their hands—walk through the gate that enclosed the building.

"Solomon is waiting outside," Dami said. She pulled a pair of cat-eye sunglasses from her purse and slid them over her eyes seamlessly. "He'll get the bags."

"Okay. Well, let's go." Hannah took a step forward and then paused. The person who walked through the gate made her heart jerk with surprise and then drum with excitement. *Lawrence.*

He was on the phone, conversing with a stern expression. Though, when he noticed Hannah, he stopped talking. He looked over her physique, then met her eyes, his stare so deep and engrossing, she tensed.

"Right. This again," Dami said. "Is this going to happen every time you two see each other?"

"Um . . . I . . . um." Babbles. It was all Hannah could produce. Her mind slowed, delayed in speech and action. She waited for her senses to return. It came gradually, like droplets filling a bucket.

Drop—sense of self. *Drop*—sense of awareness. *Drop*—good old-fashion common sense. *Drop. Drop. Drop.* Every ounce returned.

Hannah turned to her sister. "Sorry." She cleared her throat and breathed for the first time since seeing him. "I—"

"You couldn't help it. Yeah. I know." Dami rolled her eyes. "You two are obviously hot for each other, and that's exactly why he's here."

"Um . . . I don't understand."

"I texted him, told him we were done shopping, so here he is. Have fun." She waved goodbye and charged forward, toward the gate.

"Wait." Hannah seized her arm. "You're leaving?"

"Well, yeah. I think he wants to take you to an early dinner."

Dinner. Alone. Hannah pictured the scenario—a dim, intimate setting, a table small enough to keep two bodies snug, and an endless supply of wine that would eliminate every ounce of her wits. It was a setup disguised as chatting and eating when, in truth, it was foreplay. Was she ready for that—to be alone with Lawrence with no one and nothing to disrupt them? The reality was more nerve-racking than the fantasy that had played in her mind last night.

"What's the problem?" Dami assessed Hannah's tense expression. "Why do you look so nervous? You two are obviously into each other, so relax. Enjoy some time alone. Get to know each other, get cozy and . . ." She wiggled her eyebrows suggestively. "Do as your heart or your body desires."

Hannah laughed, her anxiety lessening. Flo had given the same advice, though she was more blunt in her delivery.

"Do you have a boyfriend back in San Francisco?"

"No."

"Then what's the issue? If there's no one in San Francisco, go for it. You look remarkable in that dress. You deserve a man who will worship you in it. And there he is." Dami glanced at Lawrence, who still stood by the gate. "Now, try to have fun. See you later." She strutted away, waved goodbye to Lawrence, and left.

Dinner. Alone. It would happen now.

Lawrence approached Hannah, one hand hurriedly stuffing his phone into a pocket. "Hey." He stood in front of her, so close to touching but not. "You look . . ." He blew out a breath. "Stunning."

Stunning. She loved the way his lips moved around the word, the way his accent touched each syllable.

"How was it—shopping with Dami?"

"Good." She reconsidered. "Actually, more than good. It was great. She's really sweet."

"I'm glad you had a good time. You must be hungry. There's a restaurant here. We could get something to eat."

"Yeah. I would love to."

"This way." With a hand on the small of her back, he led her to the rear of the building. It was a light touch, but even with the simple gesture, Hannah felt like she was on fire. It took every bit of resolve to stand upright.

They walked along the side of the cube-shaped building until they reached its rear—a bamboo-framed garden area. With the vibrant straw mats and multicolored thatched furniture, the outdoor space had an Afro-funk ambiance that combined traditional African esthetic with the hip. People huddled around tables, eating, drinking, chatting, and laughing. There was a reasonable distance between each set of tables and chairs and between strangers who mingled within their groups, but even so, there was a sense of intimacy in the atmosphere, a silent acknowledgment of kinship that unified.

"Here." Lawrence pulled out a chair at a table for two, and Hannah settled into it. He sat across from her, sporting a boyish grin.

"Mr. Bankole," a waiter said, approaching the table. "Good evening, sir." He tilted his head at Lawrence and then turned to Hannah. "Good evening, ma."

She had been called ma or madam too much since arriving in Nigeria. She wasn't used to the formality but presumed it was a part of the culture.

"Here you are." He handed them menus. "Can I get you started on drinks?"

"Yes. Please," Lawrence said. "I'll have the elderflower mojito."

The server turned to Hannah. "Ma, what can I get you?"

"Um . . ." She studied the list and picked the drink labeled with the prettiest words. "The passion sunrise."

"Okay, then. I will be back soon with your beverages." He

marched away, through the glass door and into the dim indoor dining space.

"This place is amazing." She looked around for a moment, then her eyes landed on Lawrence.

He sat quietly, a wide smile on his face as if the simple pleasure she got from the environment gave him some immense joy. "I'm glad you're happy. I know yesterday must have been overwhelming for you."

"Yeah. It was a lot, but today has been much better."

The server returned with two glasses on a tray and distributed the order accordingly, the red-and-orange beverage to Hannah and the translucent beverage to Lawrence. "Have you decided on what you would like to eat?"

"Um . . ." She scanned the extensive menu, unsure of what to choose. "Why don't you order, Lawrence. I'm good with anything."

"Sure." He only glanced at the menu before placing the order. "For appetizers, we'll have the sautéed snails and the grilled calamari *suya*. For the main course, catfish with grilled plantain, the coconut-and-lime barbecued prawns, and *jollof* rice."

"Yes, sir." The waiter jotted down the order and left.

Lawrence's focus settled on Hannah. He smiled, and she returned the gesture. It was happening—foreplay. Dinner. Alone. Though, they weren't entirely alone. They had caught the attention of various people in the outdoor eatery. The glances were subtle—not as obvious and intrusive as it had been with Dami. Nonetheless, it was discomforting.

"Does it ever stop?" Hannah asked, leaning into the table and whispering. "Do people always stare?"

"Oh. You've noticed?"

"It's kind of hard not to. It's been happening all day."

"Yeah. It wasn't always like this." He took a sip of his drink. "Chief had always been a well-known businessman, but the family wasn't in the public eye until Tiwa started dating a Nollywood actor."

"Nollywood?" She raised an eyebrow.

"Yeah. The Nigerian equivalent of Hollywood."

"Oh. Got it."

"Yeah. He was a very popular actor, and they dated for about six months when she was twenty-four. Even after the relationship ended, she was still a subject of interest. Then Dami started deejaying and started posting far too much on social media, and then Shola became this influencer, attending fashion shows in Paris and New York and all that. Things just escalated from there."

Hannah sipped the sweet, fruity drink that tasted just like its name—passion sunrise. "What about you? What did you do to gain the public's attention?"

"Absolutely nothing. I promise. I was just minding my business, and—"

"And you got drawn into the madness?"

"Exactly. I got sucked in by association."

Now, it seemed the same was happening to her.

"Here you are." The waiter appeared with plates. He placed them in the center of the square-shaped table. "Enjoy."

The skewered calamari, coated in an orange-brown powder, looked delicious. Hannah expected to see shells on the plate of sautéed snails. To her surprise, there were none. Just dark strips of meat.

"That doesn't look like a snail." She frowned. "I've had escargot before. My best friend, Flo, took me to this French restaurant and that doesn't look like what I had."

"You can't really compare the two. The French use small snails. Nigerians use much bigger ones. We cook them differently too—shell off and guts out." He picked up a fork, pierced one snail, and examined it. "I suppose they don't look much like snails now."

That fact would make eating them easier for Hannah. She picked up her cutlery, stabbed the snail covered in chili peppers, and popped it into her mouth. It had a slight crunch to it—unlike the slippery escargot she once forced down her throat. The snail was spicy, packed with flavors Hannah couldn't discern. "This is delicious."

"You know, this was your father's favorite restaurant," Lawrence said. "We would sit here for hours, eating and talking." He smiled—a firm line across his face rather than the curve that usually lifted his cheeks and made his eyes gleam. "He was a wonderful man. I'm sorry you didn't get an opportunity to know him." He extended his hand across the table. His fingers met hers; he touched them lightly, a gentle introduction before he took her hand and held it. "And I'm sorry he didn't get an opportunity to know you."

She squeezed his hand, grateful he had offered it. "You know, I met him once."

"Really?"

"Yeah. When I was eight."

Hannah only had a hazy memory of the encounter. But she still recalled the hushed phone conversation her mother had behind a closed door days before the visit—how her brash voice gradually shrunk and broke as she pleaded. "She's your daughter. She's always asking about you, Wale. Sending money isn't enough. She . . . she needs you. Please. Just see her." A week after that conversation, her mother announced her father was in town and wanted to meet. Hannah picked the prettiest dress in her closet, one with a pink sash bow that matched the ribbons around her puffy pigtails.

When they arrived on the eleventh floor of a fancy hotel, her mother knocked on a door. A man answered—tall, dark-skinned, handsome, her father. He towered over Hannah, a grand figure. She contemplated cowering behind her mother, but then he crouched, low enough that their faces aligned. He watched her intently, as if searching for traces of himself on her face. When he seemed satisfied with his examination, he smiled and extended a hand. "You must be Hannah."

It was strange, but Hannah couldn't recall anything after that. It was as if someone had plucked the memory from her mind. When she returned home that night, her mother had explained that the excitement of meeting her father had caused her to experience the moment too quickly. She had compared it to scarfing down a sundae and then realizing, once the bowl was empty, that she couldn't remember the taste because she had eaten it too quickly, without enjoying the flavors.

"So," Lawrence said, "he never reached out again after that one time?"

"Yeah." It still confused her. "According to my mom, the visit went well. He was happy to see me. She thought things would change going forward, but . . ." Hannah shrugged. "Nothing changed."

Years went by and nothing changed. Even though Hannah should have hated her father, she didn't. She couldn't bring herself to it. When she was a child, her mother would always say, "You can't hate someone free of charge. You have to pay a price—give something of yourself." She said this often while doing chores around the house or running errands or making dinner after a long day, constantly reminding herself not to hate the one person deserving of her hatred. It wasn't an easy thing to do, but she did it. And that decision, which she seemed to make every day, allowed her to be an exceptional mother and teacher and human being. And because Hannah wanted to be a woman like her mother, she had grown up repeating the same words. It was a reminder and a warning. She would have to give something of herself to hate her father. And she chose not to. The only emotion she held on to was resentment. Resentment didn't take up much room in her. In a way, it was the lesser evil.

She was twenty-eight and still resentful, but the emotion was half of what it used to be because the person deserving of it was dead. He was gone. What use was her resentment now, especially when another sentiment sat at the sidelines, waiting to take its place?

"Would you tell me about him?" she asked Lawrence. The curiosity that had caused her to ask about her grandparents and about Dami's occupation was present again, hungry and persistent. "What was he like? Did he have any hobbies?" She didn't release his hand, and he didn't attempt to release hers. She loved how her body quickly identified their interaction as something more than platonic. Her pacing heart knew this, her flushed skin was well aware of this, and the subtle pulse between her thighs was a result of this knowledge.

"Reading," Lawrence said. "Your father loved reading."

"Really?" Hannah leaned into the table. "I love reading." There it was—a shared interest between father and daughter. "What did he like to read?"

"African and African American literature mostly. He has a collection in his home office. I could show it to you."

"Yeah. That would be great." She beamed. "Thank you."

"Of course." His thumb caressed her hand with feathery strokes.

Music played lightly in the background. The sky had dimmed, but lamps brightened the space with a warm glow that further enriched the ambiance. Dinner. Alone. It was exactly what Hannah had pictured. The moment was near perfect until a large drop of water splattered on her forehead. That was the only warning the sky gave before it opened and released a burst of rain.

Squealing customers gathered their plates and rushed indoors. Hannah and Lawrence stood as well, their hands still clenched. When they made a move toward the restaurant, she stumbled. He gripped her arm and pulled her to himself, his quick reflexes preventing her from hitting the ground.

"You okay?" Water streaked down his face; the shiny droplets made his lips appear lustrous and alluring.

"Yeah." She inhaled sharply. The scent of dry soil hung in the air. She loved that smell; she breathed it in deeper and huddled against Lawrence's chest. She felt, through his wet shirt, the hard build of his body—the muscles, the definition, the strength. Her heart flapped erratically like the wings of a bird taking first flight. Her hair, weighed down by water, wilted over her face. Slowly and gently, he slid the tresses behind her ear, then flattened his palm on the nape of her neck.

Inhale. Exhale. She had to remind herself to breathe. It was necessary when they stood so close, subject to each other's full, unrelenting attention. Everything else—her dead father and her newly extended family—seemed trivial. The chaos of the world faded so they could have this moment.

He drew his lips near, slightly puckered, so close to touching hers when a shrill voice sounded over the patter of the rain.

"*Oga!* Madam!" It was their server, racing toward them with two umbrellas. "Please come inside." He suspended one umbrella over their heads. "The rain is very heavy, sir. You can eat inside."

"Thank you." Lawrence took the umbrella even though there was no use for it. They were drenched and unbothered, grinning at each other.

His arm curved around her waist and they walked inside.

SEVENTEEN

HANNAH

Hannah's damp, multi-print dress stuck to her body. Her soggy hair matted to her scalp. The smell of dewy earth was fresh on her flushed skin. She felt wonderful. They hadn't shared a kiss, but they were sharing a car ride, and Lawrence was playing a sensational selection of Nigerian music.

With each exuberant beat, Hannah shuffled in the leather seat. She found it difficult to sit still even though her movements didn't quite match the rhythm. Lawrence laughed, then showed her a simple hand routine more suited for the tempo.

"What's this one called?" she asked upon the start of a new song.

"It's 'Home' by Yemi Alade."

It was a love song—gentle yet still with that buoyant beat that roused her movement. Lawrence watched her, briefly taking his eyes off the road to offer a smile that had many layers to it.

Hannah wanted to study that smile, put it under a microscope, decipher all the meaning in it.

When the car stopped inside the Jolade estate, she stepped

out and didn't move until he stood beside her, close enough that his hand grazed hers as they walked inside.

"I'm sorry dinner got interrupted," he said when they entered the great hall.

"You don't have to apologize." The acoustics in the open space made her voice weightless. "It wasn't your fault it rained. Besides." She turned to him. "I had a great time."

"Even in the pouring rain?"

"Especially in the pouring rain." Taking a step forward, she closed the gap between them until they stood chest to chest. "That was the best part."

He offered that smile again, the one with layers of meaning; it slanted to the left, made his eyes shrink at their corners and made Hannah's breaths just a little scarce. His hand rested on the small of her back, pressed into her spine.

A smile, a touch, a stare, words spoken and unspoken. Hannah calculated these sweet, simple, little gestures that had occurred since their first encounter. Each had been gradually nurturing the connection between them, adding weight to something that was once so light.

"What happened to you two?" Dayo's orotund voice sounded unexpectedly, startling Lawrence and Hannah. "You're soaking wet." He approached them with an erect posture—always poised, always businesslike, especially in another well-fitted three-piece suit.

"We got caught in the rain," Lawrence answered. His collected tone didn't indicate what had almost occurred as they stood in the pouring rain.

"Oh. I see." Dayo looked between them, at the closeness of their bodies, at Lawrence's hand on Hannah's back—comfortable and possessive. "Well." He cleared his throat. He did not pry. "Hannah, I dropped by to see how—"

Tiwa barged through the living room doors suddenly and marched toward Dayo. When she stopped at his side, she glanced at Lawrence and Hannah. Her lip curled upward. "Urgh." She turned her attention to Dayo. "Can we talk?"

"Not now. I'm having a conversation with Hannah."

"Seriously?"

"Yes. Seriously."

An intense moment of silence followed. Tiwa and Dayo glared at each other, their eyes having a conversation their mouths did not.

"Anyway," Dayo said, ending the wordless exchange. "Hannah, I wanted to see how you're adjusting. How's everything going?"

"Great." She glanced at Lawrence and smiled. "Everything is great."

"Wonderful." Tiwa rolled her eyes. "You have her answer. Now, can we talk?"

Her nagging didn't have much of an impact on Dayo. He dismissed it, not even turning to acknowledge her. "Hannah, I'm actually not the only person who has been waiting to speak with you. Jumoke, your father's younger sister, is here. She has been waiting for you." He motioned toward the living room, but Hannah did not move. "Is there a problem?"

"Um . . . I'm a mess." She signaled to her wet clothes. "Maybe I should get cleaned up before meeting her." First impressions were once in a lifetime.

"How about saying a quick hello? She has been waiting for an hour and has become rather restless, and may I add, somewhat irksome."

Hannah contemplated briefly, then bobbed her head. "Okay. Sure." She followed Dayo into the living room, Lawrence close at her side and Tiwa dawdling behind.

The room was packed, every member of the family present.

"Auntie Jumoke." Dayo addressed a woman who sat with her back to him, speaking with Iya Agba and Sade. "This is Hannah."

The woman quickly abandoned her conversation and spun around. "My dear." She stood and walked forward. A loose-fitting dress draped her stout figure; the purple lace fabric matched the scarf on her head. "My beautiful girl." She cupped Hannah's cheek. "I'm your father's sister. Jumoke. You may call me Auntie."

"Sure. It's nice to meet you. Auntie."

Since Hannah could remember, her family tree had only ever consisted of two people—her and her mother. Though, it was expanding now. This sudden growth made her surprisingly happy.

"It's so wonderful to meet you, to see you." Auntie Jumoke beamed. She had skin like Tiwa—dark brown with bronze undertones.

Hannah noted something else about her appearance—a feature she saw whenever she looked in the mirror or at the picture of her father. She saw that feature again, while looking at her aunt—a nose with a short bridge and wide base.

"We have the same nose," she said.

Auntie Jumoke drew her attention to the center of Hannah's face. "Yes. I suppose we do." She smiled and hugged her niece. "My dear, you're wet." Even with that knowledge, she didn't pull away.

Hannah settled into the tight embrace; the duration of it didn't bother her. She enjoyed the comfort Auntie Jumoke's plump figure and soft, warm skin provided.

When they separated, Hannah blinked sharply, then squinted, seeing her aunt with fresh eyes. For a moment, she was no longer someone she had just met but someone she had met before . . . somewhere. She didn't have a solid memory to support this idea, but her instincts felt certain.

"You look really . . . familiar. Like we've met somewhere before."

"No, dear. Your father only told me about you a few weeks ago. Besides." She cupped Hannah's cheek tenderly. "I would definitely remember meeting you."

"Yeah. Of course." Hannah nodded and disregarded her inkling.

"Anyway," Auntie Jumoke went on, "we were just picking the *aṣọ ẹbí* for your father's funeral."

"*Aṣọ ẹbí*?" She had heard those words before—at breakfast that morning. "What's *aṣọ ẹbí*?" The instant Hannah asked, she caught Sade rolling her eyes.

"Jumoke, we do not have time for a lesson," Sade said, her tone flat. "Please let us pick one, so I can carry on with my day." She obviously had the same tolerance for Hannah as Tiwa.

"If your schedule is too full and you cannot provide time to pick *aṣọ ẹbí* for your late husband's funeral, then please leave. There is the door. Use it. Go and occupy yourself with something far more important."

Auntie Jumoke stared down Sade with a fierceness that even Sade cowered to. Her eyes dropped, and she stayed seated.

"Hannah." Her tone was bubbly again, her eyes free of that intimidating fierceness. "To answer your question, *aṣọ ẹbí* is like a uniform Nigerians wear during events and celebrations. A family usually picks one material and everyone makes an outfit with it. Then they wear it on the day of the event to represent solidarity."

"Oh." Interesting. "Will I be wearing an *aṣọ ẹbí*?"

"Yes, of course. You are a part of this family, my dear. In fact, why don't you choose the one we will use." She directed Hannah to the yards of materials spread out on the chair. They were stunning, each with various patterns and colors.

"There aren't any black ones. It's a funeral."

"Your father died at sixty-five. He was mature. Traditionally, we only wear black when a person dies young."

"Oh. I see."

"Well, go ahead," Auntie Jumoke urged. "Pick one. We have been going back and forth for days. Some say they like the red, some say the green, some blue. I am tired of arguing. We will go with whatever you choose. And that is final!"

Those last words were not for Hannah but for the people in the room—Sade, Tiwa, and Shola—who grumbled. The others seemed unconcerned. Dami absentmindedly flipped through a magazine, Segun scrolled through his phone, and Iya Agba sipped tea gingerly.

"Go ahead, dear. Choose."

Hannah studied the selection. The burnt-orange fabric with detailed floral embroidery and touches of pearls caught her attention. "That one. It's gorgeous."

"Yes. Good choice." Her aunt picked up the material and held it in the light. "Your cousins will love this."

"Cousins? I have cousins?"

"Yes. Two girls and two boys. They are currently not in the country, but they will be here for the funeral."

And the family tree continued to expand.

"I have already told them about you, and they are very—"

Tiwa's deafening screech interrupted Auntie Jumoke.

Everyone turned to her, watching as she gaped at her phone.

"What? What is it?" Sade stood and scurried to her daughter. "What's wrong?"

"This is." She extended the phone to her mother, who looked at the screen and then at Hannah and Lawrence.

"What is it? Let me see." Auntie Jumoke snatched the phone, looked at the screen, and again at Hannah and Lawrence.

The phone went around the room, each person mirroring Sade and Auntie Jumoke's reactions. When the device reached Lawrence, he and Hannah peered at what had stunned everyone.

It was a picture of them in the rain—their bodies pressed together, their lips almost touching. It was a beautiful shot—like a scene out of a romantic movie. Though, there was nothing romantic about the caption that accompanied the photo. *Romance within the Jolade Family: Cute or Incestuous?*

Hannah couldn't bear to raise her eyes and look at the others in the room. The exposure was embarrassing and unfortunate. The privilege of exploring their attraction and connection privately had been revoked with a single snapshot.

"If you think hooking up with Lawrence will make you a real part of this family, think again. You don't belong here." Tiwa's voice echoed in the silent room.

Lawrence and Auntie Jumoke reprimanded her, but it changed nothing. Tension gathered in Hannah's throat. She wasn't sure if she was going to break down, scream, or vomit. Whatever the case, she had to be alone.

She rushed out of the living room. In the great hall, footsteps trailed her.

"Hannah, wait," Lawrence called out.

She increased her pace, made it halfway up the stairs before he caught her arm.

"Please don't be upset," his voice was so tender, so sweet. "Don't let Tiwa bother you. She's just being . . . Tiwa. And the blogs are just looking to get clicks with ridiculous headlines. Of course we aren't related. Chief Jolade didn't even adopt me. The blogs are just doing what they do best—stirring up gossip. Don't let it upset you."

She pressed her eyes closed and expelled a rough breath. "It isn't just about the blog."

It was about what Tiwa had said.

Her comment took Hannah back to when she was a teenager, studying the picture of her siblings, imaging herself among them, knowing she would never fit in. Tiwa was right. Hannah didn't belong here—not with these people, not in this world. She had to disregard her curiosity and focus on the only reason she'd come—to attend a funeral. She couldn't get caught up in anything else. Not even whatever was happening between Lawrence and her.

"I came to Nigeria for my father's funeral. That's it. That's the only reason I'm here. This wasn't part of the plan."

"What wasn't part of the plan? This?" He took her hand, intertwined their fingers, and squeezed. The center of their palms pressed together. "It wasn't part of my plan either, but it is now." He climbed two steps, so their bodies aligned—chest to chest, face to face, as close as they had been in the rain.

Though, unlike that moment, every trying factor in Hannah's life—her dead father, her newly extended family, the intrusive media, Tiwa's words—was now loud, hectic, aggressive like a swarm of wasps. She couldn't ignore the buzzing; it clouded her judgment, amplified her insecurities, and forced her to retreat to safety.

"I think we should just stay away from each other." She pulled her hand from his. "I'll be leaving in a few days anyway. I'm sorry."

She turned and climbed up the stairs as quickly as her heels allowed, forcing herself not to turn around. Not to look at him.

EIGHTEEN

SHOLA

You don't belong here.

Tiwa's words to Hannah, only minutes earlier, ran through Shola's head. She understood how it felt to not belong. She understood being ostracized and ridiculed for being different. She'd learned all of this at sixteen when her father enrolled her and Dami in a prestigious all-girls boarding school in England.

Shola had lived in Nigeria her entire life. The people and the culture were all she'd ever known—her understanding of normal. While she had gone on holiday with her family many times, those trips were brief, and her normal was always intact, waiting for her return.

Living in England threatened Shola's normal, not only because she'd left her country, but because the people in her new home—some ignorant and some prejudiced—made her normal seem abnormal.

It started with the assumptions. Because Shola was from Nigeria, her classmates assumed she couldn't speak English very well and that she attended the school on a scholarship. Then the questions started. One teacher, unable to pronounce Shola's full name, asked if she would like to assume another name, a nickname—something English. She'd suggested Sara.

On a Sunday afternoon, Shola and Dami had worn dresses made with *ankara*; the patterns and colors were so different from the pastel dresses the other students wore. After noting the disparity, a supervisor had approached the twins with a forced smile and a straight, rigid posture and said, "Darlings, did you really think this dress was an appropriate choice for afternoon tea?"

Questions and assumptions were prejudice wrapped up so neatly in passive aggression, only the person it was directed to was aware of it. Any other person would have explained it away.

The bullying, however, was unmistakable. "You don't belong here. Go back to your country," students would say whenever adults were out of earshot.

In their shared room, Shola and Dami cried. On the phone, they told their parents in Nigeria everything. They were tired and wanted to come home. Shola remembered listening to her father breathe as she waited for his answer. Frankly, she had expected him to buy them tickets home immediately. Instead, he'd cleared his throat.

"No," he'd said sternly. "You both are staying exactly where you are."

"But, Daddy—"

"Listen to me. I know it isn't easy. I didn't expect that it would be. And that is exactly why I sent you there."

"You sent us here to be humiliated?" Dami snapped.

"No." He fell silent for a moment, and then he sighed. "My loves, there is a world beyond ours. There are people who, because of their ignorance or prejudice, will indirectly or directly discriminate against you. Unfortunately, the world is full of people like this. Some learn and change and some never do. But it is not your responsibility to educate them. The only responsibility you have is to yourself—to hold on to your pride, your culture, who you are despite the people who will tell you, in so many ways, that who you are is wrong."

"So you sent us here to teach us a lesson?" Shola asked, a quake in her small voice.

"Yes. A lesson that both Tiwa and Lawrence learned in the same way. And a lesson you will learn too and carry with you all your life."

Back then, Shola had been livid. But with no other choice, she'd learned the lesson her father intended her to. She'd done it with her sister. Together, they dealt with the assumptions, the questions, and the bullying. At first, Shola questioned her worth. Then she fought those thoughts with the confidence her father had instilled in her at a young age. It was hidden under layers of insecurity, but she dug it out, dusted it off, and wore it like a goddamn crown. By the last term of school, the bullying stopped, prompted by the wave of diversity and inclusivity and #Black-LivesMatter. Being woke was suddenly trendy, even for those skilled at neatly wrapping up their prejudice in passive aggression.

While in university, Shola learned that often, there was an unsaid rule about diversity—you could be different but not too different, black but not too black, Nigerian but not too Nigerian. True diversity required shrinking your identity to be half of what you were—just enough that your difference wasn't threatening and didn't make others feel uncomfortable and didn't disrupt the manufactured ecosystem already in place. That was when Shola and Dami became more adamant about being unapologetic and unabashed about who they were.

Dami started to wear her natural hair—each strand combed into an Afro rather than tamed in a plait or hidden beneath inches of straight weave. At the same time, Shola wore the stunning *ankara* dresses at the back of her closet. She took pictures in these dresses, posing at several England landmarks, merging her culture with another. She posted these pictures on Instagram, eventually gaining a large following and creating a brand as an Afrocentric fashion influencer.

Shola didn't think much about the events that shaped her, but she did now because of what Tiwa had said to Hannah.

You don't belong here.

Shola had caught the distraught look on Hannah's face, and it had felt like looking at a reflection of her sixteen-year-old self. No one deserved to hear those words. She should have said something the instant Tiwa uttered them. Instead, Shola had sat unmoving and mute—too overwhelmed to express her shock, disgust, and anger.

Auntie Jumoke had gone home and everyone else to their rooms, but Shola still sat in the living room, regretting not reprimanding Tiwa. But more than that, regretting how she'd been treating Hannah. Whatever resentment she'd once felt disappeared. It was displaced anyway. Truthfully, Shola was angry at her father, not at Hannah.

Hannah had done nothing wrong. Hannah was her sister, who now possibly felt like Shola had all those years ago—worthless and like an outsider.

And absolutely no one deserved that.

NINETEEN

HANNAH

After a warm shower, the earthy scent of rain left Hannah's skin, replaced with the floral scent of honeysuckle. She slipped on pink pajamas and curled under the duvet with her phone pressed to her ear, waiting to hear her mother's voice.

While it was 8:00 p.m. in Lagos, it was noon in San Francisco. Her mother was likely in the teacher's lounge on her lunch break. Hannah was counting on that. When the ringing stopped, she exhaled.

"Hey, Mom." She attempted to sound upbeat, but her voice shook.

"Honey?" Her mother's delicate tone sharpened. "What's wrong?"

"I . . . I just . . ." Hannah wanted to tell her everything that had happened since they last spoke. Instead, she said what weighed on her most. "I miss you, Mom. So much."

"Oh. I miss you more." Her voice lost its edge. "Do you want to hear something funny? Today, I planned on dropping by your place with dinner. I had everything planned—lasagna, wine, and cheesecake. But then I remembered you weren't here." She laughed and then sighed, as if each chuckle had taken a lot out of her.

"I wish I were there. Lasagna, wine, and cheesecake sound really good right now."

"Is everything okay?" The edge returned to her mother's voice. "You don't sound like yourself."

"Um . . . well, I—"

A knock at the door cut Hannah off. Immediately, she pictured Lawrence on the other side. Even after what she had said to him, she still hoped to see him. Sometimes emotions were so damn fickle.

The knock sounded again, and Hannah sat up. "Mom, there's someone at my door. Can I call you back?"

"Sure. We'll catch up later."

Hannah ended the call and climbed off the bed. After pulling the door open, she tensed, surprised.

"Hi." Shola fiddled with the hem of her pajama shorts. "Can I come in?"

"Um . . ." Hannah was perplexed but decided to do what she'd done since landing in Nigeria—hope for the best. "Yeah." Her voice cracked. She cleared her throat, smoothed out all the kinks inside her. "Sure."

In the room, Shola settled on the chaise longue at the foot of the bed.

Hannah sank into the cushioned seat, closer to the edge than to Shola. "Is everything okay? Did you need something?"

"I actually, um . . ." She shoved her fingers through her hair, and the gold trinkets on the long locks rattled. "I came to check on you."

"Check on me? Why?"

"What Tiwa said earlier was horrible. Despicable. It was completely uncalled for. Are you okay?"

Hannah had not expected that. She regarded Shola, trying to reconcile the two versions of her—the person who had been cold to her at breakfast and the person who sat beside her now, her sincerity both blatant and compelling. "Yeah. I'm fine. Thanks for asking."

They sat in silence for a while. It was awkward. Shola twiddled her thumbs, while Hannah looked through the window and at the velvety darkness that veiled the sky. As she considered the best way to break the silence, Shola spoke.

"Dami told me you're a writer. What kind of stuff do you write?"

"Mostly lifestyle pieces."

"That sounds interesting. If you don't mind, I'd love to read some of your work."

"Yeah. Sure."

Again, Hannah was surprised—not just at Shola's turnaround, but at herself. Downstairs with Lawrence, she had agreed to forget her curiosity and focus on the sole reason she had come to Nigeria. But as she watched Shola, whose face was so identical to Dami's, she remembered again how fickle emotions were, how quickly things could change.

"Dami told me you're a fashion influencer," she said, welcoming her curiosity, feeding it.

"Yeah. I am." Shola dug a hand into her pocket, pulled out her phone, and worked her thumb against the screen. "Here."

Hannah took the phone and scrolled through the Instagram page. Her eyes broadened while admiring the vibrant, whimsical pictures. In each shot, Shola wore extravagant Nigerian attire while performing distinctly English activities.

The most captivating image was in a tearoom. Shola sat among women in pastel dresses, all posed as if enjoying afternoon tea. Shola, however, with a teacup in her hand, wore a ruffled gown with bright African prints. The massive head wrap covering her hair matched the multicolored, multi-patterned dress. The picture, and others on the page, was an exquisite juxtaposition of cultures. Each of them—whether taken at the polo club or against the backdrop of Big Ben—was glamorous and boldly depicted Shola's culture, which she flaunted proudly.

"These are brilliant."

"Thank you. The one thing Dad taught us was to be proud of our culture—no matter where we went."

Hannah wished she had gotten the same lesson. Though to be proud, she would first have to know what it meant to be Nigerian, and she didn't know that. Another missed lesson.

"Segun is still trying to figure out how to be proud though," Shola said. "His fake American accent used to piss Dad off."

"Fake?"

"Yeah. He's lived in New York for only a few months. He does not have an accent. But he sure as hell can fake one."

"Why would he fake one?"

"He's young. I think he's just trying to figure out who he is."

Segun had grown up with everything Hannah didn't have—a connection to his culture, a father who taught him to be proud of that culture—and he was still uncertain of who he was. Hannah always believed having her father in her life would simplify things. She imagined not shying away from questions about her ethnicity, but answering them confidently. She imagined that a father and a connection to her heritage would make her more certain of who she was. But that wasn't the case for Segun. How was she so sure it would have been the case for her? She dismissed the thought and focused on the pictures.

"Wait." Hannah's mouth dropped open. "Is that Lupita Nyong'o and Naomi Campbell?"

"Yeah. Paris Fashion Week."

"You're sitting in the front row. With them." She examined the photo closer, marveling.

"So . . . um . . ." After a brief pause and a sharp inhale, Shola went on. "Sorry I've been such a bitch to you. I was angry at Dad. He lied to us for years. I was upset and needed to process. I'm sorry." She wore the apology on her face—on her brows that furrowed, her lips that bent in a tight frown, and her earnest eyes.

"Don't worry about it. Forgiven and forgotten."

"Thank you." Shola's face brightened instantly. "So . . ." She shuffled toward Hannah until their knees touched. "How was shopping with Dami? Get anything good?"

"Yeah. Basically everything in there." She pointed at the walk-in closet where all her new and expensive clothes hung, courtesy of Mary.

It still felt strange, owning such pricey things. She had walked out of the boutique in a three-thousand-dollar dress, but could she wake up in the morning and put on another dress with the same price tag when there were less privileged people just across the bridge? Were the Jolades aware of this imbalance? Did they do anything to help the less fortunate in their country? Or did they hide away in their guarded paradise?

"Looks like you got some good stuff. Sorry I missed it."

"It's fine. Maybe we can all do something next time."

Shola thought for a few seconds. Her eyes wandered then stilled. "Dami and I are getting our hair braided tomorrow. You should come to the salon with us. You could get your hair braided too."

"Yeah. That sounds fun. I would—"

A knock at the door cut Hannah off. Again, she hoped it was Lawrence. In a shaky voice, she permitted entrance and held her breath.

"Hey!" Dami's bubbly, singsong tone resounded as the door

cracked open. She entered the room, paused, and looked from Hannah to Shola. "Are we having a sleepover? 'Cause I'm so here for it." She squealed, raced forward, and threw herself on the bed. Dents misshaped her Afro, once the perfect circle.

"Well?" She propped up on her elbows and looked at her sisters. "What are you guys waiting for? *Oya*. Come *na*!"

Hannah and Shola shared a playful look then jumped on the bed. They laughed as they bounced against the plush comforter.

"Isn't this fun?" Dami asked once both girls were settled— Shola to her left and Hannah to her right. "My followers would die to see this." She lifted her phone and angled it at their faces.

"No pictures," Hannah protested. "After today, I just . . ."

"Right. I get it." Dami set the phone aside. "For what it's worth, it was a good picture. It kinda reminded me of that scene from *The Notebook*."

"Oh! I love that movie," Shola said. "You know, I made Dad watch it once." She chuckled. "And he said he wasn't crying, but I swear there were tears in his eyes."

The twins spoke about their father, recounting memories—so many memories. Hannah closed her eyes, listened, and envisioned herself in each scene.

"Do you remember how he used to go on about this house?" Dami asked.

"Urgh." Shola rolled her eyes. "How could I forget?" She cleared her throat, deepened her voice, and took on a thick Nigerian accent. "'This house is a part of our family legacy, just like the businesses. After all, I built it with my own hands, poured my sweat into it.'"

"What?" Hannah frowned. "He built it himself?"

The twins laughed.

"As if." Shola's voice returned to its normal pitch. "All he did was hire architects, a construction crew, and interior designers.

But manual labor aside, Dad put a lot of work into this house. We were eight when he bought the land, nine when construction started, and eleven when it was done. He was so particular about every detail."

"He obsessed over it," Dami added. "But that's because he wanted to create a palace and a home and a haven, not just for us but for our children and theirs. That's why this house meant so much to him. And that's why it's always going to stay in our family."

They spoke for hours, laughed for hours, held back tears for the same duration. Though, Hannah's grief differed from the twins. While they mourned the man they knew, she mourned the man she never knew, the man who seemed like an amazing father.

Soon, their loud, vivacious voices softened to whispers that eventually died out. They fell asleep, their limbs sprawled over each other, snoring and sighing and sleeping so deeply, no one heard the knock at the door or the gentle voice that called out, "Hannah."

TWENTY

HANNAH

Just as she had in the boutique, Hannah looked in the mirror and saw a different version of herself—one that would have existed had she known her father and lived in his world.

She touched the straight cornrows that ran from her hairline to the crown of her head. The rest of her curls puffed out where the plaits stopped. She had never worn her hair in cornrows or braids.

When she was a child and her hair grew thicker and longer, her mother had taken her to a black hair salon, where a group of women listed the best products and methods for maintaining curls. Her mother learned quickly and mastered a meticulous hair care routine. Once a week, Hannah would place her head over the kitchen sink while her mother worked shampoo then conditioner then oils into her hair. She would then style Hannah's floral-scented hair into puffy pigtails or a high ponytail or simply allow the springy curls to fall to her chin.

When Hannah grew older, she spent hours watching hair tutorials on YouTube, learning new techniques for her 3C curl pattern and new styles that went beyond her mother's range. Bantu knots, cornrows, Senegalese twists, and box braids were achievable with a trip to a salon, but for Hannah, there was a sort of pain in that process—in sitting before a hairstylist, alone and clueless.

It had always seemed like she needed a community for the experience—aunties, cousins, sisters with a similar hair texture, who were familiar with all the styles hair like hers could hold and who, through their own experiences, could share techniques, ones she didn't have to research, ones that were passed down.

When Hannah started working at *Teddy Girl*, she had written an article about how sharing beauty rituals bonded the women within a family and a community. Throughout her life, Hannah and her mother had bonded over many things, but never their hair because of the vast differences—straight strands and tight coils. So Hannah had given up on having that familial beauty bond, as she'd called it in her article. But then upon arriving at the salon with her sisters, Shola had leaned into her and said, "I have the most amazing mixture of rosewater and peppermint oil that I use whenever I get my hair braided. It keeps my scalp hydrated, and it smells amazing. Remind me to give you a bottle when we get home."

Shola, likely believing she had said nothing significant, didn't know what that moment meant to Hannah.

Now, the hairstylist, a young woman with fast hands and a sharp mouth, slicked Hannah's baby hair with a fruit-scented gel, then clipped gold beads on each cornrow. When she stepped back, she smiled and admired her handiwork without the slightest hint of modesty.

"Ah!" she said, bumping her shoulders to a song only she could hear. "I have done it again *o*. See how hair fine. Madam Hannah, you look good *sha*. In fact, this one pass good. You look"—she kissed her fingertips, then fanned them out—"perfecto."

"Thanks, Jenifa." Hannah turned in the revolving chair, viewing the style from various angles. "Honestly, this is the prettiest my hair has ever looked."

"I've only known you for three days, but I'm gonna go ahead and agree with that statement!" Dami shouted from the far end of the salon, where she was getting a pedicure. "You look damn good, sis!"

"Yeah. You really do."

"Thank you." Hannah turned to her right, where a hairstylist added finishing touches to Shola's long braids that were identical to Dami's.

"I'm finished, ma. I hope you like it." Unlike Jenifa, Shola's stylist smiled modestly, loosened the apron around her waist, and paced to the receptionist counter.

Shola's phone on the vanity buzzed. She looked at the screen but didn't answer the call. "It's just my boyfriend. I'll call him back later."

"You have a boyfriend. That's nice. What's his name?"

Shola beamed. "Ben. He's the best." She eyed Hannah. "Do you have a boyfriend in San Francisco?"

"No. I don't."

"Oh. Okay." She inspected her hair in the mirror, then took a selfie. After uploading the picture to Instagram, she turned to Hannah. "So, speaking of Lawrence."

"What?" Hannah frowned, confused. "Literally, no one was speaking about him."

"Well, I am now." She sat up straight and smiled. "You're into him, aren't you? You fancy him just a little or a lot."

"Do you and Dami take turns playing cupid, or is it more of a team venture?"

"Well, excuse us for trying to give two people a chance at love."

"Love?" Hannah scoffed. "Okay. That's a bit much."

"What? It's not like you have someone back in San Francisco, so what's the problem? Did the stupid blog post get to you?" Her eyebrows drew together. "Listen, Hannah. As a Jolade, you might appear in a blog occasionally. You're just getting a heavy dose of attention because you're fresh meat. Things will die down. Eventually. But don't push Lawrence away because you're a little freaked out."

"Push him away?" What did she know?

"He told me what happened yesterday—how you broke things off before they even got started. He tried to play it cool and act like he wasn't hurt, but he was. You know, he really likes you."

Hannah loved hearing that—confirmation that her feelings were reciprocated. It allowed her to be candid about her emotions. "I like him too. I really like him but . . ."

She only had five more days left in Nigeria. What was the point of starting a relationship that would end the moment she got on a plane to San Francisco?

"But what?" Shola urged. "If you both like each other, what's the issue?"

Hannah narrowed her eyes. "Why does this even matter to you? Why are you and Dami so determined to set us up? Isn't it a little weird for you guys—the fact that Lawrence and I like each other?"

"I don't see why it would be. All that matters is that you two light up whenever you see each other. And with everything this family is currently going through, it's nice to see some glimpse of happiness—even if it's just between the two of you. Besides." She slipped a lock of braid behind her ear and grinned. "You should know that I'm sappy as hell. I'm sort of a hopeless and shameless romantic, and seeing you crazy kids together brings me so much damn joy." She huffed and sagged into the chair, her hands pressed to her heart, and her eyes skyward and elated.

Hannah couldn't help laughing at Shola's far-off, dreamy stare. She hadn't expected it, but her sister was playful and goofy. And what was even more unexpected was how considerate she was.

"So tell me." Shola jerked upright, serious again. "What's the real reason you're pushing Lawrence away?"

"I'm going home in a few days. What's the point?"

"Live for today and let tomorrow worry about itself. Dad used to say that a lot. Maybe you should stop speculating about the future. You're here and he's here, so just go with the flow. Whatever happens, happens."

"Really? That's not very comforting."

"Okay. Think about it this way." She slapped her hands together and leaned into Hannah. "In the scenario where you carpe diem, you get to be with the incredible man you have feelings for. And in the scenario where you overthink things, you're alone and likely very miserable. Which do you prefer?"

Hannah tipped her head side to side, weighing the scenarios, but the answer was simple—indisputable. "Carpe diem," she said, smiling.

"Well, there you go." Shola mirrored her sister's smile. "Carpe the damn diem."

TWENTY-ONE

HANNAH

At a little past eight at night, Hannah and the twins stepped into the great hall. They had gone from the salon to a restaurant for a late lunch and then to the seamstress for the *aṣọ ẹbí* fitting.

"Well, well, well." Segun came down the stairs in a slow stride. "So, y'all went to get your hair braided and just left your boy out." He reached the landing and eyed each of them. "'Ight." He slid a hand over his cornrows that weren't as neat as Hannah's. "I should be mad, but"—he looked over his sisters, this time with a faint smile on his lips—"y'all look good. Especially Hannah."

"Really?"

"Yeah," he said. "You're definitely pulling that look off."

"Well, I sure as hell wouldn't say that." Tiwa appeared from somewhere—the dining room, the living room, hell. It was hard to tell. She strutted forward and stopped beside Segun. "Yesterday, it was the dress. Today, it's the hair." She sneered, her gaze a blend of disdain and mockery. "I don't think I've ever seen anyone try so hard to be something they aren't. It's actually really pathetic."

Tiwa's callous voice resounded in the great hall. The words pierced Hannah deep where a similar wound was still healing. The night before came to mind—the details vivid, the emotions raw. Though, rather than turning away as she had then, Hannah stood her ground. She had run out of patience, no longer willing to excuse Tiwa's antagonizing comments.

"Look," she said, her tone firm. "I know this whole situation— me being here unexpectedly—is a lot. I get it, so I've been trying to excuse your attitude. But at this point, it just seems like you're a very miserable person. And frankly, I'm over it."

Tiwa's stunned face gave Hannah some satisfaction as she marched away. She heard the twins scolding Tiwa, but that didn't stop her from leaving. Hannah needed some space—time to cool off.

The garden was beyond the French doors in the dining room. She turned the knob and stepped out. Though it was dark, lights lined the gravel pathway; the soft glow helped her spot a stone bench. She sat down, and the warm breeze shuffled her skirt; the red material flew up then flattened on her thighs. She watched the repetitive motion, focusing on it rather than her anger. Her attention was so centered, she didn't notice the person who joined her in the garden until he sat beside her.

"Hey, Lawrence."

"Hey."

They glanced at each other, then looked at the flowers and leaves polished with moonlight. The swishing of air and chirping of crickets filled the silence that followed their greeting. Despite what had occurred between them the previous night, it was a comfortable silence—not awkward at all. They stayed quiet for a few minutes until Lawrence cleared his throat.

"I heard what happened with Tiwa. Are you okay?"

"Yeah." She shifted against the stone bench. "I'm fine."

"Do you want to talk about it?"

"She's impossible," Hannah blurted. "I hate her."

"You don't," Lawrence said resolutely, as if he was more in tune with her feelings than she was. "You don't hate her, Hannah."

"Okay. Fine. Maybe I don't hate her. But she's just so . . . ugh." Her hands fisted.

"Hey." He held her fists; his gentle touch caused each curled finger to unravel. "It's okay."

"No. It's not. She is so damn frustrating."

"Trust me. I know the feeling. When I was a child and my mother used to bring me to the Jolades', Tiwa would torment me." He chuckled. "I used to go home in tears."

"But then she stopped, and you guys became friends."

"Yeah. But it didn't happen so easily. Tiwa is a tough girl. She has a combative spirit by nature. If you want to earn her respect, be as tough as she is."

"So that's what you did when you were a kid?"

"It's what I had to do, so I could stop going home in tears." His eyes moved across Hannah's face, studying her brooding expression. "Don't get me wrong. Tiwa can be a lot. But once you get to know her, really know her, you'll see she isn't who you think she is. She's just as vulnerable as everyone else."

Tiwa? Vulnerable? Hannah had seen no traces of vulnerability. It must have been a joke. She wanted to laugh, but then she got distracted by Lawrence—by his hands that were still holding hers, stroking gently, soothing her anger.

Carpe diem.

The phrase came to mind, and she shuffled against the bench until there was no space dividing them. Their legs touched. She exhaled.

"Lawrence, I'm sorry about last night—about what I said."

"You don't have to apologize."

"Yes, I do. I had a great time with you yesterday. But . . ." She breathed heavily. "I think I got in my head a little—started over-thinking things."

"And how are you doing now?"

"Well, I think—"

"Wait. Before you continue, I just . . ." He ran a hand over his trimmed beard. "Look. I don't mean to sound like I'm in pri-mary school, but I like you, Hannah. Very much. I thought you should know. In case it wasn't obvious."

"It's obvious, Lawrence." Evident in each smile, touch, stare, words spoken and unspoken—the simplest, sweetest gestures. "I like you too. In case you've been lying awake at night wonder-ing."

"Well, since you mentioned it, I came to your room last night because I was lying awake . . . thinking about you."

She laughed and shoved him playfully. "Yeah, right."

"I'm not joking."

She noted his serious expression, and slowly, her laughter faded. "Really?"

"I knocked. You didn't answer. I thought maybe you were sleeping or maybe you didn't want to see me."

"I was sleeping." She rushed out the words. She couldn't let him believe anything else. "I must have been sleeping. Of course, I would have wanted to see you. In fact, I was hoping you would come."

"You were?"

She nodded, and he touched her—his palm to her cheek. He leaned forward, and she breathed deeply. He smelled amazing, his cologne a spicy woody blend with citrus notes. Their prox-imity increased her pulse. Suddenly, time whirled, then slowed, then stilled, lost all its relevance; they were free of its conse-quences, like treasures in a time capsule.

A kiss. Hannah sensed it was coming, and she had—since meeting him—thought about this moment constantly and had one particularly vivid dream about it. But the moment, unlike her dream, had all the bittersweet elements of reality.

Her butt ached against the stone bench—bitter.

The heels she had been wearing all day pinched her toes—bitter.

Some unknown insect whipped past her ankle—bitter.

Lawrence was so close—sweet.

His head tilted, and their mouths aligned—sweet.

His lips, smooth and supple, touched hers. That was the sweetest part.

Fantasies or a vivid dream couldn't compare to this. Their lips parted. They exchanged breaths—something given, some-thing taken. The kiss was tender and slow and perfect. His tongue worked against hers, stroking leisurely until the need for more made each stroke more intense, more desperate. His hand came to her thigh just as the wind blew her skirt up. She wrapped her arms around his neck and pressed their chests to-gether. A soft moan seeped through her lips, a hoarse groan through his. The wind whistled, the crickets chirped. There was an accord with all the sounds—a symphony of nature and de-sire. It was only the sharp clearing of a throat that seemed out of place. The sound reoccurred even as Hannah tried to ig-nore it.

"Um . . . guys? Guys!"

Hannah and Lawrence jerked apart and turned in the direc-tion of the voice.

"Hey," Dami said, grinning. "So, I'm glad this is happening.

Yay. But maybe it can happen somewhere else—maybe a room, a bathroom, a closet. Anywhere but here. 'Cause you guys have an audience." She directed their eyes to the glass doors where Iya Agba, Shola, Segun, and Mary stood, their smiling faces eerily illumined by moonlight. "Yeah. They've been enjoying the show."

"Oh my gosh." Hannah turned away, her hand shielding her flushed face. "That's so embarrassing." Far more than the blog post had been. Though, unexpectedly, she giggled rather than cower away. "How long have they been standing there?"

"Long enough. I had to come out here before things got really heated."

"Wait." Lawrence glared at Dami. "So you were watching too?"

"Um . . ." Her guilt-ridden gaze shifted from left to right. "We're having a movie night. You guys should come." It wasn't the slickest attempt at changing a topic, but it worked nonetheless.

"Oh," Hannah said, her eyes wide with interest. "That sounds like fun. What are we watching?"

"*The Wedding Party*. It's a Nollywood movie. It's great. Hannah, you'll love it. It starts in twenty minutes. Change into your pajamas and join us. Bye." She trotted toward the house and opened the door, giving way to whistles and applause that erupted from Shola and Segun.

The door closed, and it was quiet again.

"By the way," Lawrence said. "I forgot to tell you how much I like your hair." He touched it—ran a finger along the cornrow closest to her ear. "You look beautiful." His finger dropped and trailed the soft contour of her cheekbone.

"Thank you." She leaned forward and pecked his lips. "I

guess we should go inside. Don't wanna miss movie night. You know, I've never seen a Nollywood movie. I'm curious."

"Well." Lawrence stood and extended a hand to her. "We should get you a front-row seat, then."

"A front-row seat?" She accepted his open hand and stood. "How about a back-row seat instead? Just so I can alternate between watching the movie and kissing you without drawing too much attention."

He grinned and squeezed her hand. "Yeah. I like that idea."

TWENTY-TWO

HANNAH

Hannah realized it had been naive to assume something simple or remotely average when Dami mentioned movie night.

With the Jolades, things were never ordinary.

She sat beside Lawrence in the last row of a fifteen-seat home theater with a fully stocked snack bar. Shola, Dami, and Segun sat in front of them, munching on popcorn and candy. Everyone wore pajamas, as per Dami's dress code.

"Are you enjoying the movie?" Lawrence whispered into her ear. His breath smelled sweet and fruity, courtesy of the Skittles he had been eating.

"Yeah. It's great. I love it."

It was a hilarious and lively film centered on the wedding of two people from different Nigerian tribes. Hannah loved the portrayal of the cultures—the clothes, the music, the dancing.

"Hannah! Hannah!" Dami called from where she sat. "This is my favorite part! You're gonna love it."

"How about you just let her watch it," Shola shouted.

"How about you both be quiet!" Segun snapped. "I'm trying to sleep."

"Then go to your room! Gosh!" the twins said together.

The yelling stopped.

Hannah regained her focus and leaned into the massive screen, totally immersed. The closing credits rolled a little after eleven. Everyone left the theater except for Segun, who had fallen asleep with a Twizzler dangling from his mouth.

Lawrence walked Hannah to her room, just as he had on her first night. He pushed the door open, and she stepped inside, while he remained in the hallway.

"Um . . . are you going to come in?"

"Hannah, I—"

"Come in, Lawrence."

He entered. He'd been waiting for an invitation—for permission. He wasn't presumptuous. Hannah liked that.

The door closed, and they were alone—safe from prying eyes.

"I didn't stick to the plan," she said.

"And what plan was that?"

"To do this." She stood on her toes and kissed him. "While we were watching the movie."

"Yeah. You completely ignored me." He pouted. Though it wasn't a convincing portrayal of sadness. "I think it's only fair you make it up to me somehow."

"Okay. And what do you have in mind?"

"Just one simple thing—answer a question."

It wasn't the request Hannah had hoped for, but she allowed it. "Okay. Ask."

"Why did you wear this?" His fingers dropped on her shoulder, on the spaghetti strap of her tangerine-orange camisole.

"Because Dami asked everyone to wear pajamas," she answered. "And these, as you might have noticed, are pajamas."

"And you decided to wear this specific one." He looked down

at her legs, at the matching shorts with lace trimming. "When you knew I would sit beside you."

"I'm not sure what you're implying." Her lashes fluttered. A coy smile appeared on her face. "I simply wore my pajamas."

"And I'm simply trying to get the truth out of you."

"And what truth do you presume that is?" she asked.

"That you wore this little ensemble because you wanted to distract me, drive me crazy."

"Me?" She gasped, an over-the-top expression of shock that lacked all sincerity. "I would never. "If the mundane things I do drive you crazy, then . . . oops."

"Hannah, nothing you do is mundane—not a damn thing."

Their lips locked instantly. This kiss, unlike their first, didn't start slow and gentle. They didn't ease into it—they dove into it with full intensity.

He grabbed her ass. She slipped a hand under his T-shirt and ran her fingers along his chest. Their breaths turned heavy. Their hands moved swiftly, eager to explore. Hannah tugged on the drawstring on his sweatpants and undid the knot.

"Hey." He stepped back suddenly—away from her hands— and exhaled. "It's getting late. I should go."

He wanted to leave. She had moved too fast, been so caught up in the moment and strictly acting on the basic instinct to feel. "Lawrence . . . I . . . I'm sorry. I didn't . . . I wasn't thinking."

"Hey. Relax." He kissed her briefly—just enough to assure her everything was okay. "We're in a packed house. I don't want us to get carried away. We have time, Hannah."

But they didn't. She would leave in a few days. The thought depressed her.

"What are you doing tomorrow?" he asked. "Do you have any plans with the twins?"

"No. None that I know of."

"Then would you like to spend the day with me?"

Not a few hours. Not an afternoon or an evening. Not even a night. A day. A whole day. With him. "Yes. I would love to."

"Great. I'll plan something." He took her hand and planted a soft kiss on it; his lips lingered. "I guess I'll see you tomorrow, then."

"Tomorrow?" It seemed so far away. "Why don't you stay a while. We could hang out—talk." She took his hand and drew him toward the bed, not giving him the opportunity to turn down her request.

"Okay." He sat on the bed. "What would you like to talk about?"

"Well, we can start with the basics." She sat beside him. "What's your favorite color?"

He laughed. "Really? That's what you want to know?"

"Yep. Go ahead. Answer."

"Green. You?"

"Purple."

"Oh. You know, the night we met, you weren't wearing shoes. And your nails were painted purple."

Hannah slapped a hand over her mouth. "Oh, my God. You noticed I wasn't wearing shoes? I was really hoping you hadn't." Her embarrassment passed quickly as she watched him. "You remember the color of my nail polish?"

"I remember a lot of things about that night." His gaze moved over her frame slowly and suggestively. When his eyes met hers again, he smiled. "Next question."

She cleared her throat and tried to ignore the heat creeping up her skin. "Favorite movie?"

"*Jerry Maguire*," he answered. "Yours?"

"*Matilda*."

"Isn't that a children's movie?"

Hannah's face went straight. "Isn't *Jerry Maguire* a romance?"

"Sports romance," he said. "Emphasis on sports."

Hannah stared at him, her expression still deadpan.

"Okay. Fine." Lawrence laughed and tossed his hands up. "You got me. It's a romance. Shola made me watch it a few years ago, and I've loved it since."

"No judgment here." Her features softened again. "Favorite food?"

"Rice and stew."

"What's that?"

"One of Nigeria's most popular dishes. When you try it, you'll understand why. What about you?"

"Lasagna. My mom makes the absolute best." She sighed while recalling the taste.

"Tell me about her," Lawrence said. "What's she like?" He reclined on the bed, his folded arms propping up his head.

"Well, she's really sweet and always in a good mood. She's all about making the best out of what you've got—looking on the bright side of things."

"And what does she do for a living?"

"She's a teacher." Hannah rested on the bed, beside Lawrence. "At a middle school. She's taught there for years and loves it."

"What about you?" He turned to face her and placed his arm over her waist. "I have no idea what you do for a living."

She loved the weight of his arm on her; she tried not to focus on the thrill it gave her as she answered. "I'm a writer. I work at an online publication called *Teddy Girl*. It's all about female empowerment."

"*Teddy Girl*. That's an interesting name."

"Yeah. It refers to the young women in England, who were

trying to assert their independence after World War II. They had a whole movement going on with their style and their atti- tude."

"Oh. That's cool. And do you like working at *Teddy Girl*?"

"I love it," she gushed. "I get to meet and interview a lot of interesting people and then write their story. That's my favorite part—writing. But honestly, the dream is to be an editor one day." She had often imagined helping other writers shape their articles while also actively contributing to the operation of *Teddy Girl*. She craved that responsibility and imagined being a power- house like her current editor, Yín. Though, a lot less critical and strict. "Anyway." She shook away the fantasy. "For now, I'm happy as a writer."

"Well, I would love to read some of your work. I'm looking you up the moment I leave."

"Knock yourself out. I'm sure you'll be impressed."

"I don't doubt it." He drew her closer. "So. What do you like to do in San Francisco when you aren't working?"

"Well, my best friend usually drags me off to some fancy party or event."

"Like the one where we met?"

"Yeah. Like that. She usually takes an hour to network, and then we hang out—eat, drink, people-watch, and dance off- beat." The memory made Hannah smile. She hadn't realized how much she missed Flo until this moment. They'd been text- ing since she arrived, but it wasn't the same. "Anyway, I also volunteer at a community youth center. I think I spend most of my free time there."

"Really?" Lawrence slanted his head to get a better view of her face. "You volunteer with youths? And do you enjoy it?"

"Of course. That's why I do it. I've been volunteering there for years. It's great."

"Well, I think that's wonderful." He stroked her flushed cheek. "So? Do you have any more questions for me?"

"Yeah. Tell me more about what you do for a living. Tech, right? Do you love it?"

"Yeah. I do love it. I've always been interested in it. But after I completed my studies, I worked for Fortune Oil, your father's oil marketing and power generation company. I worked there for four years, but I wasn't passionate about the industry."

"Then why didn't you look for another job—something you'd love?"

"Nigeria's job market isn't like America's. There are a lot of graduates with multiple degrees, who can't find jobs. Because of the Jolades, I had an opportunity many don't, so I made the best of it—used it as an opportunity to learn."

"Oh. I see."

"Anyway, all the work I did at Fortune Oil paid off because when the tech industry started to thrive in Lagos, your father wanted to buy a start-up and grow it. And he wanted me to spearhead the whole thing." His voice softened as his eyelids flapped slowly. "And I did that with Tiwa's help. And now, we're . . . um . . ." His eyes fell shut completely, and his breathing deepened.

Hannah gently ran a finger along the lines of his serene face. He didn't stir. "Good night, Lawrence."

She thought of curling up against him and falling asleep as well. The thought soothed and excited her, but she couldn't sleep just yet. She was thirsty, a result of her Q&A.

Regretfully, she crawled out of bed, left her room, and descended the stairs. With everyone asleep, the house was unusually quiet and had an eerie aura that made Hannah's steps swift.

She hastened across the great hall and approached the kitchen. At the entrance, she heard shuffling and other sounds

difficult to discern. This didn't help the already uncanny atmosphere. Hannah's heart thumped. Her nails dug into her palm.
Afraid, she decided not to step inside, but curious, she poked
her head in for a quick peep. That was when she discovered the
source of the shuffling and the other sounds she now recognized as Tiwa moaning—Tiwa moaning while kissing Dayo.

She sat on the kitchen counter, while he stood between her
open legs. They were going at it—kissing and doing other things
Hannah couldn't make out in the dim light. Actually, she didn't
want to see the extent of what they were doing. She ducked behind the wall as Dayo pulled away from Tiwa.

"I cannot keep doing this with you," he said, his tone curt.

"Dayo, stop all this *na*," Tiwa whined. "Can't we just go back
to the way things were before?"

"Lying to your family about our relationship? Keeping it a
secret? We have already been through this. The answer is no."

Dayo and Tiwa were in a relationship, one they'd been keeping a secret. Why hadn't they told anyone? It was strange but
none of Hannah's business. Gently, she tiptoed away. It seemed
like the heated conversation would come to an unpleasant end
at any moment. She crept up the stairs, confident her presence
had gone unnoticed. As she strolled to her room, still reeling
from the discovery, a figure in a sweeping gown appeared at the
far end of the hallway. The white, long-sleeved ensemble had a
massive ruffled base that gave the illusion of a cloud.

Hannah froze, unsure of who or what was approaching her.

"What are you doing?" Sade's voice sounded just as her identity became apparent.

Right. It wasn't a ghost or anything of the sort. Just an icy
woman with a peculiar taste in sleep attire.

"Um . . . I went to the kitchen for a drink of water." *And saw
your daughter having a late-night rendezvous.* "I'm going to bed

now." She walked past Sade, keeping her distance. It seemed like the sensible thing to do.

"Why are you here?"

"Um." Hannah stopped walking and turned to face Sade. "I just told you. I went to get a drink."

"In this house. Why are you in this house? Is it because of the money?"

"Money? What money?"

"Your inheritance. The one your father left you."

"Why in the world would he leave me an inheritance? He didn't even know me."

"He knew of you," Sade said. "He was a generous man. He must have included you in his will."

"And you think that's why I'm here?"

"Why else? You have only come to collect what does not belong to you."

With every ounce of restraint, Hannah bit back a profanity. She was livid. Since coming to Nigeria, she had endured a lot from a family who was understandably shocked and confused by her arrival. She had tried to overlook so much, but her patience had run out with Sade as it had with Tiwa. Being called an opportunist pushed Hannah to the brink. She wanted to retaliate but calmed herself by closing her eyes and breathing slowly, concentrating on the subtle, seamless way air moved in and out of her body.

Breathe in. Breathe out. Slow. Easy.

When she opened her eyes, her glare was firm on Sade.

"I get it." She spoke through clenched teeth. "My father lied and cheated on you with my mom. That is unfortunate, but it is not my fault. I am the result of what he did—not the reason he did it. He hurt you, but he hurt me too. More than I can express." Her jaw relaxed, her shoulders sagged slightly. "I met him once in my life and that was it. That was it. I waited for him. I hoped he would come, but he never did. So believe me, I'm just as hurt and confused and angry. But I am not taking my anger out on anyone, so stop taking yours out on me."

Rather than walking away, Hannah kept her eyes on Sade, proving she wouldn't cower. They stood, watching each other. When Hannah's stance and glare did not waver, Sade turned and strode off.

TWENTY-THREE

✦

SEGUN

Segun stood on a step, frozen. He extended his head above the railing. When he saw his mother enter her bedroom, he climbed the rest of the steps and approached Hannah.

"Well, look at you," he said, clapping slowly. She spun to face him, and he smiled. "First, you took on Tiwa and now, Mom. All in one day." He stopped clapping. "I gotta admit, I didn't think you had it in you."

"Segun, where in the world did you come from?"

"From the movie theater, where you guys left me. Y'all couldn't even wake me up and tell me the movie was over?"

"Well, you said you were trying to sleep so . . ." She rolled her lips into her mouth and fought back a laugh.

"Haha. Very funny."

Her lips were straight again. "So." She eyed him. "You heard all that?"

"Every word." He was tempted to give her another round of applause.

People didn't go around confronting his mom. The woman was intimidating as hell. She had a soft side, but reserved it for her family—the people she loved. The rest of the world got icy, assessing glares and passive aggression glazed over with elegance. And people put up with it because of who she was. But Hannah hadn't. And it had been damn entertaining to watch.

"I wish I had gotten it on camera. It was epic."

"Well, I wasn't trying to put on a show. I was just pissed. She thinks I'm here for money—an inheritance."

"Yeah. I heard that."

"So?" She considered him, her eyebrows furrowed. "Is that what you all think?"

Segun huffed and pushed the hood off his head. He dropped on the white velvet bench set against the wall. It was more of a decorative piece in the hallway, small enough for just two people. He motioned for Hannah to join him, and she did.

"I heard what you said about Dad. How you've met him only once—how he never showed up for you. That's fucked up."

He imagined how it must have been for her—not knowing their father. He put himself in the same position but pushed the thought out of his mind almost immediately. He couldn't imagine it. He didn't want to. His father was gone now, but at least he had known him. At least he had memories, and they made his loss somewhat bearable.

He'd been staying up lately—unable to sleep, recounting those memories. He had a new appreciation for them and his father, now that he was gone. Segun remembered how he'd taught him to drive. He'd been such a patient and coolheaded teacher, even when Segun mistook the accelerator for the brake and drove into the gate. Why hadn't he appreciated his father's temperament? Why had he rolled his eyes during each of his father's lectures on business and life? Why hadn't he taken an interest in his hobbies—the many novels that filled his office shelf or his collection of old Fela records?

His father had loved music, and that was the reason Segun learned to play the piano as a child. The melodies his little fingers created used to fill the house for hours, and while his mother would beg him to stop, his father would hover over him, proudly encouraging him to carry on. Their shared love of music had connected them, but as Segun grew, it seemed to separate them. Whenever his father played Afrobeat in the car, Segun would put on his headphones and listen to hip-hop. Once, his father, trying to close the gap between them, had asked to hear a hip-hop album. In turn, he proposed Segun listen to Fela, the greatest Nigerian musician of all time. But Segun had responded, "I don't wanna hear that crap. And besides, you won't even get hip-hop, so why bother? Just do you, and I'll do me."

Why the hell had he said that? Why had he been at such odds with his father? Why had his father's passion for his culture pushed him toward another?

Whenever Segun thought of it, he came up with no good reasons. He'd just been a stupid kid set on defining himself. As the only son, he'd felt pressured to be a certain way. The weight of his father's legacy had been so grave. And although his father never asked anything of him, he'd felt that weight regardless, and it caused him to forge another identity, one that was so different from his father's. He wished he hadn't done all that. He wished he had different memories, memories of talking with his father, laughing with him, learning from him, and learning about him.

But at least he had memories. Hannah didn't even have the privilege of reminiscing and envisioning do-overs.

"I think you're here because you never knew Dad," he told her. "And this seems like your only chance to. I get it. If I were in your shoes, it's the same reason I'd be here. I would want to know him." He bit the inside of his cheek while holding back tears that only ever fell when he was alone in his room. "Even now, I wish I had known him better. Because I think I kinda blew my chance."

Hannah's eyes softened, sympathetic.

Fuck. He didn't want her feeling sorry for him or anything. Was she going to make him talk about his feelings now or hug him and make this whole situation sappy as hell? He didn't know what to expect. But Hannah said nothing. She just sighed and dropped her head on his shoulder. She stayed there, soundless. And seconds later, after Segun recovered from the shock and adjusted to her closeness, he lowered his head and rested it on hers.

They stayed that way for a long while, neither one saying a word.

It was nice.

TWENTY-FOUR

HANNAH

Beside Lawrence, Hannah had slept well. She woke up early in the morning, refreshed, and left him asleep while she got some exercise. Thanks to Mary, Hannah wore the perfect tennis attire. The pleated white dress swayed against her thighs as she walked outside.

Evergreen shrubs stood eight feet tall, surrounding the tennis court and secluding it from the pool and the garden on either side of it. Hannah stepped through the arched entrance carved into the groomed hedges, then froze. She had not expected to see Tiwa, swinging a racket at flying balls, her skirt flapping along with her side-to-side movement.

Instantly, the image of Tiwa and Dayo's late-night tryst entered Hannah's mind; she tried to push it out but wasn't successful.

The tennis ball machine emptied, and as a maid collected the balls around the court, Tiwa spun to Hannah. She straightened her stance and grimaced. "What the hell are you doing here?"

It was far too early for this—for the bad attitude and the insults that would likely follow. "I'll come back when you're done."

"Yeah. Go entertain yourself with one of my siblings who have somehow built a tolerance for you. I have not."

No matter how much Hannah tried to be civil, Tiwa never seemed to let up. Maybe Lawrence was right. She had to be just as tough. "You know what?" she said. "Why don't we play a game?"

Tiwa hissed and turned to the maid, who was still squatting and gathering balls. "Mimi, for Christ's sake, can you be fast?"

"Yes, ma! I'm coming, ma!" She ran to the machine and poured the balls into the bucket.

"Hey." Hannah approached the maid with a friendly smile. "She won't be needing this anymore. Please take it away."

"What the hell do you think you're doing?" Tiwa shouted from the other end of the court. "Mimi, don't you dare listen to her!"

"What's the problem? Intimidated by a little competition? Maybe you're afraid I'm better than you."

Tiwa laughed as if she'd heard something truly absurd. When her face fell flat, she turned to Mimi. "Give her a racket."

The maid obeyed. She rolled the machine away and handed Hannah a racket and a ball.

"Serve," Tiwa said.

"Sure." Hannah adjusted her visor, shielding her eyes from the sun. "Ready?"

"Just do it!"

"Is that what you tell Dayo when you two get it on?" The instant Hannah finished the sentence, she swung her racket.

The ball entered Tiwa's court, but she didn't aim for it. She stood, motionless. "What?"

"I said, is that what you say when you play with Dayo? Mary mentioned you two like to play together. Play tennis, of course."

"Oh. Yeah." Her enlarged eyes shrunk to their normal size. She exhaled. "We . . . we play tennis. Sometimes."

"Mm-hmm." Hannah pressed her lips together and fought the urge to laugh. "By the way, that was a score for me." In every sense. "Fifteen–zero."

The next time the ball came toward Tiwa, she didn't miss it.

They went back and forth until Hannah's swing caused the ball to hit the net.

Tiwa smirked. "Your hand getting tired already?"

"I'm fine." Hannah served again, more aggressive this time.

Tiwa returned the aggression, and soon, she was ahead.

"Fifteen–forty." Hannah bit her lip after announcing the score. This wasn't how she intended the match to go. She bounced the ball and prepared for another serve, when she saw Dayo through the arched opening, walking toward the kitchen door. Talk about a saving grace.

"Hey, Dayo!" She waved him over. When he approached her, she smiled. "Good morning."

"Good morning, Hannah." He glanced over at her opponent. "Tiwa."

"Hi." Her persona changed immediately. She was no longer the woman with a mean mug and a firm stance, determined to win a game. Now, she was a woman desperate for the attention of a man. She softened her gaze and took a more feminine stance. "What are you doing here? Did you want to see me? I could—"

"Tiwa. Please." He pressed a finger to his temple and rubbed circles into his skin as if trying to repress a headache. "I only came by to drop off some documents for your mother." He looked away from her. "I should go. You two have a good day." He hurried off while clutching his briefcase.

Tiwa stared at the departing figure, her lips pinned in a frown. Hannah didn't expect it, but she suddenly felt sorry for her.

"Do you want to continue the game?" Hannah asked. "We could stop. Or take a little break if you want."

A harshness resurfaced in Tiwa's eyes as she turned to Hannah. "If you feel like quitting, go right ahead. I'm perfectly fine!" Obviously, she didn't take any downtime. She stayed in character even while shamelessly pining over a man. "Hit the damn ball or leave!"

Hannah didn't hesitate. She served, and although Tiwa lurched forward, her racket missed the ball. Seeing Dayo had thrown her off—distracted her. Hannah used this to her advantage, and within minutes, she was ahead.

"Hey. What's going on here?" The question came from Lawrence, who stood at the sidelines.

Having an audience increased the intensity of the game. Hannah and Tiwa hit the ball back and forth. They completed one game and then another. The sun rose higher. They completed two more games. Hannah's skin turned damp with perspiration. Her throat was dry. She was so close to winning the set but also very thirsty. Her determination wavered slightly. The ball came to her again, and when she flung it over the net with her last bit of strength, Tiwa shuffled to the right only to miss it.

"Yes!" Hannah threw her arms up. "Looks like I just won!"

"You got lucky. I wasn't on top of my game today." Tiwa clenched her jaw, the sharp lines on her face defined. "Besides, I'm sure you haven't had a lot of wins in your pathetic life, so enjoy this."

To Hannah's surprise, she wasn't hurt or offended. She was just curious. Did it ever stop with Tiwa—the attitude, the insults? Was there more to her? Could she be as kind as the twins and easygoing as Segun? Maybe not. Maybe Hannah had to accept that and do what Lawrence had advised—be just as tough.

With that in mind, she approached the net with her head held high. "Maybe you would've been on top of your game if you hadn't been so distracted by Dayo, your boyfriend. Or whatever he is to you."

"What? What . . . what are you talking about?"

"I saw you two last night. In the kitchen."

A combination of shock and horror crossed Tiwa's face. It was rare, but it was there—vulnerability. It almost seemed out of place.

"Hey," Lawrence said, walking toward the two women. "That was a great game."

"Thank you." Hannah accepted the compliment with a smile. Tiwa, still stunned, did not say a word.

"Anyway, I just exhausted all my energy playing. I'm starving. Breakfast, Lawrence?"

"Yeah. Sure." He held her hand, and they walked toward the arched entryway. "I must admit, I was surprised to see you two together. Is there hope for a cordial relationship after all?"

"Who knows what the future holds. Anyway." She watched him, amused. "You kinda passed out last night. One minute you were talking and the next, you were out. How did you sleep?"

"Better than I have since I got back from San Francisco." He squeezed her hand. "I guess I should credit that to you."

"Maybe you should make a habit of sleeping with me every night." She winked, walked through the door he held open, and entered the kitchen just as her stomach growled. "I'm so hungry."

"Madam, would you like to place a request for breakfast?" the chef asked Hannah. He was a tall man, formally dressed for his role in a white double-breasted jacket. Though, his pants and toque were an African print fabric.

"No, thank you," Hannah said. "You don't have to do that. I can make my breakfast."

"It's my job, ma. It's not a problem at all."

"Um . . ." She was still hesitant.

"It's okay, Hannah." Lawrence placed an encouraging hand on her back. "Andy will make whatever you want. Just tell him. Go ahead."

"Um . . . okay." She turned to the chef. "I would like some *akara* and scrambled eggs. Please. If it's not too much trouble."

"It isn't, ma. Your breakfast will be ready in forty minutes." He turned and disappeared into the pantry.

"I still can't believe they live like this—maids and a chef. It's crazy."

"You get used to it after a while," Lawrence said. "I did when I first moved in. It definitely took some adjusting to because this place is nothing like Ajegunle."

"Ajegunle? What's that?"

"It's where I lived with my mother before she died. It's an incredibly poor part of Lagos—another world from this."

"Oh." Hannah wanted to know what life was like beyond the Jolades' fenced utopia. She was also curious about Lawrence and the life he lived before. "Will you take me there—to Ajegunle?"

"What?" His brows creased in a frown. "You want to visit a slum?"

"I want to see what it looks like. I want to see where you grew up."

Hannah understood she was asking for something that probably had a prerequisite of intimacy. Their relationship was new and lacked that element. So she was being rather bold with her request, but she asked anyway, hoping he would make an exception for her. She wanted to know him. Lawrence was worth knowing.

"Um . . ." He watched her closely then nodded. "Okay. It's not how I wanted us to spend the day, but okay. I'll take you."

"Thank you."

"Sure." His arms circled her waist. He pulled the visor off her head and planted his lips firmly on hers.

"Mmm." She clung to him as he controlled the kiss—slowly locking then releasing her lips, and then pressing smooth strokes on her tongue with his. When they separated, Hannah's chest swelled, filled with air she hadn't expelled during the kiss. *Breathe.* She had to remind herself. "You know what? You're a really good kisser."

Lawrence laughed. "Thank you. So are you." He kissed her again, and again, Hannah—utterly consumed—forgot to breathe.

TWENTY-FIVE

HANNAH

A foul stench made the humid air more intolerable. Hannah refused to display any signs of discomfort. After all, she had asked
to come here—to Ajegunle, where Lawrence once lived.

During the car ride, she had looked through the window and
watched the scenery alter as Solomon drove farther away from
Banana Island. It had been a gradual disintegration, starting
first with the way the smooth road became uneven. The car's
wheels sank into potholes, then lurched out in a manner that
made Hannah sway against Lawrence. Lampposts disappeared.
Wooden utility poles lined the streets; the loose wires connecting them sagged so low, it wouldn't take much effort to grab
hold of them. Rusty tin-roof shacks in tight clusters replaced
stunning mansions. People, yellow buses, rickshaws, and motorcycles crammed the street. There were no luxury vehicles in
sight, so the Range Rover Solomon drove especially stood out.

When the car had stopped and Hannah stepped out, the air
she inhaled confirmed the change of environment more than
anything else.

"There's a canal just ahead," Lawrence had explained. "It's

infested with waste. It's basically a sewer. That's the reason for the smell."

Now they walked toward that canal. The street was a mixture of sand and trash—mostly deflated packets with logos and colors that had faded because of exposure to the elements for what must have been years.

"I lived there with my mother." Lawrence pointed at a bungalow caked with grime. It must have been a radiant aqua blue at some point, but now its color had dulled significantly and the crooked, corroded gate that surrounded it served no true purpose. "It looked a little better back then. It's gotten worse." He didn't near the house. Rather, he watched it from afar like a child terrified of approaching the one house in the neighborhood rumored to be haunted. "My mother died in that house."

Hannah didn't know that. If she had, she wouldn't have asked to come. "Lawrence." She took his hand. "I'm so sorry. I didn't know. We can leave. Let's go."

"It's okay." He looked at her and then at her hand that was gently nudging him to turn away. "We don't have to go. I haven't been in that house since it happened, but I come here often."

"Why? Doesn't it make you sad?"

"No. Coming here reminds me of her." He observed his surroundings with acute focus as if invoking memories and watching the playback in the precise places they had occurred. A small smile touched his lips. "Look." He drew Hannah forward, toward a narrow, busy intersection. "That's where my driver used to pick me up for school."

"You had a driver?"

"Well, not exactly. My primary school was about forty minutes from here, so my mother paid a taxi driver to take me to school and bring me home every day."

"Oh. Weren't there any schools closer to your house?"

"Those weren't very good. My mother wanted me to go to a school with a better education system. She wanted me to have more opportunities."

They turned into a bend in the street and entered one of the many clusters of rusty tin-roof shacks. Hannah was grateful Lawrence had advised her to wear comfortable shoes that completely covered her feet. Her pink Puma sneakers were a sensible choice because the ground was rough, the layers of garbage as much a foundation as the drenched soil. Children in tattered clothes and flip-flops kicked a soccer ball without the slightest care. It occurred to Hannah that Lawrence had probably been one of these kids.

"Didn't the Jolades pay your mother enough?"

"They paid her well. But she used most of her salary to pay for my expensive school. She chose my education, my future over our comfort."

"Well." Hannah looked at him and smiled. "It sounds like she was a great mother."

"Yeah." He nodded. "She really was."

They arrived at an iron bridge that extended over the canal. The stench was stronger here.

"Ten naira. Pay it or you cannot cross," hollered a man at the base of the bridge. He didn't wear a uniform nor did he look the least bit professional or groomed, but Hannah quickly dubbed him the bridge patroller. He had an authority people yielded to; they slapped money into his palm before climbing the steps that ascended to the bridge.

Lawrence pulled a hundred naira from his wallet as they approached the front of the line. "For both of us," he said, extending the bill.

"*Oga*, you want change?" the bridge patroller asked.

"No. It's okay."

"Ah." His wide grin exposed his missing front tooth. "See better person. Thank you *o*. *Na* God *na* go bless you and your fine madam. Make *una* cross."

Hannah frowned as they climbed the steps. "I didn't understand much of what he just said. It kinda sounded like English, but . . ."

"It was broken English—pidgin English."

"Oh. And what did he say?"

"He said I was a good person for letting him have the change. And then he said, God bless me and my beautiful woman." He glanced at Hannah just as they landed on the deck.

"Your woman?" She pursed her lips and attempted to conceal a smile. "Is that what I am now?"

"Hey. Those were his words, not mine, but . . ." He squeezed her hand and grinned. "I'm not fighting it."

And neither was she.

"Come on." He nudged her forward, and she took a step, then paused.

Her eyes roamed over the extent of the canal and the waste that congested it. The murky water didn't flow. It sat still between ragged plank houses, emanating a revolting stink. The water was dead. Hannah had never seen such a devastating sight of poverty. People lived here. Lawrence had. She turned to him, her brows wrinkled.

"Hey. It's okay." He stepped toward her, nodding as if he fully understood her unvoiced shock, disgust, anger, and sadness. "I know." One hand cupped her cheek, and he leaned into her. With such delicate care, his pursed lips touched her forehead. "Come. I want to show you something. We're almost there." He led her down the bridge and farther along a narrow path that opened to a massive space. "My mother and I used to come to this market all the time."

A market. Hannah beamed at the lively environment. Large, colorful umbrellas shaded various products and the women tending to them. Under a yellow umbrella, there were wooden baskets filled with tomatoes and an assortment of peppers. A red umbrella sheltered various fruits—mangoes, baby bananas, papayas, pineapples. There were colors everywhere, a vibrancy that was such a contrast to the dullness of the polluted canal. Customers made purchases, bargained loudly, laughed even louder, and contributed to the vitality of the environment.

"So?" Lawrence nudged Hannah with an elbow. "What do you think?"

"This is . . ." She glanced around again and instantly found something new to marvel at. "This is amazing."

"I thought you might like it. There's a woman here who makes the best rice and stew. She's just ahead."

They ambled along, and Hannah stopped to observe and admire things that caught her interest. As she moved through the market, stares followed her. Though, it wasn't because she was Chief Jolade's daughter. These people had different priorities. Here, Hannah only stood out for one reason—she looked different from the crowd.

"Yellow pawpaw, how *na*? You fine well-well," a woman selling a range of produce shouted. "Come buy coconut from me *na*. *Dey* sweet. I no *dey* lie."

"She's talking to you," Lawrence said to Hannah. "She says you're beautiful, and she wants you to buy coconuts from her. She says they're very good."

"I like coconuts."

"Then let's get you some."

The woman offered Hannah a sample of her merchandise.

The coconut was truly delicious. Lawrence bought a couple and gave a generous tip. They walked farther and approached a wooden shed.

"And we're here. Mama Ojo's Sweet Rice."

Hannah searched for a sign, any indication that the establishment was truly what Lawrence had called it. There was no signage, but the shed was packed with customers waiting to be served.

"Ah! My friend!" The exclamation came from a petite woman. She stepped out of the shed, pushed past the crowd of customers, and jogged toward Lawrence. "Long time, no see." She hugged him, and her face rested snug against his chest. "I heard about Chief's passing. My dear, I am so sorry. How is Tiwa coping?"

"She's fine, ma. Everyone is fine. How is business?"

"Ah." She broke the embrace and turned to the shed where another woman attended to customers. "Business is very good o. To God be the glory." She faced Lawrence again and finally noticed Hannah. "Ah-ahn. Who is this? Is she your sweetheart?" She didn't give him a chance to answer. "Fine girl, how are you?" She didn't give Hannah a chance to answer either. "I am Mama Ojo. What is your name? You are his girlfriend, *shebe*? Glory be to God o. Do you know how long I have been begging him to find a woman? Years. Ah. This is good. Come." She took Hannah's hand and led her to the front of the shed, where plastic chairs and tables were set up. "Get comfortable."

Hannah settled into the chair Mama Ojo pulled out, and Lawrence sat at the opposite end.

"Ah-ahn. Why are you sitting miles from her? You young boys of nowadays. You don't know how to romance a woman. *Oya*. Come and sit beside her."

He changed his position promptly.

"Eh-heh. Now, put your arm around her. Like this." She took his arm and placed it over Hannah's shoulders. "Eh-hch. Now, whisper sweet things into her ear. I cannot tell you what to say. I have done enough. Let me go and bring your food."

Alone, they said nothing about Mama Ojo's comments or actions. They could hardly get a word in between their laughter.

"Ah-ahn." She returned with two foam plates and two bottles of Coke. "What is so funny? Why are you both laughing like two hyenas in love?"

Hyenas in love. It was one of the strangest things Hannah had ever heard. It caused her and Lawrence to laugh even harder.

"Well, here is your food. I hope you enjoy it." She placed the plates and drinks in front of them. "Try not to laugh while you eat *sha*."

"Yes, ma. Thank you." Lawrence cleared his throat and reached into his pocket.

"Don't even try it," Mama Ojo said, a hand on her hip as she took a serious stance. "Just put your money away. I am not taking it. You already know that."

"But, ma—"

"Look. You and Tiwa are the only reasons my son is currently in university. I owe you both everything. You especially. So please. Take the food. *Abeg.* Or I will just make a scene in this market. Do you hear me?"

He hesitated but nodded. "Yes, ma."

"Good. Fine girl." She turned to Hannah. "I hope you enjoy my food."

"I'm sure I will."

Mama Ojo smiled and returned to her customers.

"So, what do you think?" Lawrence picked up a plastic fork. "Looks good, doesn't it?"

Hannah examined the bed of white rice topped with tomato

stew. Fried plantains were on the side—brown and crispy. "It looks really good."

"Then let's dig in." He mixed the rice and stew then ate. "Mm. So good." He tossed his head back. "The absolute best."

"Well, I want to see what all the fuss is about." She scooped stew-coated rice into her mouth and while chewing, smiled. "Okay. I see it."

They ate in the bustling marketplace, saying very little as they consumed their meals.

After taking a sip of Coke, Hannah leaned into the unbalanced plastic chair. "So. Mama Ojo said you and Tiwa are the reasons her son is in university. What did she mean?"

There was a plantain in Lawrence's mouth, which he chewed considerably slow as if intentionally delaying his answer. "It's nothing," he said after swallowing.

"It seemed like it meant everything to her. What was she talking about?"

He drank from his bottle of Coke and sighed. "Tiwa and I started sort of a . . . a charity. It's called Rise and Shine. We sponsor children in this community and others like it around Lagos. We send them to some of the best schools in the city, schools they otherwise wouldn't have access to. A bus picks them up every day—takes them to school and brings them home."

"Like your mom did for you with the taxi."

"Yeah." He nodded. "Then we help them get scholarships to universities in Nigeria and around the world. When they graduate, we assist them with internships and job placements—many in your father's companies. Anyway, Mama Ojo's son is at Yale—third-year premed."

"Wow. That's amazing, Lawrence. What you're doing for them . . . is . . . is incredible."

"It's the right thing to do. These are smart kids. They have a lot of potential. Tiwa and I simply provide the resources."

"Tiwa. Huh."

"Yeah. I brought the idea to her and your father a few years ago, and they were immediately on board. But Tiwa spearheaded the whole thing. She's very hands-on. She comes down here and gets to know potential candidates. Dami and Shola are also involved in their own way. They donate regularly and have helped partner us with some incredible sponsors."

Two nights ago, Hannah wondered if the Jolades did anything to help the less fortunate in their country. This morning, she questioned if there was more to Tiwa. She had the answers now, and it made her smile. There was so much more to the Jolades.

"Are you ready to go? I can call Solomon and tell him to pick us up."

"No. Not yet. Let's walk around a little more. I like it here."

"Yeah. So do I." He took her hand, and they stood.

"Are you going?" Mama Ojo shouted from her post at the shack. "Okay. Bye-bye. Fine girl, take care of that boy *o*! He is a very good boy!"

Gazing at Lawrence, Hannah disagreed with Mama Ojo.

No, she thought to herself. *He's an incredible man.*

TWENTY-SIX

LAWRENCE

Lawrence was used to the hustle and bustle of the market. He found it comforting. A part of him still associated it with home.

"My mother sold secondhand clothes in this market," he told Hannah as they walked hand in hand, leaving the produce section and approaching sheds filled with colorful, patterned textiles.

"Really?" She looked up at him, and her eyes narrowed and adjusted to the sun's glare.

"Yeah. But it wasn't a stable business. Some days, she sold a lot. Some days, she didn't sell enough. So she looked for a steady job and found one with the Jolades."

"Where was her shed?"

"She didn't have one. She usually just found a free spot, spread a big cloth on the ground, and displayed her merchandise over it. That was it."

"Really? Just like that? Find a spot and set up a business?"

Lawrence laughed. "I know. It must sound ridiculous. In America, people need licenses and permits to start a business.

In Nigeria, depending on the type of business and its location, none of that is necessary. Anyone can start a business. You don't need much—a good spot at the market, a bucket to balance on your head, or a sturdy wheelbarrow to push around."

"Like the street hawkers."

"Exactly. Here, everyone's an entrepreneur. Because of the high unemployment rate, it's sometimes the only way people can survive. It was how my mother took care of me until she found a better alternative."

They walked through a narrow pathway, each side lined with fabric shops.

"Believe it or not, my mother was a university graduate. But in Nigeria, that doesn't count for much when no one's hiring. She was so smart. She wanted to work as an engineer. When the opportunity never came, she found other means."

It surprised Lawrence how much he spoke about his mother with Hannah. While he thought of his mother often, he didn't speak of her much—not even with Tiwa. He felt a satisfaction in keeping his memories to himself. But sharing them with Hannah gave him a greater satisfaction. Maybe it was because a single mother had raised her too, and she understood the sadness and joy that came with that.

"Can I ask you something?" Hannah squeezed his hand and drew his attention away from a woman forcing a dress over a mannequin.

"Of course. Go ahead."

"Do you ever feel . . ." Her eyes darted in thought. "Guilty?"

"Guilty. For what?"

"For the life you had with the Jolades after your mother was gone?"

The question slowed Lawrence's stride. The people behind

them rushed ahead, their plastic bags swinging against their quick legs. The loud chants meant to attract customers, the tenacious haggling of traders, and Afrobeat from a stereo were a few of the sounds Lawrence became oblivious to. The bustle of the market continued, while he thought about Hannah's question.

"Yes," he answered. "I've felt guilty." He had never told anyone this, but he would tell her. "When I started living with the Jolades, it was hard not to feel guilty. My mother was gone, and suddenly, I had everything—everything she wanted to give me but couldn't. I couldn't enjoy the perks of being a part of that family without feeling guilty."

Lawrence's life with his mother had been so different from his life with the Jolades. For one, waste congested their neighborhood in Ajegunle, even spilling into the open gutters that lined the streets. In the rainy season, the water, having no channel to run through, would pour into the streets and flood it for days. Banana Island, however, was paved with smooth concrete. Iron gates with elaborate designs surrounded the base of mansions. On the clean streets, strategically placed palm trees sprouted out of trimmed, green grass. Within the Jolade estate, maids served him. In the beginning, it had been hard to accept their service without thinking of his mother, without even crying. For many years, he felt displaced. He hadn't been born into privilege. He'd gained it only by circumstance. The most unfortunate circumstance. His mother's death had been the gateway to his privilege. The guilt ate at him.

"I feel guilty too," Hannah said.

"Why?"

"My mom has given me everything. Everything she possibly can. I love her more than anything in the world. I trust her more than anyone. It's always just been me and her and now . . ." She

ran a hand over her braids; her fingers reached farther to tousle
her curls.

"And now you have your siblings."

She nodded. "It's not like I came here wanting to know them
or anything. I just came for the funeral but . . ." She paused and
exhaled. "I hung out with Segun last night while you were
asleep. We talked a little, and it was nice. And I went shopping
with Dami, and she's just so sweet. And Shola is just as sweet.
And I can't help being curious, wanting to know about my siblings and my father. Being in this country and in that house,
makes it so hard not to want . . . more." She murmured the last
word—*more*—as if it were a bad word and then bit her lip as if
punishing herself. "And I feel guilty for that. I feel like I'm be-
traying my mom. After everything she did to raise me alone,
I shouldn't want to know anything about the man who abandoned us."

"But you do."

Slowly, she nodded.

"Hannah." He stopped walking and faced her. "Even though
it was difficult for me to adjust to my life with the Jolades, I
eventually did. I knew my mother would be happy and at peace
because I had everything she ever wanted to give me. And she
secured it before she passed. It might have been unintentional,
but she did." He smiled fondly. "Her dedication to her job and
kindness to the Jolades is the reason they took me in. She secured my welfare without even knowing it."

"Yeah," Hannah said, nodding. "I suppose she did."

"Now, your mother asked you to come here, right? She
wanted you to be here?"

"Yeah."

"Then maybe she was trying to secure something for you—
give you something she knows you need."

Hannah's eyes shifted as she considered. When she met Lawrence's gaze again, the uncertainty was gone. "Yeah," she said. "I guess so."

"Then there's absolutely no reason to feel guilty. She wanted this for you."

"Yeah." She smiled. "I suppose you're right. Thanks."

"Of course."

He wanted to kiss her. God, he wanted to kiss her so damn bad. He felt a relentless pull to her, and he couldn't credit it to chemistry alone. Doing that cheapened it. Whatever was going on between them, whatever he felt was beyond attraction. Yes, the attraction had come first—during their encounter in San Francisco. But the emotions had started during their second encounter—the moment she stepped into the Jolades' living room and their eyes connected. He'd felt it since then—small doses of emotions gradually accumulating as they spent more time together and even when they were apart.

He could list the reasons he cared about her—she was funny and kind and passionate and open-minded, willing to try new things and even visit a slum. Those were the rational reasons, but then there were the irrational reasons—reasons Lawrence couldn't grasp or explain. He cared about Hannah because something beyond his understanding compelled him to. That was it. It was sensible and insensible, the rational mixed with the irrational. And the combination, coupled with attraction, created an irresistible pull.

He leaned forward to kiss her, but a brash, objecting voice jolted him back. Suddenly, Lawrence was aware of the chaotic setting—the people, the noises, and a woman sitting on a stool in her shed, her legs crossed and her stare disapproving.

"No be for here *na una* go romance *o!*" she said, suppressing a laugh. "If you want show you madam say you love am, come buy fine cloth for am."

"What did she say?" Hannah asked.

Lawrence faced her and tried to contain both his embarrassment and amusement. "She said here's not the best place to kiss you. But if I want to show you that I like you, I should buy you clothes."

"Hmm." Hannah looked over his shoulder and into the shed. The woman on the stool gestured to her merchandise. "You know what, I like the way she thinks." She grabbed Lawrence's hand and drew him into the modest space.

The shop owner, pleased to have customers, pulled yards of fabric off the rack. Hannah pressed each to her chest and spun around as if wearing a dress with an elaborate flare. Her smile was radiant. Her eyes, gleaming. Lawrence stood back, watching and admiring, and felt another dose of emotion drop and pool inside him.

TWENTY-SEVEN

HANNAH

"I had a great time today," Hannah said to Lawrence as they stood at the base of the staircase in the great hall.

It was a little past six in the evening. Their day together was over. Would they go their separate ways now—she to her room and he to his? It seemed only appropriate to end the day another way, with another activity. She kissed him gently—a silent proposal he was very receptive to.

His arms wound around her. The kiss deepened, became more sensual and ardent. Their current location wasn't ideal for the activity they had in mind, but common sense escaped them until a sharp voice called out to Lawrence and forced them apart.

Tiwa marched toward them, wearing her signature expression—a mixture of boredom and irritation. "I need to speak to her. Alone. Now."

"To me?" Hannah pointed to herself, baffled. "Why?"

"Yeah. Why?" Lawrence looked between the two women. "Is everything okay?"

"That's between me and her, so if you don't mind giving us a minute."

"Um . . . I—"

"It's fine." Hannah squeezed his arm and nudged him forward. "I'll catch up with you."

"Okay." He moved toward the living room, his steps hesitant as he turned and glanced at the women.

"What is it?" Hannah asked Tiwa once they were alone. "What do you want to talk about?"

"You said a lot of shit this morning, so I need you to tell me exactly what you think you saw last night."

To Hannah's surprise, she had forgotten about Tiwa and Dayo's late-night rendezvous. Her day with Lawrence had been eye-opening and had even made her believe there was more to Tiwa. But now, she was skeptical.

"What I think I saw?" Hannah shook her head. "No. I definitely saw you and Dayo kissing. Definitely. Don't bother denying it."

Tiwa expelled a deep breath. "Have you told anyone—Lawrence, Dami, anyone at all?"

"No. I haven't."

"Well, you can't. Ever." It wasn't a plea, but a demand. "Seriously, if you tell anyone, I'll—"

"You'll what?" Hannah folded her arms and waited for Tiwa to complete the sentence.

She did not.

They stood, glaring at each other.

"Is everything okay here?" Lawrence's head poked out of the living room. "Are you two all right?"

"Yeah. Everything's perfect!" Hannah answered, overly chipper. "We were just having a heart-to-heart. We have a much better understanding of each other now." She left Tiwa brooding and walked to Lawrence.

"Well, that's great. It's about time." He looked genuinely

happy about the news. If only he knew. "Anyway, Auntie Jumoke is here." He took Hannah's hand. "She wants to see you."

"Sure. Let's go."

In the living room, everyone was present. They were chatting and laughing, but their attention quickly veered to Lawrence and Hannah, who held hands. There was a moment of silence where Hannah expected someone to say something, but no one said a word—no disapproval, no endorsement. Just a simple acknowledgment of what now was—Hannah and Lawrence were a couple.

"Hannah." The voice came from Sade, who sat on a sofa in one of her infamous sweeping gowns, looking like the grande dame of the manor. "How are you? How was your outing with Lawrence?"

It was a question—not an insult or an accusation. Just a simple question accompanied by an expression that was neither condescending nor callous. Everyone in the room, including Tiwa, appeared equally confused by Sade's behavior. What had inspired it? Hannah had an inkling. Maybe the conversation they'd had the night before had brought Sade to a certain realization. Whatever that was, Hannah did not know. But it must have been good, since Sade was actually smiling at her.

"I'm doing fine. Thank you for asking. And my day was wonderful. Lawrence took me to a market in Ajegunle."

"You what?" Auntie Jumoke sprung to her feet. "Ajegunle? Lawrence, is that your idea of a romantic date? What kind of nonsense is that?"

"Actually, I really loved the market. It was great."

"What the hell is Ajegunle?" Segun asked, his words slightly muffled by the lollipop in his mouth.

"It is a slum. And it is certainly not the right place for my niece. My dear, are you okay?" She held Hannah's chin and tilted it to new angles while searching for evidence of harm.

It was strange, but as Auntie Jumoke offered an assessment, an image flashed in Hannah's mind. Actually, several images flashed in her mind—broken, disoriented pieces. Like she was putting together a jigsaw puzzle, she assembled the pieces, interlocking them until a picture formed. A memory. It was old, buried deep in her subconscious, but Auntie Jumoke's simple touch had unearthed it.

"I was right." Hannah's voice cracked. "We've met before. In the hotel. That first time I met my father, you were there."

Auntie Jumoke took a step back and cleared her throat. "My dear, I have already told you. We have never met. You must be confused."

"No. I'm not. I remember. I remember what you said to him." Hannah started shaking. She didn't feel Lawrence's hand anymore. She only felt the anger coursing through her with the intensity of thunder. "He wanted me. You told him to leave me."

She remembered it well now. After their introduction at the door, Hannah's father had invited her and her mother into his suite. They sat on a sofa, and he asked Hannah simple questions—favorite color, best friend, favorite movie. He was kind. He was funny. He was attentive. He gave Hannah a gift—a stuffed bear in a pink tutu. Fifteen minutes into the visit, her mother received a work call that she took in the hallway. Auntie Jumoke appeared shortly after, stepping out of a room in the suite.

"Well." She held Hannah's chin and tilted it in angles as she inspected her face. "She's beautiful. She looks like you."

"I know," Hannah's father had said, smiling proudly. "I don't know why I waited so long to see her."

Hannah moved to the carpeted floor to play with the stuffed bear, and Auntie Jumoke approached her brother.

"You know why, Wale. If Father discovers what you've done, he will disown you. He trusted you to come to America for business—to be responsible. But look at what you did. You dishonored your wedding vows. And with a white woman. To make matters worse, there is proof of it. He won't forgive this, Wale. He will cut you out of everything—the businesses, your inheritance."

"Oh God." He rubbed his shaved head and grunted. "Jumoke, what do you suggest I do, then?"

"Forget about the girl. No one can know about her. You cannot have a relationship with her."

"Ah. No. I cannot do that—not after seeing her." He watched Hannah, her red, puffy dress flared out on the floor. "She's mine. I cannot deny her—not anymore. I will deal with Father."

"Then you are a fool," Auntie Jumoke hissed. "You send the girl's mother money every month. Don't you?"

"Yes. I have since she was born."

"When Father cuts you off, you won't be able to provide for her and the rest of your family."

"Then I will get a job." His tone was firm, resolved. "I will work for someone else."

"And who will hire you? A father disowning his son and removing him from the family business sends a clear message. Once the news gets out, no one in Lagos will want anything to do with you."

As he absorbed his sister's words, he watched Hannah, and she watched him. Regardless of the distance between them, she had heard every word. She was old enough to understand the conversation but too young to plead her case. She could only think to say one thing. She stood and approached him, the bear tucked under her arm.

"You're my daddy," she said, eyes wide and imploring.

He nodded, and tears touched his eyes. "Yes." He crouched so their faces aligned. "Yes, I am."

Even at her age, Hannah had known it was goodbye. Her father had not chosen her. It was heartbreaking—too much for an eight-year-old to bear, so automatically some part of her contained the memory, prevented it from spilling and tainting all her sweet, naive youthfulness. The memory had been sealed away until Auntie Jumoke made the simple mistake of holding Hannah's chin—just as she had twenty years ago.

"Auntie." Dami stood gingerly from her seat. "What's Hannah talking about?"

"Yeah." Shola stood next, beside her twin. "Did you know about her this whole time?"

"I . . . I . . . well . . ." She mouthed words, sampling her lie before uttering it. "I thought—"

"Just answer the question," Sade said. "Yes or no. Is Hannah telling the truth?"

"Yes. She is."

Everyone voiced their shock with gasps and exclamations. Hannah was speechless, disheartened, and exhausted. She turned to leave, eager to be alone, but Auntie Jumoke gripped her arm.

"My dear, please. At the time, I thought it was for the best. But I was wrong. I regretted it, and he regretted his decision as well." She sighed and released her grip. "When you were sixteen, he contacted your mother and—"

"Wait. What?" Hannah's brows drew close, her face tightened. "No. He didn't."

"Yes. He did. He tried to make amends and have a relationship with you. He wanted to be in your life, but your mother would not allow it."

"No. My mom wouldn't do that. If he had contacted her, she would have told me. She tells me everything. She keeps nothing from me."

"I am telling the truth. I swear."

Hannah didn't know what the truth was. It had been fragmented and distributed among different people—her auntie, who was only now confessing; her father, who had taken his truth to the grave; and maybe even her mother, who she wanted to give the benefit of the doubt. Hannah only had mere scraps of the truth—scraps she had been trying to survive on for years.

"My dear." Tears dripped from Auntie Jumoke's regret-filled eyes. "I am sorry. We should have found another way. We should have stood up to our father. He was a difficult man, but we should have stood up to him. For your sake. I am so sorry. I wish . . ." She sniffed. "I wish I could fix things."

"Well, it's too late for that now. There's nothing you can do."

The damage had been done. An apology or wishful thinking could not undo it. It couldn't right what had been done to Hannah. It couldn't console her in this moment when she was furious and distraught. Her pulse raced. Tears gathered at the corners of her eyes. A painful lump formed in her throat as she suppressed a cry. She turned away and rushed out of the room, a hand pressed over her trembling lips.

ALONE, HANNAH SHOVED CLOTHES INTO HER SUITCASE. Her movements were hasty, clumsy, and frantic. She had to get away—to someplace where she could clear her head. Solomon could drive her to a hotel or maybe to the airport. Yes. The airport seemed like the best option. She opened the drawer in the nightstand and grabbed her passport.

"Hannah."

She turned to the open door where Lawrence stood. "I told you I wanted to be alone."

"I know, but . . ." He glanced at the suitcase and then at the passport in her hand. "What are you doing? Where are you going?"

"Home. Back to San Francisco." She slung her handbag over her shoulder and marched to the door, rolling the suitcase along.

"Hannah, wait." He stood in the doorway and prevented her exit. "Just wait."

This would be the hardest part, leaving him sooner than expected. "Lawrence, please just move out of the way. I need to get out of here."

"I know you're upset. This whole situation is fucked up. But please. Please don't go. Okay? Stay."

"I . . . I . . ." Her voice shook, her chest tightened, something tickled her throat. *No.* She wouldn't cry—not here, not in front of him. She tried to focus on inhaling and exhaling, but the tickle in her throat sharpened. Fighting it was useless. The cry broke free—cracked, hoarse, and heavy with pain.

Lawrence held her as she sobbed. He stroked her back and pressed kisses atop her head.

"I can't stay here." She panted against his chest. "It's just . . . it's too much."

"Okay. Then let's get you out of here." He grabbed the suitcase and took her hand.

Minutes later, after Lawrence had packed a bag for himself, they left the estate.

TWENTY-EIGHT

HANNAH

Hannah was on a plane after all. Though it wasn't bound for San Francisco but Akwa Ibom, a state in the southern part of Nigeria.

After leaving the estate, Solomon had driven her and Lawrence to the airport. Lawrence had spoken on the phone during the drive, detailing flight plans to someone on the other end. At the time, Hannah was clueless about their destination and wasn't particularly concerned with the details—only relieved at the prospect of putting distance between herself and her aunt.

When they arrived at the airport, she noticed they weren't at a terminal but an aircraft hangar. There was a sleek jet with its door open, ready for boarding.

"What's going on?" she had asked Lawrence. "What are we doing here?"

"Running away." He had stepped out of the car, opened her door, and extended his hand. "Are you coming?"

There was nothing to contemplate—Hannah trusted him completely. She took his hand, and they ascended the steps of the luxurious plane.

The cabin was spacious with tall ceilings and a sumptuous leather and wood interior. The seats were large, each generously spaced apart rather than crammed together like in a commercial plane.

Hannah sat upright on a plush sofa. "Lawrence," she had said, still inspecting the space, "where are we going?"

"Akwa Ibom. It's another state. You'll like it." He sat beside her and pointed past the four-seater dining table. "There's a bedroom back there if you would like to lie down."

"No. Thanks. I'm fine here."

Hannah sat on the sofa for the length of the seventy-minute flight, later relaxing by curling into Lawrence's side.

Now, as she looked through the oval window, she saw the outline of the landscape between parting clouds. Specks of light dotted the night—a sign of a metropolis below.

"Sir, madam," a petite flight attendant said, "please fasten your seat belts. We will land shortly."

Hannah spent the thirty-minute car ride from the airport looking through the window. She tried to make out the new environment, but it was dark—a little past ten at night, and the only thing visible was the woodland on both sides of the road.

The driver—a short, lean man—stopped the car at a security gate. Lawrence offered his full name and received access. The trees continued along the road, then gradually thinned until a massive structure came into view. Bright lights surrounded the building and highlighted the words etched into the display plaque—Ibom Hotel & Golf Resort.

"*Oga*, we have arrived," the driver announced as he pulled up to the front doors.

Lawrence and Hannah stepped into the resort; a bellhop rolled their bags after them. The lobby was magnificent. Tall columns—with wooden barrels at their base—took up room in the expansive space. Giant vases held red and white bamboo sticks, and African-inspired art hung on the walls.

The manager welcomed Lawrence and Hannah, then escorted them to a suite on the second floor. When the door closed behind them, Hannah stood in the living space where a floor-to-ceiling window revealed a dark expanse of trees.

"The view is better in the morning," Lawrence said. "You'll see." He directed her to a room designed with warm earth tones. "You can sleep here."

You—not we. She frowned and turned to him. "Where will you sleep?"

"There's another room."

He wasn't presumptuous. Hannah knew that about him and respected it. Though, she wanted him to presume just a little because she didn't have the energy or the guts to ask for what she needed—him.

"I'll see you in the morning, Hannah." He pressed his lips to her cheek then pulled away. "Get some rest."

That would be impossible. She couldn't rest with him so close and so out of reach. Her initial reaction to run back to San Francisco alone had been a mistake. Hannah needed Lawrence. His care, his attentiveness, his confident assertion that everything would be all right, made her feel better. Every moment with him lessened her anger—even the long periods when they said nothing and just allowed their closeness to feed their connection. Separate rooms would do Hannah no good. She wanted to tell him that, but held her tongue and watched him walk away.

She took a shower in the en suite and then pulled a nightdress from her suitcase. The bed was snug with sheets that had a delicate vanilla fragrance. She closed her eyes at 11:30 p.m., then sat upright an hour later. She hadn't slept—not even for a minute. Restless, she skimmed off the bed and tiptoed out of her room, then across the living space to Lawrence's room.

At the closed door, her bare feet flattened on the floor. *Knock or walk away?*

Hannah considered the two options briefly but chose neither. Instead, she gripped the doorknob and turned it. It was a daring move. Lawrence could be asleep or undressed. Her daring move suddenly seemed thoughtless. She decided to turn back, but Lawrence called her name.

She froze.

Shit.

After gathering courage, she poked her head through the break in the door.

He sat upright in bed, his head resting against the wooden frame and his legs covered by a blanket. The room was dark, lit only by the glow of the moon. Hannah couldn't determine his facial expression. Was he happy to see her or unsettled by her lurking in the middle of the night?

"Is everything okay?" He sounded concerned.

"Yeah. Everything is fine."

"Are you sure?" He flung the blanket off his legs, preparing to stand.

"Yes." Quickly, she entered the room. "I promise. Everything is fine. I just couldn't sleep."

"Oh." He sighed, a deep exhale that released the strain in his voice. "You must have a lot on your mind. Do you want to talk?"

She nodded and neared him. The right side of the bed was still neat, without the slightest wrinkle in the sheet as if he had been reserving the spot for someone. For her.

"What's running through your mind? I'm sure it's a lot."

"I just . . ." She blew out a breath and settled beside him. "I just keep thinking he wanted me. He wanted to be my dad. If

Auntie Jumoke hadn't convinced him to stay out of my life, I would have had a father. But why did he even listen to her? Why couldn't he just make the decision on his own?" She gathered the white bedsheet and squeezed it in her fist. "I'm just so angry at her. And at him too. But . . ." She loosened her grip. "I'm kinda happy because I know my dad wanted me." She smiled, and tears trickled out of her eyes. "I've always wondered."

For years, it had been the same questions. *Why didn't he come? Why doesn't he want me?* She thought she would never get the answers, but she had them now.

"I'm happy I know. But even so, it's bittersweet. Then there's my mom. Has she really been lying to me?" Hannah bit her lip. "I don't know what to believe. It's just all very frustrating."

"You should talk to her."

"Yeah. But I think it might be best to do that when I get home—a face-to-face conversation."

"I'm so sorry you're going through all this." With his thumb, Lawrence wiped her wet cheeks. "I wish I could fix it—make it better somehow."

"You're making it better right now. Just by being here." She watched him. The moonlight coming through the terrace door shone on his brown skin. "How come you're awake?" she asked.

"Well, it's a little hard to sleep when I'm here and—"

"And I'm in another room—away from you." Close but out of reach.

"Yeah. But after everything that happened today, I thought you wanted space."

"To be honest, I just want to be with you." She smiled, then slipped under the duvet and rested her head on a pillow.

Lawrence reclined flat on his back without saying a word. His arm came around Hannah, and he gently drew her to his chest. Immediately, she felt the comfort and protection she needed. She held on to him, her ear against his thumping heart that no doubt matched the erratic rhythm of hers.

Hannah hadn't dated in a long time. She missed this. She missed being touched and wanted but hadn't realized it until Lawrence. She had learned to disguise her loneliness as something else, call it a different name and repurpose it. Lawrence, however, unmasked her loneliness, stripped away all the things it was not until it was real, raw, undeniable, painful, bleeding.

Hannah was lonely; her body and her heart were starving and deprived.

That, she could no longer ignore.

TWENTY-NINE

HANNAH

Sunlight flooded the room and forced Hannah's eyes open. She sat upright and looked at the view through the terrace door. Gently, she glided off the bed, not wanting to disturb Lawrence as he slept.

After sliding the glass door open, she stepped onto the terrace. Past the iron railing, there was a wide expanse of dense, lush palm forest that extended over mountains and valleys. There was so much rich green huddled together, surrounding the resort. Hannah had seen nothing like it.

"It's beautiful, isn't it?" Lawrence said, stepping through the door. He stood behind her and looped his arms around her waist.

"It's one of the prettiest things I've ever seen."

"I thought you might like it. I come here whenever I want to get away. It's the perfect escape."

"Yeah. It is." She turned and looked at him. "Thanks for bringing me."

"You're welcome." He planted his lips on hers—a soft open-mouth kiss that ended with him gently biting her lip.

"Mmm." She licked the spot his teeth had scraped. She needed more of that—more of him. "Do we have to go back today? I don't want to. Not yet."

"Well, Dami and Shola have both sent me a hundred text messages this morning, demanding I bring you back as soon as possible, but . . ." He smiled. "I told them we'll be back tomorrow."

"Really?"

He nodded, and Hannah sighed, relieved and grateful.

"This is great." She bounced on her toes, her body unable to contain her excitement. "So, what's there to do around here?"

"There's a spa and a pool. There's also an eighteen-hole golf course—one of the biggest in Africa. It's very impressive."

"I don't golf, but I would like to spend some time outside." It would be a shame if the environment went unexplored.

"Then I have the perfect activity for us, but first . . ." He brought his lips to hers and kissed her slow and sweet.

THE RESORT PROVIDED THE BICYCLES HANNAH AND LAW-rence pedaled along a curvy pathway enclosed with acres of green forest. Biking was the best way to experience the scenery up close. They rode side by side, and there was something so youthful and carefree about the activity. Hannah pedaled with her arms waving in the warm air. The alarm on Lawrence's face made her shake with laughter. He was a more cautious biker.

"You're somewhat of a daredevil, aren't you?" he said as they climbed off their saddles and pushed their bikes along the path.

"Well." She eyed him coyly, then grinned. "There's a lot you don't know about me." And for a moment, she wondered if he would ever get the opportunity.

She would leave in three days. Once in San Francisco, where

would their relationship stand? Where would she stand after meeting her siblings and knowing what she now knew about her father? Would she carry on with her life as though nothing had happened in Nigeria, persuading herself to be content with what she had in San Francisco? Hannah had done that for years, convinced herself she needed nothing more. But she did. Being in Nigeria forced her to confront this truth.

"Hey." Lawrence squeezed her shoulder. "Is everything okay? You've got that look on your face."

"What look?"

"The one where you frown and tighten your lips and shift your eyes as if you're trying to solve a complicated mathematical equation."

Hannah wondered how long it had taken him to notice her habit—something that would have gone unnoticed by others.

"I'm guessing you've got something on your mind?" He considered her. "What's going on? What's bothering you?"

"It's just that . . ." She sucked in air, then expelled it forcefully. "I only have a few days left in Nigeria, and I'm not sure what's going to happen once I leave. There's still so much I don't know about my father and his culture—*my* culture. There's still so much I don't know about my siblings. And I want to know them. I've always felt kind of incomplete without them, without him—like I'm missing pieces of who I am."

She expected Lawrence to say something. He said nothing. For a few minutes, there was only the wind whistling through the leaves and insects chirring. Their bicycles crunched against the sandy concrete as they rolled them along the pathway woven through the golf course. Hannah followed his unspoken lead, dropping her bike and strolling up a hill. When they reached the highest point in the golf course, her eyes widened. From her stance, she saw the line where the cloudless blue sky met the coarse green earth. It was breathtaking.

"My father died in a car accident before I was born." Lawrence turned to her. "Growing up, I was so curious about him. I would ask my mother so many questions, and she would answer them the best she could." He smiled—a lackluster smile. "Every time she told me something about him, I mimicked him—his personality or his interests. She told me he was a mechanic, and the next day, I was screaming I wanted to be one too. My mother, the very intelligent woman she was, saw right through me. Do you want to know what she told me?"

Hannah nodded.

"She told me something I will never forget. She said, 'You don't have to rely on your father to determine the kind of man you want to be. You don't have to rely on anyone but yourself.'" He took Hannah's hand and squeezed it gently. "It's rational to be curious about your father—to want to know everything there is to know about him. It's natural to want to know about your siblings too. Our culture and our family and the people in our lives can help shape who we are, but ultimately, I think it's up to us to decide who we want to be—to rely on ourselves and no one else. Do you get what I mean?"

Hannah nodded. "Yeah. I get it." And she did, but in a way that confused her further—made her uncertain of what she truly needed. Though, she didn't admit her uncertainty. She needed time to think about Lawrence's words, but for now she just leaned into him and watched the landscape, focusing only on the simplicity of earth and sky and nothing else.

THIRTY

HANNAH

After almost two hours in the spa, Hannah returned to her suite tranquil. Though the instant she walked into the living space, tension seized her and she froze in place. With wide eyes, she considered the woman and man who stood beside a tall rack of clothes.

"Um . . ." Hannah gripped the cord on her plush robe. "Who are you? And what are you doing here?"

"I'm Felicia," the woman answered, cheerful. Her burgundy hair flowed over her shoulders in soft waves, the color stunning against her cocoa brown skin. "And this is James." She motioned at the young man beside her. "We work at a boutique in town. Mr. Bankola asked us to bring you something to wear."

"What?" Hannah shook her head, muddled. "Why?"

"He said he has a special night planned for the two of you," James answered. His eyebrow shot off its base, and he smirked. "He thought you might need something to wear."

"Really?" As tension eased out of Hannah, she smiled and surveyed the suite. "And where is he?"

"That, we don't know." James shrugged. "But he wants you to meet him in the lobby at seven thirty."

That was in two hours. And it seemed like too far away, especially since Hannah had expected to see him the moment she entered the suite. But he had other plans, and the not knowing was thrilling. She would play along.

"Okay. Let's see what you've got."

"Of course, ma." Felicia pulled an A-line dress from the rack. She showed it off, and Hannah shook her head.

"What about this?" James presented a lengthy strapless dress. "What do you think?"

"It isn't really my style." But it didn't take her long to find something fitting. It was an emerald-green slip dress that would likely come to her knees. "It's perfect."

"Wonderful," Felicia said. "I'm glad you chose that because I have the perfect shoes." From the lower level of the rack, she picked a pair of strappy heels. "What do you think?"

"Oh." Hannah held the metallic copper shoes. "They're gorgeous."

"Absolutely," James confirmed. "With that dress and those shoes, you're going to look incredible. He won't be able to take his eyes off you."

Hannah was counting on exactly that.

WITH THE CORNROWS UNDONE, EACH OF HANNAH'S ginger-blond curls puffed free around her head. Her skin, dusted with a copper bronzer, gleamed in the emerald slip dress; the satin material dipped low and gathered at the base of her spine. There was more skin than fabric, and she wanted it no other way.

She descended the grand stairs gracefully, with as much

speed as her four-inch heels allowed. When Lawrence appeared
at the base, warmth crept up Hannah's cheeks.

He stood erect, his hands behind his back, his gaze fixed
on her.

"Hi," she said at the landing.

"Hey." He leaned forward and pressed a kiss to her cheek.
His palm flattened on her back that curved in response to his
touch. "You look exquisite."

"Thank you. And you look . . ." Her eyes swept over him.
"Very handsome."

Which was an understatement. His dark blue suit fit his
build flawlessly. He looked as elegant as he had that night in
San Francisco. It was funny to think that only a few days ago,
they had been strangers at a cocktail party. And now, here they
were. What a difference thirteen days made.

"So. What exactly do you have planned?" she asked him.

"First, dinner." He took her hand and led the way. "Are you
hungry?"

"Very."

They had dinner outside in a straw cabana; strings of tiny
lights hung from the roof and gave the illusion of fireflies. The
weather was a perfect balance between mild and breezy. Hannah looked up at the palm trees that hovered above them, their
branches so tall, it almost seemed like they were touching the
stars. The setting was romantic, and the flames in the torches
emitted a soft glow that enhanced the ambiance.

"This is beautiful," she said, marveling. "I can't believe you
had this set up for me."

"Why can't you believe it?"

She looked at him and shrugged. "No one has ever done anything like this for me—nothing even remotely close."

She'd had three serious boyfriends in the past, and none had

even attempted to be romantic. Hannah had accepted her part-
ners as they were. She had never asked for too much, afraid her
demand would cause another man to deem her unworthy and
walk out of her life. That fear prevented her from ending her
relationship with Marc when he'd initially cheated. It caused
her to normalize his inattentiveness and selfishness and dishonesty and live with it. It caused her to tolerate so much from him
and every man she had ever dated—to endure a relationship
rather than enjoy it. Now, as she looked around the setting and
then at Lawrence, she regretted every decision her fear had
caused her to make. Flo had been right. She deserved better.

"Hannah." Lawrence reached across the table and took her
hand. "I know we've known each other for only a short time,
but—"

"But it feels like much longer," she said. "Doesn't it?"

He smiled. "Yes. It does."

The cool night air brushed her skin just as her temperature
spiked. Her body reacted whenever he looked at her with so
much warmth and regard.

"I want you to know that I care about you," he continued. "I
care about you very much, Hannah."

"I care about you too. So much."

She meant it, but again, it was an understatement.

"By the way," he said. "I read some of your articles."

She stiffened. "You did?"

"Yeah. Why do you look so surprised? I told you that I
would."

"Yeah. But I didn't think you would actually get around to it."

None of the men she'd dated had ever gotten around to it.
They'd made the promise to read every article she'd ever written, but in the end, they'd read none.

"Well, I got around to it," Lawrence said. "There was one you wrote about intergenerational trauma. You covered how an un-treated mental health disorder affected three generations of women. It was brilliant." A smile lifted the corners of his lips. "You're brilliant. Seriously, Hannah. You're such a talented writer."

For a moment, Hannah was confused. *Why did he read it?* she asked herself. *He didn't have to. He shouldn't have bothered. I would have been fine with it.* Then she had to intentionally adjust her mind-set to understand that her current situation with Lawrence was normal. This was how a relationship was supposed to be. The man she was dating was supposed to take a genuine interest in her passion. He was supposed to put an ef-fort into making her feel special and cared for. This was normal.

"I'm happy you read it and liked it," she said. "Thank you."

"Of course." He glanced at the watch on his wrist. "Did you enjoy your dinner?"

"Yeah. The salmon was delicious." She brought her wine-glass to her lips and sipped while watching him. "So. What's next?"

"That depends." He arched a brow, a challenge in his eyes. "Are you tired?"

She placed the goblet on the table and grinned. "Not even a little."

"Then I suppose we should get going."

Lawrence led Hannah through the hotel, around corners on the first floor, until they arrived at a nightclub. The space was dim. Colored lights shone on the stage where a band played Afrobeat.

"Let's sit." The club was crowded, every seat taken, except for two in the front. The table between the two chairs had a re-served sign on it, but Lawrence claimed the spot without a sec-ond thought, pulling a chair out for Hannah and then himself.

Once settled, Hannah—like the rest of the audience—listened to the band. The lead musician was spirited, his vocals bold and raspy. He danced in big, jerky movements and alternated between singing and playing the saxophone.

"Your father loved music," Lawrence said into her ear. "His favorite singer was Fela Kuti. He was a legendary Nigerian musician, known worldwide. When Fela died, his son took over his band."

Hannah turned to Lawrence. "Is that his son performing?"

"Yes. Seun Kuti."

She focused on the musician again. He sang about Nigerian youths chasing the American dream. "Tell me who *dey* dream for Africa?" he bellowed. "Who *go* manifest the vision of so many lost generations?" He performed as if his words weren't enough to convey his message, as if he needed to use every ounce of his being. He rolled his shirt off and tossed it aside. Sweat glazed his tattooed chest. He closed his eyes and bounced back and forth, moving in accord with the Afro melody created by the trumpet, the guitar, the piano, and the drums.

"He's incredible," Hannah murmured to herself.

The song ended, and the instruments eased into a new upbeat tempo. The two backup dancers gyrated. They wore small pieces of African fabric around their chests and their waists. White tribal paint covered their exposed skin. As they moved, the layers of coral beads on their chests swung.

"Are you having a good time?" Seun asked the crowd, who cheered. "This is important to me, man! Are you having a fucking good time here tonight?"

The crowd roared louder, some even rising to dance.

Hannah laughed, giddy as she turned to Lawrence.

"Are you having a good time?" he asked, amused.

"The best!" she said.

"I think there's room to make it better." He took her hand and directed her to stand with him.

Hannah wanted to object. She wasn't much of a dancer. Instead, she allowed Lawrence to take the lead as he had all night.

He stood behind her; his arms circled her stomach. Her stiff spine relaxed into his chest, and she swayed along with him. She closed her eyes, feeling both the music and the beat of his heart. The combination soothed her. Then Lawrence lowered his hand. His fingers slid between the slit in her dress. He stroked her thigh, and heat and tension gathered inside her—immense, uncontainable, and desperate for release.

"I'm ready to go." She turned to him, and they watched each other intently. She didn't explain why she wanted to leave, and he didn't probe. It wasn't necessary. The message was clear— clear enough for Lawrence to take Hannah's hand and lead her out of the club.

They left quickly; the music faded behind them.

Inside their suite, Hannah slipped off her shoes, and he did the same. Their eyes never left each other. Their need increased with every moment they did not touch. Hannah loved the anticipation; it was as much a part of foreplay as kissing and fondling. When Lawrence reached to pull her close, she turned and walked into the bedroom. He trailed her.

It was dark. The moon beaming through the large windows produced the only light. Hannah sat on the bed, and when Lawrence crouched before her, she watched him expectantly.

They had slept in the same bed twice now and nothing had happened. Two nights ago, caution and a full house had restricted them. The night before, she'd wanted to be held and comforted. But tonight, she wanted something else, and there was absolutely nothing standing in the way.

Lawrence placed a finger on the strap on her shoulder. He traced it, slipped it off, then pressed his lips to her bare shoulder.

Hannah's breathing quickened as a warm sensation hummed through her body.

He pulled back, his attention now on the single strap that held the dress in place. He looked at Hannah, a question in his smoldering stare. When she answered with one sharp nod, he freed her shoulder of that last strap. The satin material slipped away and revealed the curve of round breasts. Lawrence tensed; his jaw flexed as he held Hannah's tan nipple between two fingers.

His touch was slow and coaxing. He built tension and anticipation, then defused them with gentle kisses and firm strokes. The eagerness to be together was still there—fiercer than ever, but they controlled it, understanding the significance of the moment, knowing it had to be savored with unhurried, deliberate movements. Like their first kiss, they existed outside of time—unbothered by its pace.

Clothes landed on the floor—hers and then his. He slipped on a condom. He wasn't presumptuous, but he had come prepared. He had hoped for this just as she had, and that made Hannah smile as she straddled him.

Their eyes locked as they moved against each other. Moonlight bathed their naked bodies with a pale, shimmery glow—his strong, muscular frame and her lean, delicate limbs.

As the sensation of a climax built, Hannah felt overwhelmed with emotions—old ones that had suddenly intensified and new ones that were raw and in need of nurturing.

She wrapped her arms around Lawrence's neck, pressed her chest to his, and clung to him, desperate to be closer than she already was, wishing their budding relationship could be more than what her seven-day stay in Nigeria permitted.

It has to be more than a fling. She communicated this with every part of her body and hoped he understood, hoped he agreed, hoped he didn't want to let her go just as she didn't want to let him go.

Ever.

THIRTY-ONE

HANNAH

When Hannah walked into the great hall on Thursday morning, a piercing screech shocked her. She flinched and instinctively drew closer to Lawrence. The sound hadn't alarmed him. He was probably used to it. This, however, was the first Hannah had heard the twins produce such a deafening noise. She credited it to excitement. They smiled as they raced toward her.

"You're back!" they said, embracing Hannah. "We missed you!"

"Hey." Hannah held them—one arm around Shola and the other around Dami. "I missed you guys too."

"I went to your room and all your stuff was gone," Dami said. "You took all your clothes and none of the new ones. I was genuinely worried, Hannah. Worried you were terribly dressed wherever you were."

"Seriously, Dami," Shola said. "That was your main concern?"

"No. Of course not. But it was definitely a major one."

The twins released Hannah just as Sade and Iya Agba descended the stairs, a faint haste in their elegant movements.

"Hannah, my dear," Iya Agba said. "How are you? We were very worried about you."

"Yes. We were," Sade added, soft-spoken. "I hope Lawrence took good care of you."

"Oh, I'm sure he took real good care of her." Dami's eyebrows wiggled as she nudged Lawrence with an elbow. "What exactly did you two get up to?"

"Dami, mind your own business," Iya Agba snapped. "*Tatafo.*"

No one said another word or acknowledged that the answer to Dami's question was apparent on Hannah's flushed face.

"Hey, sis." Segun ambled past his family. His attention shifted between Hannah and his cell phone. "You're back. 'Ight. Dope."

It wasn't a welcome as heartfelt as the twins, but it meant a lot to Hannah regardless. Segun had called her sis. She liked the sound of it. When he disappeared into the living room, Hannah looked at the people who surrounded her. She expected another person to appear at any moment.

"She isn't here," Sade said. "Auntie Jumoke is not here. I asked her to give you some space."

Hannah released a repressed breath. "Thank you."

"But we have a surprise for you." Dami clapped and squealed. "After the whole Auntie Jumoke drama, we wanted to cheer you up, so we got you a surprise." She bounced in place, barely containing her enthusiasm. "Are you ready to see it?"

"Um . . ." Hannah turned to Lawrence, a question in her eyes.

He shrugged—just as clueless as she.

"It's really not necessary. I don't need . . ." She looked at Dami, who impatiently awaited clearance. "Okay. Sure. Where's this surprise?"

Everyone turned to the double doors that closed off the dining room. Hannah followed their stares and watched the doors part to reveal what was truly a surprise.

"Mom?"

"Honey." Hannah's mother stepped out of the dining room. Her eyes turned misty as she approached her daughter and held her. "Gosh. I missed you."

Hannah settled into the embrace. It was comforting and familiar. She held her mother tight and inhaled the scent of her shampoo. "I missed you too, Mom. So much."

"Nothing like a mother's touch to make everything better," Shola said.

"Actually, I think it was Lawrence's touch that made everything better," Dami added.

The twins giggled even as Iya Agba scolded them in Yoruba.

When Hannah broke the embrace, she looked in her mother's eyes and suddenly recalled Auntie Jumoke's accusation.

She still didn't know what to believe and wasn't ready to ask for answers. Maybe she feared hearing the truth. Now, with her mother in Nigeria, there was no way to avoid the truth or even delay it.

"Mom, what's going on? What are you doing here?"

"Well, school is out for the summer, and when Tiwa called me and—"

"I'm sorry." Hannah shook her head. "What did you say? Who called you?"

"I did." Tiwa stepped out of the dining room—her hands behind her back as she strolled forward with a smirk. "When the twins suggested cheering you up with a surprise, I thought what better surprise than your mother."

"Yeah," Shola chimed in. "We thought seeing her, someone familiar, would make you feel better."

"Exactly," Tiwa continued. "I know how much Auntie Jumoke upset you. She made some serious accusations about your mother, but you just kept defending her. It was so sweet." She pressed a hand to her chest as if truly touched. "Well, I believe there's some tea waiting for me in the kitchen. Enjoy your surprise, Hannah. You really deserve it." She waved goodbye and strutted away.

Hannah's body tensed. She was livid. While the entire family genuinely believed they were doing something nice, Tiwa's intention had been vindictive, all part of the high-school-mean-girl act she had not outgrown.

"What's going on?" Hannah's mother asked, flustered. "What was Tiwa talking about?"

"Mom, give me a minute. Okay? I'm just gonna run to the kitchen."

"Hey." Lawrence placed a comforting hand on Hannah's back. "I don't think that's the best idea right now."

"Don't be silly. Just stay here with my mom. Get to know her, and I'll be back in one minute." Hannah forced a smile and marched off before he could say another word.

In the kitchen, she looked past a two-tiered cake and saw Tiwa on a barstool—legs crossed as she sipped tea leisurely.

"Oh. Hi, Hannah." She grinned. "What do you think of the cake? I asked Chef Andy to bake it to further commemorate your mother's arrival."

Hannah approached Tiwa steadily—fists clenched at her sides, words plenty in her mouth. "Were you so set on pissing me off that you disregarded the feelings of your family? Did you even consider how bringing my mom here would affect them?"

"Come on. I'm not heartless. Of course I spoke to them, and everyone was on board." She placed the porcelain teacup on its saucer and hopped off the stool. "I think my mother was a little curious about yours—you know, the other woman. Shola and Dami thought seeing her would make you feel better and stop you from going back home. Segun was . . ." She chuckled. "Well, Segun is Segun. He couldn't have cared less. As for me, after all the drama with Auntie Jumoke, I thought a surprise visit from your mother—who you would likely not want to see—would be incredibly entertaining. I was right."

"I . . . you . . . ugh." Words jumbled in Hannah's mouth. She sorted through them and got out a few sensible sentences. "What in the world is wrong with you? Whatever issues we may have, you should have left my mom out of it. You had no right to call her—to bring her here. Or to say what you just did out there."

"And you had no right to interfere with me and Dayo. You know what they say about payback." She slid the tip of her finger along the base of the cake, gathered a cluster of pink icing, and popped it in her mouth.

"I wasn't interfering. I just saw what I saw."

"Yeah. And you planned on telling everyone. For all I know, you've already told Lawrence."

"I haven't. And I wasn't planning on it. But you know what? I've changed my mind. It's time everyone knows about your little affair." Hannah pivoted, and as she marched to the door, a mushy clump collided with the back of her head. She stopped, stiffened, and turned around to see the ridged hole in the two-tiered cake.

White and pink icing covered Tiwa's clawed hand—evidence of what she had done.

"Are you kidding me?" The words were loud even through Hannah's clenched teeth. "Did you seriously just throw cake at me?"

Tiwa licked the icing off her finger. "Maybe."

For days, Hannah had tried to exercise patience and tolerate Tiwa, to suppress her anger with every bit of resolve.

She was done with that.

Swiftly, she charged forward, plowed her fingers into the cake, and smashed the gathered clump in Tiwa's face.

Tiwa stood motionless—dumbfounded. She hadn't expected Hannah to retaliate. But her shock wore off fast, and she wiped icing from her eyes and dug both hands into the golden loaf.

Things escalated quickly. Chunks of cake flew around the room, hitting faces and limbs and kitchen appliances. When Hannah lost her balance and slipped, she brought Tiwa down with her, and the two squealed and scuffled over the cake-smeared floor.

"What in God's name is going on here?"

Hannah and Tiwa froze. They looked at the doorway where Iya Agba stood, the whole family—including Hannah's mother—behind her. The twins giggled behind their hands, while Segun chuckled. Hannah's mother was silent, but her wide wandering eyes proved she was both confused and shocked. Lawrence's face, however, was blank, his emotions unreadable. Iya Agba's and Sade's emotions were obvious, unmistakable. They were furious.

"Are you both mad?" Iya Agba took a small step into the kitchen, not nearing the white tiles grimy with cake. "What is the meaning of all this? Eh?"

"Um . . . I . . ." Hannah bit her lip, taking in the sweet buttercream icing into her mouth. *Damn it.* How had she allowed this to happen? No words could lessen the degree of her humiliation. She felt her cake-coated cheeks redden. She turned to Tiwa, whose eyes were low as if she too, now with an audience, realized the shame in her behavior.

"Get up." Sade took a cautious step forward. "Both of you. Now!"

Hannah and Tiwa sprung to their feet. They swayed before regaining their balance.

"What nonsense!" Sade gathered her long gown in her hand, protecting it from the mess on the floor. "Fighting like common ruffians. And on the day before your father's funeral." She said nothing for a few seconds, only glared at the guilty parties whose heads hung low. "Have you both forgotten you are sisters?"

Hannah and Tiwa glanced at each other, then quickly turned away.

"Okay. Well, it seems like you have. Maybe spending some time together will jog your memory."

"Spending time together?" Tiwa's head snapped up. "Mommy, what do you mean?"

"You both will clean this kitchen. Together." She held up her hand just as her daughter attempted to protest. "Do not say a word. Start cleaning. And don't even think about asking Mary or anyone else for help." She turned away and ushered everyone out. "Let's go. You too, lover boy," she said to Lawrence, who made a move to enter the kitchen. "Out."

He turned away and followed the others, leaving Hannah and Tiwa alone in the mess they had created.

THIRTY-TWO

HANNAH

Hannah dragged a towel along the kitchen counter and eyed Tiwa, who handled a broom with disgust and uncertainty. Hannah turned on the faucet, and as water drenched the towel, she cleared her throat.

"I still can't believe you threw cake at me. What are you—five?"

"Well, what did you expect me to do?" Tiwa stopped sweeping and braced a hand on her hip. "You were going to tell everyone about me and Dayo."

"I wasn't going to say anything, you psycho." She turned off the faucet and drained the wet cloth. "I was bluffing."

"Bluffing? You were walking to the door like you were on a goddam mission to destroy my life."

"I was messing with you." Hannah sighed, fatigued in every sense. "I wasn't actually going to do it. It's not my place to inform people about what's going on between you and Dayo. That's none of my business."

They watched each other, a wariness in their regard. After a moment, they looked away.

"Your mom seems nice," Tiwa said while hurling a chunk of cake into a dustpan.

"What's your point?" Hannah asked, her tone flat.

"Maybe you should talk to her about what Auntie Jumoke said."

"Maybe you should tell everyone you're having a secret fling with Dayo."

Tiwa's head spun to Hannah. Though her hair, thick with cake, didn't move along with her swift motion. "It's not a fling."

Hannah frowned, puzzled. That was not the response she had expected. An insult? Yes. A patronizing statement? Absolutely. A correction that lacked Tiwa's signature flavor of bitchiness? That was an utter surprise.

"It's not a fling, okay? When you call it that, it makes it sound cheap and fleeting."

"And it isn't?"

"No. Of course not. I love him." The instant Tiwa said the words, she flinched. "Oh my God." She dropped the broom and sat on a barstool. "I've never said that before—not to him, not even to myself. Shit. *Love.* How the hell did that happen? What am I going to do? Do I tell him . . . that I love him?"

Hannah's confusion deepened. "Are you asking for my advice?"

"What? No. Why would I ask for your advice?" Tiwa scowled and shuffled against the stool. Though as the tension left her face, she watched Hannah. "Okay. Fine. Yes. I'm asking."

For the sake of her sanity, Hannah decided not to dwell on the moment and the peculiar turn it had taken. "Yeah," she said. "Of course. Tell him how you feel, and while you're at it, tell everyone else too. Honestly, I don't understand why you're keeping it a secret to begin with."

"Because he was one of our father's closest friends."

Our. It was one word, but with it, Tiwa acknowledged something she hadn't before—the fact that she and Hannah were related. Sisters.

"How close were they?"

"Close," Tiwa answered. "They were friends for years. Dayo was always at our house—for dinners and birthday celebrations. I grew up calling him uncle, for Christ's sake. And then one day, everything changed." She groaned. "When everyone learns we've been seeing each other, they'll have a lot to say—my mother especially. I just want to be with him without all that complication."

"So you two are gonna continue sneaking around? The other night, he said he didn't want to do that anymore."

"Seriously? Were you also eavesdropping? How much of our conversation did you hear?"

"Just enough. Now listen." Hannah clapped her hands together and took a stern stance. "If you really love him and think this is the real deal, come out with the truth. It's definitely an unconventional situation, but everyone deserves to know. You have to give them a chance to react and adjust to it. You have to be honest with them. If not, you might lose Dayo. And do you really want that to happen? Because I'm sure some other woman will happily take that Idris Elba look-alike off your hands."

Tiwa watched Hannah with a deadpan expression, and then slowly, a smile tugged the corners of her lips upward. "He does look like Idris, doesn't he?"

"So much."

It happened suddenly—an outburst of chuckles from Tiwa, who doubled over, and Hannah, who tossed her head back. The laughter was loud and warm. When they settled, Tiwa sat up straight and huffed.

"I'm sorry about your mom," she said, her voice gentle. "I took things too far."

"Yeah. You really did." Hannah rubbed the wrinkle between her bent brows. "Now, I have to deal with things I'm not ready to deal with."

"Well, maybe just talk to her and see what she has to say."

"Yeah. I guess."

They returned to cleaning in silence.

As Hannah dragged a wet mop on the floor, she paused and turned to Tiwa. "Why have you been such an ass to me? I mean, I understand being shocked and having to adjust. But everyone seemed to have adjusted. Everyone's been great, and you have been . . . horrible."

Tiwa dropped the dustpan and broom on the floor and sighed. "Yeah. I know."

The admission was unexpected.

"The truth is, I was angry at Dad for lying, and I suppose I just took it out on you."

That seemed to be the common excuse.

"And when my anger wore off, I didn't know how else to act around you. I didn't know how to connect with you." She looked away and blinked rapidly. "Everyone seemed to be connecting with you, and I . . . I just couldn't. And that made me act out a little . . . a lot. And then I thought you were going to tell everyone about me and Dayo, so I called your mom and made everything between us even worse. I really messed up." She sniffed, and tears trailed down her cheeks. "I'm supposed to be your big sister, and I . . . I . . . messed up everything. It's not what Dad would have wanted."

Hannah didn't allow shock to delay her reaction. She hurried across the kitchen and wrapped her arms around Tiwa. "It's okay."

"I'm sorry." Tiwa sank into the embrace; her face nestled against Hannah's neck.

"Seriously, it's fine. I'm over it." And she sincerely was. Anger and resentment were pointless once Tiwa had apologized.

"Hannah, is this strange?"

"Is what strange?"

"Us hugging."

"Oh. Yeah. Very. It's very strange. But." Hannah tightened her grip and smiled. "We'll get used to it."

THIRTY-THREE

HANNAH

After a thorough wash, Hannah's hair was clean—no evidence of the cake brawl that occurred earlier. The air in the bathroom was dense with mist and the scent of a berry body wash. Hannah tightened the cord on her robe and stepped into her bedroom, where she flinched, startled by an unexpected visitor.

"Mom."

"Hi, honey." Hannah's mother sat on the snow-white chaise longue—back straight, hands in her lap, blond hair cascading over her shoulders. "Got all the cake out of your hair?"

"Yeah. I think so." She shifted her weight from one leg to another. The impulse to hug her mother was strong, but she resisted.

"So, what was all that about with you and Tiwa?"

"It's nothing. We talked. We're good now."

"Okay. Well, can we talk?" She tapped the empty spot beside her and motioned for her daughter.

Hannah hesitated for a moment, then sat. It was awkward. She toyed with the cord on her robe and looked straight ahead—at the silver picture frames on the wall. The disconnection between her and her mother was undeniable. The pressure to speak made the silence between them more daunting.

"Hannah, I—"

"I met my father's sister, Jumoke. She told me he contacted you when I was sixteen. Is that true?"

Her mother opened and closed her mouth repeatedly, chewing on words, tasting them, deciding if they were fit to utter. In the end, she remained silent.

"He wanted to be a part of my life, and you didn't let him. Is that true, Mom? Please. Just tell me the truth."

"Hannah." She shifted and faced her daughter. "I hadn't heard from him in years. All he ever did was send money. Then one day, out of the blue, he called me. He said he wanted to be part of your life. And I—"

"And why didn't you tell me?"

"I didn't tell you because . . ." She rubbed the length of her straight nose and blew out a rough breath. "Do you remember when you were eight and met your father?"

Hannah nodded.

"It was a good visit. You two were connecting. I thought he was ready to be a part of your life, but suddenly something changed. I don't know what." She shrugged, and when her shoulders fell, they sat lower than they had before. "He just backed out. He disappointed you, and I couldn't let that happen again.

"So when he called and told me he wanted to be a part of your life, I didn't trust him. How could I? So I told him to stay away from us. I told him you wanted nothing to do with him. I lied."

Unable to remain seated, Hannah stood and paced while processing her mother's confession. "You lied to him." She stood still, her fingers on her throbbing temple. "But you lied to me too."

That was the most painful part. Hannah didn't understand why her mother had kept the truth from her. They told each other everything, and she'd hidden this for years.

"Mom, how could you keep this from me?" Her voice shrunk, the sound faint and shaky. "We're supposed to tell each other everything. You should have told me he reached out, and we would have made a decision together."

"As your mother, I had to make the decision. I hated lying to you, but I had to. I was worried he would hurt you again." Tears glossed her gray-blue eyes. "I did what I thought was best. I protected you. That's all I've ever tried to do." She pressed a hand over her mouth and hunched over.

As Hannah listened to her mother's muffled cries, she contemplated where to direct her anger. Who could she blame for this mess? Auntie Jumoke? Her father? Her mother? Each of them was at fault to some degree. But what did it matter now? Placing blame and being resentful changed nothing.

Hannah had already lost her father, but Auntie Jumoke was a stranger she still wanted to know. And her mother was all she had ever known. Hannah couldn't direct blame at the one person who loved her unconditionally and who had raised her all alone—always kind, always supportive, always devoted. Hannah didn't know how to blame her mother for protecting her, for doing what any good mother would have done.

"Mom. It's okay." She knelt at her mother's feet and held her. "It's okay."

"I'm sorry, honey. I am so, so sorry."

"I know." She pressed kisses on her mother's cheek. "I know you are."

They held each other for a long while, and then they separated, sniffing and wiping each other's flushed, wet cheeks.

"Come. Sit. Tell me how you've been doing."

"Sure. But first." Hannah sat on the empty spot on the lounger, her expression pinched. "You met Sade, his wife. How was that?" She imagined it must have been awkward and tense. How had her mother handled it?

"I spoke to her before you arrived. I thought it was necessary."

"Oh? And how did that go?"

"I told her the truth—that I didn't know your father was married. He didn't tell me until I had you."

"And what did Sade say?"

"Something I didn't expect." Her eyes wandered as she thought on it. "She said, and I quote, 'I don't blame you for what happened. I only blame him. And since he is dead, let the sleeping dog lie.'"

Hannah's eyes expanded. "Really? She said that—even the sleeping-dog bit?"

"Yeah. I was surprised myself, but she's been very cordial, considering the circumstances. But enough about that." She flicked her hand as if shooing off a fly. "I want to know how it's been for you, being here with your siblings."

"Um . . . it's been good."

"You don't sound so certain. What is it? What's the problem?"

The problem was that guilt often limited Hannah's curiosity. She wanted to know her father and her siblings but didn't want to hurt her mother in the process. She thought of her conversation with Lawrence. He'd understood her conflict so well, related to it even. He'd given her wonderful advice, and at the time, it had been enough. But now, Hannah realized she wasn't satisfied with what he had said. She needed to hear from her mother.

"Mom, can I ask you a question?"

"Of course. Anything."

"Are you okay with this?"

"With what, honey?"

"With me wanting to know them and him. If it hurts you, even a little bit, I'll have nothing to do with them. I promise."

"Hannah." Her mother's voice was soft, honeyed, drawing out each syllable with so much warmth and tenderness. "Why do you think I wanted you to come here? Why do you think I devoted an entire weekend to convincing you to come? Hmm?" She held her daughter's chin, ensuring their eyes locked. "Listen to me. I want this for you. Seeing you with them makes me so happy. Hearing the twins talk about you this morning brought tears to my eyes. They adore you."

Hannah laughed as she blinked back tears.

"That's all I've ever wanted for you—to be a part of his world as you are mine."

Part of two worlds. The idea was so new to Hannah. She had never had the option before. There was only one world, and she had forced herself to be satisfied with it. But now, there was a second, and it was fascinating, and she was eager to claim it completely and be a part of it. She would have to figure out what it meant to live within these two worlds, but for now, she didn't dwell on that. She simply embraced it.

"Thanks, Mom."

"Of course." She pressed a kiss to her daughter's cheek. "Now, will you please tell me about this boy? Lawrence. What's going on there? Are you guys dating?"

"Yeah. I guess we are." Hannah sighed, slightly dazed at the thought of him. "He's the best. He's sweet. And generous. And attentive. And . . . I'm going to fall in love with him, Mom." She paused and considered her words but didn't retract them. "Yeah. Any moment from now, I'm going to fall in love with Lawrence."

She'd felt it the night before—the beginnings of that emotion, budding inside her. Soon, it would grow wildly and coil through every part of her like a vine.

It was only a matter of time.

THIRTY-FOUR

HANNAH

Hannah descended the stairs in search of Lawrence. As she neared the landing, she looked through the windows. The sky was turning a molten brass hue at the gradual loss of sunlight.

A few hours had passed since she saw him last. She'd checked his room before coming down, but he hadn't been in there.

"Mimi," Hannah called out to a maid, who was walking toward the living room. "Hey. Have you seen Lawrence? I've been looking for him."

"No, ma. I haven't, but he might be in the office."

"Office? Where's that?"

"I'll show you." Mimi led Hannah past the living room and to a door at the far end of the extensive hallway. "Here, ma. This was Chief's office. *Oga* Lawrence is probably inside."

"Oh. Thank you."

"No problem." Mimi cracked the door open, then walked away.

Chief Jolade's office. Lawrence had intended to bring Hannah here, but must have forgotten. Eager to see the space, she pushed the door open and stepped into the room that had a mild fragrance of leather. The smell exuded from the cocoa-colored furniture—the executive swivel chair behind the massive mahogany desk and the three tufted couches that enclosed a coffee table.

Hannah scanned the floor-to-ceiling bookshelves that covered two walls. With one finger, she tilted a book out of perfect alignment and read the cover.

"*Their Eyes Were Watching God*." She smiled, remembering her copy back in San Francisco—old and tattered after being read too many times. Her father's version, however, was a first edition in impeccable shape. She slipped the book into its former position and picked another. "*The Bluest Eye*." Another book she had read, and another first edition in the tasteful collection. When her finger fell on the third book, she frowned at the peculiar title. "*An Orchestra of Minorities*." She read the premise and was intrigued.

It was as if her father, with no words at all, had given her a book recommendation. She sat in the chair behind the desk. Cool, smooth leather pressed against her skin. Her father once sat in this chair. This had been his space—filled with books he had read and loved. Hannah instantly felt close to him. Physically, he was gone. But if by some chance, remnants of him lingered in this room, she was here with him and he with her.

As Hannah opened the book, she heard shuffling. Her alert eyes shifted to one of the three tufted couches, where Segun lounged. She hadn't noticed him until now, as he struggled to an upright position.

"Um . . . what are you doing here?" he asked, rubbing his drowsy eyes.

"Well, I wanted to read some of this book. I had no idea anyone was in here." She watched him with a raised eyebrow. "What are you doing?"

"Sleeping and hiding from my mom. She wants me to cut my hair for Dad's funeral tomorrow." He slid a hand over his cornrows. "I ain't doing that shit."

Hannah had been unaware of Segun's fake American accent until Shola mentioned it. Since then, she'd noticed that the intonation had an overstated flare and lacked steadiness as it swayed between who Segun was and who he was trying so hard to be.

"Well, I'm heading out. Can't risk bumping into my mom." He stood. "Gonna head to the studio and drop some lyrics on a beat."

"You make music? I didn't know that."

"Yeah. I'm a rapper. Wanna hear one of my tracks? It's dope."

"Okay. Sure." How could she pass up the opportunity? She closed the book and offered her complete attention. "Play something."

"Really? You wanna hear it? You . . . you ain't gotta do that." It seemed like he'd suddenly lost grip on his confidence. "In fact, just forget it."

"I want to hear it, Segun. Seriously."

"'Ight." He cleared his throat. "Imma play it. But I'm still working on it so . . ." He set his phone on the desk just as a beat sounded.

Hannah listened attentively. She bobbed her head to the up-tempo soundtrack, and then stopped when a brash, choppy voice rapped out of sync with the beat.

It was bad. Terrible. Definitely a disgrace to the hip-hop genre. Hannah's eyes widened, narrowed, wandered around the room—did everything but meet Segun's gaze. If she could avoid eye contact, she could lie successfully.

Wow. That was amazing. You're so talented. You've got a new fan. She rehearsed the lies and prayed for the acting chops to pull it off.

"Hannah, you don't like it. Do you?"

"Um . . . I love it, Segun. You're . . . um . . . amazing." *Just stare at the wall and avoid eye contact,* she coached herself. "You're so talented."

"Don't lie to me." He stopped the music and rammed the phone into his pocket. "Just be honest. I'm bad, aren't I?" Segun waited for an answer Hannah did not offer. He dropped into the chair across from her, his face in his hand. "In New York, I wanted to perform at this club. I played one of my tracks for the manager. He said I wasn't good. He said he couldn't put me up onstage. In fact, he laughed. So I bribed him. Gave him five grand." He slammed his palm against his forehead. "I'm so fucking stupid."

This was the perfect time to insert a lie. He could use the false boost of confidence, but Hannah couldn't voice the words.

"Dad never supported this—me wanting to be a rapper. He never got it. But I guess I didn't want him to get it. I didn't want him to get me." He rubbed the early growth of a beard along his jaw. "You know, we both loved music. But I got into hip-hop because it was so far from what Dad liked and who he was. Hip-hop let me be my own person, completely different from him.

"Now, I feel like this whole rapper persona has completely fucked with me. I don't know how to be anything else but this . . . this . . . caricature." He looked far off—his stare distant and empty. "I don't even know how to be a proud Nigerian man—a man like . . . like Dad."

"Is that the kind of man you wanna be, then—a man like our father?"

"I don't know. Maybe. You know what they say—like father like son. Maybe I shouldn't have fought it so much when he was alive. It wasn't like he was a bad man or anything."

Hannah leaned into the table, her chin in her palm as she watched Segun and at the same time, thought of Lawrence. "Someone told me something recently." She looked upward as she paraphrased. "They said we can't rely on anyone to determine who we wanna be. We can only rely on ourselves."

Lawrence's words seemed to float in Hannah's head, not yet settled. She thought she would share them with Segun, hoping he could make something of them that she couldn't.

"Who told you that?" he asked.

"Lawrence."

He snorted. "You sure he didn't get that from a fortune cookie?"

Hannah laughed. "Yeah. I'm sure." She studied her brother, who expelled a long breath. "Are you okay?"

"Yeah. I am." His tone relaxed, the false American accent receded slightly, giving way to a delicate Nigerian accent. "Thank you."

"For what?" she asked.

"The other night and even now. For just listening, for not saying too much." He shrugged. "Sometimes, you're not really looking for a pep talk or a lecture or any of that shit, you know?"

"Yeah. I know."

He smiled, shifted the chair back, and stood. "Well, I should probably leave, so you can get back to reading. I'll see you later?"

"Yeah. Sure." Hannah was enjoying Segun's company. She loved his personality—how coolheaded he was. It had always made her feel comfortable. She wanted to spend more time with him, but when he closed the door, her attention returned to the book.

"Hey." Lawrence's head appeared through the break in the door after she'd read only one line. "Segun told me you were in here." He entered the room, and she blushed.

A few hours ago, cake completely covered her. She hadn't recovered from the embarrassment. As she stood and approached Lawrence, she avoided making direct eye contact.

"Hi." She watched him through flapping lashes.

"Did you get a chance to speak with your mother?"

She nodded.

"And is everything okay with you two?"

"Yeah. We talked. Everything's great."

"Good." He smiled and playfully tugged on one of her curls. "And I see you're cake-free."

"Yeah. I was very thorough."

"Were you? Are you sure you didn't miss a spot? Maybe"—he pressed his lips to her neck—"here."

"No." She giggled. "I think I got that spot."

"Well, you must have missed a spot. Maybe somewhere under here." He slipped a hand under her floral blouse, and she squirmed as his warm palm skimmed her stomach. "Okay. I think you got everything." He pulled his hand out, and his expression tensed slightly. "By the way, I spoke to Tiwa. She said you guys worked it out. Should I believe her?"

"Yeah." The reconciliation was still fresh in Hannah's mind. She and Tiwa were now friends or sisters or the awkward, indefinable something in between. That was nothing short of a miracle. "Cake throwing was very therapeutic."

"Well, whatever works. I'm just happy you two are finally

getting along." He smiled. "Now, can I take you and your mother to dinner?"

"Yeah," she said. "That sounds wonderful."

And although it did, Hannah left the office reluctantly, not quite ready to leave the room that made her feel closer to her father than she ever had.

THIRTY-FIVE

HANNAH

Hannah had only ever been to one funeral. Flo had invited her for moral support when a relative passed. Hannah remembered the atmosphere—the smothering grief that oppressed her even though she hadn't known the deceased. That feeling was absent on the day of her father's funeral. The sadness was still there, signifying what the day meant, but it wasn't overwhelming; it gave way to other emotions, allowing for laughter as she and her sisters got dressed in Tiwa's bedroom.

The midafternoon sun shone through the windows and drenched the space with a brilliant glow. A makeup artist highlighted Hannah's cheekbones with a bronzed champagne shimmer, while another defined Tiwa's lips with a red liner. A woman who was especially skilled at manipulating fabrics added pleats to the burgundy *gele* on Shola's head. Hannah's *gele* was smaller and fashioned into a rose.

"Madam, I'm done." The makeup artist stepped back to view Hannah's face. "You look very beautiful. I hope you like it."

"Thanks, Nancy." Hannah rose and walked to the full-length mirror, where Dami stood in a one-shoulder gown that fitted her slender figure precisely. The burgundy *gele* on her head formed a perfect circle that framed her small face. "Dami, you look gorgeous."

"Thank you." She turned and faced Hannah. "And you look . . . wow. I don't have the words. Here." She moved aside and positioned Hannah in front of the mirror. "Just look."

And Hannah did. She looked at herself—at the rose-shaped *gele* on her head and the mermaid-style gown with double straps that drooped off her shoulders. Then she inspected the tasteful makeup that didn't overpower her features but delicately enhanced them. She was stunning. Was it appropriate to look this beautiful for a funeral? In Nigeria, apparently, it was.

"Well, look at you," Tiwa said. She strutted toward Hannah, her long leg peeking through the slit in her straight gown.

"Look at us," Shola added as she neared her sisters. "Aren't we a sight?"

They were in unique gowns that represented their differences but still, with the burnt orange material Hannah had chosen, unified them.

"Do you think Daddy is watching?" Dami asked. "Do you think he's . . ." She pressed her teary eyes shut. "Happy? Happy we're all finally together with Hannah and stuff?"

"Of course," Tiwa said. "He's happy. And proud of us." She took her younger sister's hand. "But remember that even though we're mourning Daddy today, we're also celebrating him— celebrating the life he lived and the things he accomplished. Okay?"

"Yeah." Dami nodded and blinked her tears away. "Okay."

A knock sounded at the door.

"Come in," Tiwa permitted.

The brass knob turned, the door opened, and Lawrence stepped into the room. He wore a burnt orange *agbada* with white embroidery that ran from his neckline to his chest. The material wasn't the delicate sheer the women wore; it was solid and lacked the detailed floral stitching and touches of pearls. Hannah's heartbeat quickened as she ogled him blatantly.

"Hi," he said, staring at her with the same lack of discretion.

"Oh gosh." Dami rolled her eyes. "They do this every time they see each other."

"Do what?" Tiwa asked.

"Act like no one else exists. It's cute but annoying as hell."

"Right. Sorry." Lawrence cleared his throat and focused on the others. "Everyone's ready for the church service. They're waiting downstairs."

"Well, I'm ready," the twins said together.

"Then we should go." Tiwa headed for the door, and her sisters followed.

Hannah started to leave with them, but Lawrence held her arm. She paused and stayed in the room with him. They said nothing until the makeup artists left. Once they were alone, he drew her close.

"Hannah, do you have any idea how incredible you look? Seriously." His gaze shifted over her physique. "You're breathtaking."

A deep blush warmed her complexion. "Thank you." She scanned him, took in his appearance more carefully. "You look like—"

"Like a true Yoruba man?" He chuckled.

"Like a very, very handsome Yoruba man." She touched the coral beads around his neck. She was tempted to kiss him but resisted, knowing a kiss would lead to more.

"Hannah, I've been meaning to ask you something."

"Yeah? What is it?"

He straightened his back and stood tall. "Well, I know you're supposed to leave tomorrow. I know you have a life to get back to in San Francisco, but . . . but . . . would you consider staying in Nigeria a little longer? I know it's crazy, but I can't imagine letting you go quite yet. I know we've only—"

"Yes!" she blurted, eager to answer. "Yes. I'd love to stay."

"Really?"

"Yeah. Really." She locked her arms around his neck. "I can't imagine letting you go either. Not now." Maybe never.

"But what about your job?"

"Don't worry about it. I'll figure something out—ask for more time off."

"Okay. Great." His smile was radiant. "This is wonderful."

"Yeah. It is." More time in Nigeria with Lawrence and her siblings. What could be better?

The door creaked open unexpectedly, just as Hannah was about to give in to temptation and kiss Lawrence.

"Hello," Auntie Jumoke said, entering the room. "Hannah, my dear, you look lovely." Her tone was low and shaky, a result of uncertainty. "How are you?"

"Fine." And to her surprise, no longer livid. The day before, she'd chosen to let go of her anger and resentment. It was easier that way—easier to live and carry on and make the most of what she still had.

"Lawrence, can you please excuse us? I would like to talk to my niece."

"Yes. Of course." He squeezed Hannah's hand before leaving the room.

"Can we sit?" Auntie Jumoke gestured to the cushioned chairs next to a velvet ottoman.

They sat side by side, neither uttering a word for a few seconds.

"Hannah," Auntie Jumoke said finally, a slight strain in her voice as she stifled a sob. "I am so sorry for everything." She touched the sleeve of her blouse and fiddled with a pearl on the sheer fabric. "I am so sorry for hurting you—for not being a better auntie. I will apologize as much as you need me to."

No matter how many times it was said, an apology remained an apology. It didn't evolve into something else. It didn't change the past. Hannah needed no more apologies. Rather, she needed an answer to something she had been pondering.

"Auntie, I have a question for you. Will you answer it honestly?"

"Yes." She angled her body toward her niece. "Absolutely. Ask me anything."

"In San Francisco, all those years ago, you mentioned something about my grandfather. You said he would disown my father if he knew about me."

"Yes. That's right. He would have disowned him."

"Why? Because he cheated on his wife and had a child out of wedlock, or because he cheated on his wife with a white woman and had me?"

"Um . . ." She touched the folds on her *gele* and averted her eyes.

"I just want the truth. Which is it?"

"Hannah." She looked at her niece again. "Your grandfather was a very traditional man."

There it was—the answer. A traditional man who wouldn't have wanted a biracial grandchild.

"He was a very strict man. All our lives, your father and I struggled to please him—to gain his approval. Your father especially. We feared him. And we did till the day he died."

A prejudiced grandfather—another person deserving a portion of the blame. Resentment cropped up, but Hannah dispelled it. She refused to be bitter, remembering it would do her no good.

"My mom is here," she said. "Have you seen her?"

"I have. We were introduced and spoke briefly."

"You have to talk to her—explain why my father stayed away. She has no idea what happened. She deserves the truth. She deserves an explanation and an apology from you."

Auntie Jumoke nodded. "And I will give her that. You have my word." She watched her niece timidly, her eyes low. "Hannah, will you . . . will you forgive me? Please."

"Auntie." A small smile softened Hannah's face. "I already have." And it felt especially good to admit it—to finalize the deed by saying it out loud. "I forgive you."

THIRTY-SIX

HANNAH

The Cathedral Church of Christ was an architectural wonder. The immense Gothic building was light gray with clean white lines framing the arched doors and windows. Inside, the choir sang a hymn. The acoustics softened their voices, made it a weightless, angelic melody accompanied by the chimes of the organ.

The song ended and everyone took their seats—Hannah between Lawrence and her mother, who wore a burnt orange wrap dress Tiwa had provided. The priest, an elderly man with a slightly hunched back and a shaved head, stood behind the pulpit; his white cassock swayed above the marble floor.

A short sermon began, but Hannah's attention was elsewhere—on the closed cherrywood coffin that contained her father's body. He was gone. And the child in her—the one that had been waiting by the windowsill, watching cars pass by and waiting for Daddy to come home—remembered again he wasn't coming. He was never coming home.

Dami stepped onto the altar and stood behind the pulpit; her bare shoulders were covered with a shawl Iya Agba had insisted they all wear during the service. Dami turned to a page in the Bible and read.

"Romans chapter eight verses thirty-eight and thirty-nine. 'For I am convinced that neither death nor life, neither angels nor demons, neither the present nor the future, nor any powers, neither height nor depth, nor anything else in all creation, will be able to separate us from the love of God that is in Christ Jesus our Lord.'"

Shola stepped behind the pulpit next and read another short verse. Segun and Lawrence did the same. When Tiwa stepped up, she didn't open the Bible. With her back straight and her chin high, she watched the congregation.

"My father was an extraordinary man." She was confident in her statement, having the knowledge to support it.

Hannah wished she could speak about her father with the same conviction, or at least with a clear knowledge of who he'd been. She could never do that.

"Now," Tiwa said, after mentioning a few of her father's achievements. "I would like to call up my sister, Hannah, to say a few words."

Though she'd heard her name clearly, Hannah stayed seated, twiddling her thumbs even as Lawrence nudged her.

"Hannah." Tiwa's voice and that single word boomed over the microphone. "Please come up."

Was this a joke, or had Tiwa reverted to her former self? The day before, they'd had a genuine reconciliation. Hadn't they?

Heads turned to Hannah. Lawrence nudged her again, and having no other choice, she stood. Gripping the shawl around her shoulders, she walked along the aisle and stepped onto the altar.

"Are you kidding me?" she whispered. "Seriously, what do you think you're doing?"

"Relax," Tiwa said, shifting her mouth from the microphone. "Just say something—anything. He was your dad."

"I don't know what to say. What can I possibly say?" She didn't know him, nor did she have any memories to recount.

"Just speak from your heart. You'll be fine." Tiwa stepped down from the altar and left Hannah to the full attention of the congregation.

Hannah moved behind the pulpit. The assembly of unfamiliar faces stunned her and made her recede slightly. She considered returning to her seat even with the embarrassment that would trail her, but Lawrence's gaze grounded her shifting feet. Even with the distance between them, she saw the encouragement in his eyes; it propelled her toward the pulpit and forced her mouth open.

"Um . . . I . . . I didn't know my father." Her small voice, heightened by the microphone and the acoustics, filled the church. "It's unfortunate. I wish, more than anything, that I had known him. I'm sure he was a great man."

That was it. That was all she could think to say. The next step was to return to her seat, but Hannah stood fixed. Her eyes were no longer on Lawrence but on her siblings. Dami, Shola, Segun, and Tiwa. Her father's children. Bits and pieces of him were installed in them all, and looking at each of them, Hannah— for the first time in her life—got an image of who her father was. The puzzle she had been trying to put together for years was somewhat whole now, a picture that each of her siblings and even Lawrence pieced together.

"I didn't know my father, but I know the children he raised," she said with a conviction she never thought possible. "Dami is the most vibrant, sweetest person." She smiled at the sister she had long dubbed her favorite. "Her joy is contagious. Her heart is kind." She shifted her gaze. "Shola is considerate. She cares so much about the happiness of others." She looked at her brother, who wore an *agbada* like Lawrence. "Segun is so easygoing. He can make you feel welcome and loved without even voicing it. Tiwa is . . ." She fought the urge to laugh as the event that led to their reconciliation came to mind. "Tiwa is the fiercest person I have ever met—strong-willed, confident, yet tender even in her unwavering strength." She shifted her gaze to where it had been initially and smiled. "And Lawrence is generous, kind, and . . ." She shrugged. "Well, he's just perfect."

The crowd laughed lightly.

"These are the children my father raised. Each one of them carries something he must have—through the course of his life—embedded in them. Looking at them, I'm certain my father was kind, considerate, strong-willed, lively, generous, and easygoing. The evidence is so clear. In them."

And that was all she had to say. With her stare on the floor, she paced down the aisle. As she shuffled into the pew, along the row of knees, Dami stood abruptly and embraced her.

"Hannah, that was so beautiful," she said, sniffing. "I love you."

"Oh, Dami." Hannah's throat tightened just as tears soaked her eyes. "I love you too."

It was strange to say it and even stranger that she meant it. She had known her for only a few days, but what Hannah felt for Dami and all her siblings was the kind of love that didn't require deep fostering. It was just there, sealed in DNA, rooted in the deepest parts of her—in blood and bone, fibers and fragments, heart and soul.

What followed Dami's embrace was simultaneous. Half the row—Shola, Segun, Tiwa, and Lawrence—rose and held Hannah in a huddle of overlapping arms.

As Hannah clung to them, each carrying parts of a father she never knew, she sighed and allowed her tears to fall freely.

A BRASS BAND OF TWELVE PLAYED A MELLOW AND DARK tune while marching behind the suited pallbearers, who propped the coffin on their shoulders. In the cemetery laden with green grass, groomed shrubs, and tombstones, Hannah and the rest of the family walked on the paved path, steps behind the band.

The sun's shine diminished. The air cooled as evening approached. The path eventually brought them to their destination. They gathered around the hole in the ground. The priest read verses from the Bible and then said a prayer. The coffin sank into the ground. Dami and Shola sobbed. Tiwa comforted her sisters, placing an arm around each of them. Large Gucci sunglasses covered Sade's and Iya Agba's eyes, but tears slipped from under the thick frames and onto their cheeks. Hannah held her mother's hand. It was comforting to have her near. They mourned differently from the others, and that understanding kept them close as the coffin disappeared into the earth.

THIRTY-SEVEN

HANNAH

While the funeral ceremony had been a farewell, the reception was a celebration of a man who lived. Hannah understood the distinction now. Her attire no longer seemed inappropriate; it was fitting for the reception location—a stunning waterfront garden.

A little past seven, the sun had already set. Strings of lights brightened every inch of the venue—the large stage with the band, the straw kiosk where bartenders mixed drinks, and the groomed shrubs and pastel-colored flowers between the circular tables.

Hannah sat with her mother, her siblings, Lawrence, Dayo, Sade, and Iya Agba. Auntie Jumoke occupied the next table with her husband and children, who Hannah had met at the church.

As servers cleared the tables of dinner plates, the MC swaggered onstage. "Ladies and gentlemen," he said into the microphone. "I hope you enjoyed your meal. As we are here to celebrate the late Chief Wale Jolade, I would like us to welcome his son, Segun. He has a special performance dedicated to his father."

The crowd applauded, but the family, Hannah included, was

confused. What special performance? Segun stood and walked to the stage, addressing no one's bewilderment.

"Um . . . what is he doing?" Dami asked.

"I have no idea," Shola answered. "But I saw him talking to the band earlier. I guess we're about to find out why."

"I don't know what is happening," Iya Agba said. "But if that boy gets up on that platform and does that hip-hop hooray nonsense, I will deal with him."

Was he really about to do that? Rap? From what Hannah had heard the day before, she was positive Segun didn't have the talent and was also positive he had embraced that fact. But he stepped onstage, pulled up the sleeves of his *agbada,* and took a seat behind the electric piano a musician had been playing moments ago.

Iya Agba continued with the threats, while Sade fixed steely eyes on her son. Then Segun began to play the piano. He produced slow, gentle notes that seamlessly evolved into something more danceable. The tune was familiar, but there was a distinct African flair, especially with the inclusion of the *shekere* and the talking drum.

Hannah couldn't determine the original song until Segun sang, and his smooth, soulful timbre caressed the words to "One Sweet Day." The connection between his heart and his voice was clear, evident in each riff and run. The song didn't mimic the slow tempo of the original, but it was just as emotive.

The performance was a perfect bridge between R&B and Afrobeat. Segun had created something novel—like nothing Hannah had heard before, and she and the rest of the family were mesmerized. Iya Agba's threats stopped. Sade's gaze softened, growing mournful and then proud. She wiped a fallen tear and leaped to her feet, clapping as Segun played the final notes on the piano. Everyone—the family and guests—stood and applauded energetically, as it truly was a performance worthy of a standing ovation.

However, someone at the table was missing. Tiwa. Hannah spun around and caught her rushing away. Concerned, she followed her through the exit and then to the railing that overlooked the lit Lekki-Ikoyi Bridge. She approached her from behind, then stood beside her.

"Hey. Are you okay?"

Tiwa tilted her head from Hannah's view. "What are you doing here?"

"I saw you leave, so I followed you. You're upset. What's wrong?"

"It's nothing. I'm fine." She sniffed. "Just go back to the party."

"Hey." Hannah edged closer. "You know, you don't always have to be so tough. It's okay to let go sometimes." She placed her hand over Tiwa's. "Tell me what's going on."

"It's just that . . ." Her voice shook. "He's gone. Dead. And I've been trying to stay strong for everyone, but then Segun sang that song. And I just couldn't be . . ." She didn't complete her sentence, didn't admit to being weak, human. It just wasn't in Tiwa's nature to fully succumb to that emotion. Even as she fell into her sister's open arms, her vulnerability seemed measured.

As she cried, Hannah said nothing. She didn't search for the right words, understanding that Tiwa simply needed a moment free from the facade she always assumed. Hannah gave her that moment, and when it passed, Tiwa stopped sobbing and cleared her throat.

"I had no idea Segun could sing like that," she said. "He's really good."

"He's amazing," Hannah added. "I was blown away."

"Yeah. Me too." Tiwa dabbed her wet cheeks with her fingers. "So, on another note." A smile spread across her face. "This morning, I told Dayo that I love him."

"Really?"

"Yeah. And I plan to tell everyone about us soon. Because honestly, these past few days without him made me realize how important he is to me—how much I love him. We've wasted so much time hiding and caring what other people will think. I'm not doing that anymore."

"That's great, Tiwa. I'm happy for you."

"Yeah. Thanks." Her stare shifted to the bridge. "So . . . you're leaving tomorrow."

"Yes." Hannah didn't want to correct her. Not yet. "I am."

"Well, do you have to? Could you maybe stay? For a little longer?"

"You want me to stay?"

"Yeah. I really do."

"Oh. Well, okay. Sure. I'll stay."

Tiwa's mouth dropped open, caught between a laugh and a gasp. "Seriously? Just like that?"

"Actually, I already decided to stay a little longer. Lawrence asked me this morning, and I said yes. I just thought I'd mess with you."

"You little devil." Tiwa shoved Hannah playfully. "You're lucky it's time for the family dance."

The MC had made the announcement, calling for members of the Jolade family to step on the dance floor.

"I seriously hope you haven't forgotten the dance lesson we gave you last night."

"Of course not," Hannah said confidently. "Don't worry. I've got this."

The two-hour lesson had served as entertainment for Tiwa and the twins, who laughed as Hannah attempted to perfect the

Gbeku and the *Zanku*. Now, as she approached the dance floor where the rest of the family gathered, she proved the lesson hadn't been futile. Flawlessly, she nailed one move and then another, and the twins squealed, their shrill voices audible even through the music.

"Well, look at you," Lawrence said, bopping toward Hannah with all the finesse of an experienced dancer. "I see those lessons worked."

"She had great teachers," the twins boasted. "You're welcome!"

As guests joined the Jolades on the dance floor, Hannah extended a hand to her mother, who took it reluctantly.

"Honey, you know I'm more of an observer not a dancer."

"It's okay, Mom. Just sway or do a little shoulder bop."

It was all her mother could do, but it sufficed.

The music elevated, the bass became heavier. Guests showered the family with dollar bills. Some directed their aim at Hannah.

"What in the—"

"It's a Nigerian tradition," Hannah said before her mother could finish the sentence. "The twins explained it to me yesterday." And it felt good to explain it to her mother, to have gained some knowledge of her culture she could confidently impart.

The dancing carried on, the atmosphere was buoyant, and Hannah, in that moment, was happier than she had ever been in her life.

THIRTY-EIGHT

HANNAH

Hannah blinked the weariness from her eyes as Dayo entered the living room and sat before the family. It was only noon, and no one had truly recovered from the previous night, but they gathered, regardless, for the reading of the will.

Hannah was unsure why Dayo had insisted she be present for it. Despite what Sade had said a few nights ago, Hannah was certain she didn't have an inheritance. And that was perfectly fine. She didn't feel entitled to her father's wealth. Maybe she would have felt differently if she'd grown up with him or worked alongside him like Tiwa and Lawrence. But that hadn't been the case. So again, Hannah wondered why she wasn't in bed like her mother.

"I'm sure this will only take a few minutes," Lawrence said, squeezing her knee. "Hang in there."

She held back a yawn and nodded.

"Okay," Dayo said. "The last will and testament of Chief Wale Jolade."

Everyone seemed tense as Dayo opened a file and read.

"My dearest family," he began. "It gives me so much joy to

envision all of you together with Hannah—my family finally complete."

At the mention of her name, Hannah became alert. The fatigue left her eyes, and she looked at Lawrence, smiling.

"This isn't the type of reunion I wanted," Dayo continued reading, "but it is the only one permitted after I made so many mistakes. I wanted to bring all of you together so that you could hopefully connect and be a family. I am sorry for the secrets I kept for so long. I am sorry for hurting all of you. But know that I love you all. So much. Know that I am proud of each one of you. And know that every decision I made in this will was well-thought-out and intentional. I hope you will respect it." Dayo turned the page. "The executors of the estate are Tiwa and Lawrence."

No one seemed surprised by the news except for Lawrence, whose eyes went wide.

"They will run Jolade Group of Companies. All my children will become members of the board of directors, as stated in appendix four."

Hannah flinched. He'd said all my children. That meant her. She was confused, and before she could process, Dayo carried on. He mentioned properties in Nigeria and overseas, all divided between Sade, Lawrence, Hannah, and her siblings. And then before she could process that, Dayo carried on about money. So much money—millions of dollars. What was Hannah supposed to do with all of that? Her father had given it to her, but could she accept it? Would she be stupid not to?

With it, her life would change. That much was certain. She could pay off her mother's mortgage and give her the opportunity to retire early and travel the world—to explore all the places she'd always wanted to. Hannah could also make donations to charities, including the Youth Hope Center. The building that housed the center was old. It could use a lot of upgrades. There were so many possibilities, but there was still that question: could she accept the inheritance? Accepting it felt like taking something that belonged to her siblings and Sade and Lawrence.

"I can't take it," she blurted. "I can't take any of it."

Everyone turned to her, their stares inquiring.

"I don't understand," Dami said. She shuffled to the edge of the couch and studied Hannah, who sat across from her. "Why can't you take it?"

"Because it's not mine. It doesn't belong to me."

Sade had told Hannah this a few nights ago, after accusing her of coming to Nigeria strictly for an inheritance. Hannah wondered if everyone else felt the same—if they believed she was taking something that didn't belong to her. Looking around the room, she focused on each of them and tried to read their expression.

"It does belong to you." Sade's tone was mellow. "Hannah, I know what I said the other night. I was wrong." Tenderness washed over her features, even reaching her eyes. "You are his daughter. You have every right to be in this house and every right to your inheritance. I know he didn't do much for you—he didn't give you everything you needed. But let him give you this."

Hannah was speechless and touched. She hadn't expected that from Sade. She looked at her siblings, who all nodded, agreeing with their mother.

"Shall I continue?" Dayo asked.

Hannah turned to him and smiled. "Yeah. You can continue."

"Okay." He looked at the sheet of paper in his hands. "For the last property, the most important property. The Jolade family home."

"Well, we already know who gets the house," Segun said. "Obviously, it's Mom."

"Segun, please let me finish." Dayo returned his focus to the paper and read. "This house means so much to me. This is a place with so many wonderful memories, a place that has always brought us all together. And I hope it will continue to bring all of you together as a family. This house is willed to my daughter Hannah."

In an instant, Hannah was the center of attention. She looked around the room and tried to decipher the stares she received from everyone, including Lawrence. Was he as shocked and perplexed as she? Too much had happened all at once. Her head was reeling. Had she heard Dayo correctly? Had he really said her name? Maybe he'd said Shola or Tiwa or Dami—anyone but her.

"What the hell do you mean she gets the house?" Tiwa rose to her feet and scowled. "My mother gets the house."

Everyone looked at Sade, who sat unmoving, a bewildered expression on her face. They waited for her to speak, but she was clearly stunned into silence.

"Dayo, are you sure of what you're reading?"

"I read exactly what is in your father's will, Tiwa."

"But that can't be," Shola said, rubbing her forehead. "That makes no sense. Why would Dad leave Hannah the house?"

"That is exactly what I would like to know." Tiwa's voice took on the bitter edge it had before—before she and Hannah had reconciled. "Why the hell would he give her the house? She isn't even a part of this family. You told us to be nice to her, to get to know her, and then we would get our inheritance. You didn't say anything about her getting the goddam house! Our house!"

"Tiwalade, enough," Iya Agba said firmly.

Her attempt at censoring Tiwa was pointless. Hannah heard the truth and processed it, and in an instant, everything became clear.

It had all been a lie. Everything had been a lie. They had put up an act, tolerated her so they could be rewarded with their inheritance. At the realization, Hannah's chest squeezed, her heart strained by so many emotions all at once. She felt foolish. She felt betrayed and used and worthless. That was the hardest emotion to bear, feeling like she meant nothing to the people she had come to consider family.

She shifted away from Lawrence and eyed him as if she didn't recognize him. She looked at the rest of them and stood. "I guess that explains it." A thickness built up in her throat, but she pushed her words out. "Shopping, the sleepover, movie night. Everything." She did not wipe the tears that came down her cheeks; there were too many. "You were just doing it for money."

"Hannah—"

"Don't." She held up a hand, silencing Dami. "Don't bother. You got what you wanted, didn't you? While you're at it, you can have mine too. I don't want any of it—not this house, not the money. Nothing. Because you're right." She turned to Tiwa and watched her even as tears blurred her vision. "I am not a part of this family. It was stupid of me to think otherwise."

For the third time since her stay began, Hannah rushed out of the living room on the verge of tears. As she marched toward the stairs, she heard Lawrence behind her. She spun around to look at him.

"Leave me the hell alone," she shouted, even as her voice trembled. "You got what you wanted, didn't you? What else do you need me for?"

"Hannah, listen to me. I didn't know about the condition of the will. I swear."

"Don't stand there and lie to me."

"I'm not lying." He ran a hand over his face and groaned. "Hannah, I know this is a lot, but I need you to trust me. After these past few days together, I'd like to think that you know me. So, give me the benefit of the doubt here. Please."

She wanted to. She wanted to believe him. After everything that had happened between them, she wanted to believe him so desperately. She searched his eyes for proof he was telling the truth, but she didn't know what it looked like. Was his crestfallen expression proof, or was he just a good actor?

Memories of their time together—their first kiss, their day in Ajegunle, their nights in Akwa Ibom—played in a loop in her mind. She slowed them down and looked through each frame with a sense of detachment, trying to spot a moment of insincerity in their interactions. What part had been a lie? She'd been completely genuine. From the moment she'd met Lawrence in San Francisco, she had felt an attraction that developed into something deeper. But what about him? What did he truly feel for her? Had their time together really been a lie—an attempt to get his inheritance? Still, she inspected her memories and looked for clues of dishonesty on his part. She found none. But maybe she didn't want to find any. Maybe she didn't want to see what was so clear. Lawrence, like the Jolades, had used her.

"I never want to see you again," she told him. She had to force the words out over a sob. She had to mean them. She had to convince herself that it was the right thing to do, even as her heart broke. "You're a liar. And I want nothing to do with you."

She turned and rushed up the stairs, devastated and regretful.

She shouldn't have come to Nigeria. It was the biggest mistake she had ever made.

THIRTY-NINE

TIWA

The morning after the reading of the will was quiet—quiet and at the same time, loud like the deafening ring that comes after an explosion. The commotion of the previous day was gone. Now, there was just the ringing—the aftermath of everything Tiwa had said humming in her ears.

She sat upright in bed, recounting the scene.

After Dayo made the announcement about the house, she'd been stunned and puzzled like everyone else. Though, no one had made the mistake she had. She bit her tongue at the recollection. She should have done that before, held her tongue with every ounce of restraint. Her impulsiveness had pushed Hannah out of their lives. She shoved her fingers into her hair and disheveled the perfect bob.

"Tiwa?"

Her head snapped up and turned to the door where Dayo stood. "Hey. What are you doing here?"

"I wanted to check on you." He stepped into the room and shut the door.

"Why? I'm not the person you should be checking on. Try Dami or Shola or Segun. Try Lawrence. I'm the one who fucked everything up."

"Well, I'm checking on you." He pressed a kiss to her forehead and sat on the bed. "How are you doing?"

"Why aren't you angry with me like everyone else? I deserve it."

"I know you regret what happened."

"It doesn't matter if I regret it. What happened, happened." She bit her tongue again, punishing it. Punishing herself. "Segun and the twins won't even speak to me. Lawrence left. He went back to his place." That was the true punishment—her family shutting her out. And of course, Hannah's departure.

She'd packed right after Dayo read the will and left with her mother, even as Shola and Dami pleaded with her to stay. Iya Agba's mediation hadn't counted for much either.

Tiwa had gone to Hannah's room after. There was no trace of her, except for the designer clothes that hung in the closet.

Her absence struck Tiwa deeply—more than she thought possible. They were just getting to know each other, and Tiwa had hoped they would have more time. There was so much she wanted to tell Hannah, so much she had kept to herself since learning they were sisters. For one, Hannah smiled like their father. Tiwa noticed this whenever she would watch her with reserved curiosity. She should have mentioned it long ago, but stubbornness had kept her mouth pinned.

"Can I ask you something?" Dayo said.

"Sure."

"What did you think was going to happen with Hannah owning the house? Did you think she would throw you all out?"

"Um . . ." Tiwa thought briefly, then shook her head. "No."

"Then what was really the issue? Why did you react the way you did?" He studied her, a slight pinch between his eyebrows. "Did you think she didn't deserve it?"

"I was confused. I still am. I know what this house meant to my father. I know what it means to us." She pressed a finger to her forehead and sighed. "Hannah didn't grow up here. She doesn't have the memories we have. This house means more to us than I imagine it means to her. It's our home. And I just don't understand why he would give her our home."

"Tiwa." He held her hand. "Do you remember what your father said in his will before stating who gets the house?"

"No. Not entirely."

"He said this house has always brought you all together as a family. He hoped it would continue to do that. That was why he left it to Hannah."

Tiwa cocked her head. "I don't get it."

"He didn't want the funeral to end and have things return as they were—with Hannah apart from you all. He believed that if she owned the house, she would always have a reason to come back. And the house would connect all of you. That's why he gave it to her."

Tiwa's face fell into her palm, and she groaned. Dayo's explanation made perfect sense. Why hadn't she thought of that? Why hadn't she even tried to understand and respect her father's decision? After all, he'd asked them to do just that—respect his wishes. And she hadn't. Shame mingled with her remorse.

"Damn it." She lifted her head and met Dayo's gaze. "What do I do? How do I fix this?"

"Give her a call, love." He squeezed her hand. "I'll give you her number. Talk to her. And when you do, be honest with her. It's not the time to act like you're made of stone. Show her how sorry you are."

Tiwa nodded. "Okay. I can do that."

"I'm sure you both can work it out."

"Yeah. I really hope so." She considered him and couldn't resist smiling. "I love you, you know."

"Yeah. I know." He pressed a kiss on the back of her hand. "I love you too."

"Thanks for checking on me."

"Of course." He looked over her body, the part the duvet didn't conceal. One strap of the black nightgown hung off her shoulder; the sweetheart neckline dipped low. He leaned into her, and she pressed a hand to his chest and kept him back.

"Dayo, I need to tell you something."

"Okay. What is it?"

"I spoke to my mother late last night. She couldn't sleep and wanted to talk about Hannah."

Given that Tiwa couldn't sleep either, she'd been sitting in bed when her mother barged into her room.

"Was she upset with you?" Dayo asked.

"Yeah. And disappointed. She told me to fix things with Hannah." Tiwa had pissed off her entire family. The staff were likely pissed as well. Maybe it was sensible to get her own cup of tea until things died down. "Anyway, we also talked about something else."

"What?"

"Us. I told her about us, Dayo."

He frowned and watched her inquisitively. "Um . . . what exactly did you tell her?"

"I told her we've been seeing each other for months. I told her we're in love."

"Okay . . ." His wide eyes urged her to continue. "And what did she say?"

"She said she had a suspicion."

"What? What do you mean, she had a suspicion? How?"

"She noticed the way we look at each other." Tiwa laughed. "And the way you say my name."

"How do I say your name?"

"Apparently, like a man who's madly in love."

He chuckled, then leaned forward and kissed her gently. "Well, I am," he said, smiling, "madly in love."

"And it would appear that I am too."

And she truly was. Dayo was everything she was not—calm, patient, slow to anger. In a lot of ways, he reminded Tiwa of her father. And in a lot of ways, he made her aware of her faults. Without judgment or rebuke, he alerted her to all the parts of herself that could be better. And Tiwa knew, without doubt, that he was the man she wanted to spend the rest of her life with.

"So, when you confirmed your mother's suspicion, what did she do? How did she react?"

"Well, she wasn't completely angry. But she wasn't happy either. She has concerns and wants to discuss them further to-day." Tiwa rolled her eyes. She wasn't looking forward to sitting with her mother and defending her relationship. It was exactly what she'd wanted to avoid from the beginning. Now, she would have to do the same with her grandmother, her siblings, and even her friends. It would be like taking an act on the road. She imagined repeating the same lines. *I love him. He loves me. He didn't take advantage of me. I can make my own decisions. I want to spend my life with him. He's the one.* As true as those words were, the idea of repeating them again and again to people who needed convincing made Tiwa clench her jaw.

"Hey," Dayo said, noticing the tension on her face. "Every-thing will be okay. We'll just give everyone some time to get used to us."

"But I don't want to put our relationship on hold because

everyone needs time. I don't know how long the adjustment period will take, and I really just want us to start our lives together."

"Yeah. Me too." He beamed and interlocked their fingers. "We'll figure this out. Together. Okay?"

She sighed, nodded, and squeezed his hand. "You know, if it wasn't for Hannah, I don't think I would have had the courage to tell my mother."

"Hannah?"

"Yeah. She knew about us. She saw us in the kitchen the other night but didn't tell anyone. Then she told me to be honest with the whole family. She helped me, and I . . ."

The memory of the day before flashed in Tiwa's mind. Hannah's pained expression stood out more than anything else. Tiwa had hurt her immensely.

She had to find a way to make things right and to keep her family intact. Just as her father had intended.

FORTY

HANNAH
san francisco

Sun slipped through the slivers of space between the closed blinds. Hannah considered getting out of bed. Mornings always pressured her into doing something productive.

For four days, since returning from Nigeria, she had stayed in bed. Today, she chose differently. The showerhead spouted hot water over her tangled hair. She worked through the curls with conditioner until each lock was loose. When she stepped out of the tub and wiped mist off the mirror, she cringed at the sight of her inflamed eyes that were weary and miserable. She looked away and got dressed. A black sweat suit seemed like the perfect attire.

There wasn't much in the refrigerator but a container of raspberry yogurt that had expired a week ago. It would have to suffice as a meal.

In the luminous living room, Hannah stood and regarded the space. For the first time since moving into the apartment, she regretted the lack of blinds in the room. Though more than that, she regretted the canary yellow sofa, the fuchsia ottoman, and the mint-green bookshelf she had purchased to make her apartment appear whimsical.

It now seemed like the space was mocking her gloom with its vibrancy. She wanted to set it ablaze but dropped on the sofa, switched on the television, and dug a spoon into the pink, lumpy slush.

On the television, the women from *The Real* discussed trendy topics that didn't interest Hannah. She scooped expired yogurt onto the spoon, but a knock at the door stopped her from putting it in her mouth.

"Hannah, it's Flo! I know you're in there! Open the door!"

Hannah wasn't interested in company. "I'm busy. Go away."

"Busy doing what? Hanging out with Loni from *The Real*?" She banged on the door again. "Open up or I'll just keep disturbing the peace of this building. Then I'd probably get arrested, and then you'd have to bail me out. It would be a whole thing. Is that what you want?"

Fully aware of her best friend's temperament, Hannah succumbed. "What are you doing here?" she said, glaring at Flo in the doorway.

"I came to check on you."

"I've already told you. You don't have to keep doing that. I'm fine."

"Really?" She eyed Hannah and then pushed past her to enter the apartment. "Anyway, I brought breakfast from Blackwood. Omelet and potatoes. Yum."

"It's past ten on a Thursday. Shouldn't you be at work?"

"Took the day off." She pulled takeout containers from a plastic bag and arranged them on the ottoman. "Ew." Her attention was on the lumpy yogurt and then on Hannah. "Seriously, is this what it's come to? I'm not judging, but I'm judging."

"Then can you judge or not judge far away from here? Maybe in your apartment?"

"Ha. Nice try. You can't get rid of me that easy." She sat on the sofa and tapped the spot beside her. "Come on. You must be starving."

Hannah rolled her eyes but sat.

They ate without saying a word. The chatter on the television filled the silence until Flo cleared her throat.

"I spoke to your mom. She said you haven't been going to work. Weren't you supposed to go back on Tuesday?"

"I've been working from home." She wiped the corners of her mouth with a paper napkin and sank into the couch.

"You call this working from home?"

"I was about to get to it when you showed up."

"Hannah." Flo pushed her fingers into her auburn hair and sighed. "I know what happened in Nigeria was bad, but you can't carry on like this. It's not healthy. You need to get out of this apartment and do something—maybe help prep for the fund-raiser at the Youth Hope Center. It's happening next week. Or maybe you can just go to the office."

Hannah grabbed a quilted throw pillow and held it to her chest. "I didn't feel like being around a ton of people right now."

"Come on."

"I'm just not in the mood. Okay?" She tugged on a red thread that had unraveled from the stitching in the pillow. "I need some space."

"So you're just going to stay cooped up in here? For how long?"

"I don't know." Hannah tugged harder; the red thread loosened further. The patch of cloth it had been holding together popped free. She studied the unwoven fabric, separate from the rest. Tears threatened to fall, but she blinked them away. "They used me, Flo," she whispered. "They lied to me. Everything was a lie." No longer able to hold back tears, she sobbed.

"It's okay." Flo held her best friend and soothed her. "Shh. It's okay, Hannah."

"You know, I convinced myself I didn't want to know about my dad or my siblings." She pulled away from Flo's hold and rubbed her wet cheeks. "But the moment I got to Nigeria, I was curious. I couldn't help it. I got to know and care about them. Then I realized how much I need them—how inadequate my life has been without them, how incomplete I am without them." She shook her head. "But I think I made a mistake." With her gaze fixed on the empty takeout containers, she considered her situation. She'd been doing a lot of that lately—thinking, reconsidering, rearranging perceptions and notions so she could make sense of herself. "Yeah. I made a mistake."

"By going to Nigeria?"

"No. By expecting too much from them. By relying on them to give me something I don't think they can."

Flo squinted and studied Hannah. "And what is that?"

"I don't know."

But Hannah considered Flo's question long after she'd left. The sun set. The sun rose. Light slipped through the slivers of space between the closed blinds. Hannah wiped the mist off the bathroom mirror and examined her reflection. Court shows followed talk shows on the television. She watched but did not listen.

The question was a ceaseless echo, rattling her already troubled mind. She searched for the answer but didn't just rummage through her mind for it. She dug deep, peeling layers in search of it.

The sun set. The sun rose. The routine repeated until a new desire urged Hannah to break it.

On Monday morning, she got up, got dressed, and went to the office.

FORTY-ONE

HANNAH

Yín's office reeked of coffee and smoke. Hannah had never caught her middle-aged editor with a cigarette between her lips, but she didn't have to. The evidence of her habit trailed after her and engulfed her office that was cramped with too many live plants. An overgrown pothos spilled out of its pot and onto the carpeted floor. There was a well-groomed bonsai tree on the windowsill and a bundle of bamboo that intertwined to form the prettiest pattern. The office would have had somewhat of a serene ambiance if not for the stench of nicotine and, of course, Yín, who was forcing a chocolate-glazed doughnut into her overstretched mouth.

There was nothing calm about Yín—not the way she breathed, sucking in air deeply and aggressively as if intent on consuming it all for herself; not the way she struck the computer keys as if they were ants she was trying to kill with one stroke; and certainly not the way she bluntly criticized people's work.

Hannah had never been on the receiving end of Yín's criticism. Though, she sensed her luck had run out. She suspected Yín had called her in to critique the article she had submitted on Friday.

"I just need to send this email," Yín said. Her tongue flicked the corners of her mouth, capturing the remnants of chocolate. "Give me a minute."

"Sure. No problem." Hannah sat on the edge of her seat and bunched her pink dress in her palm; sweat seeped into the delicate chiffon material.

"Okay. Done." Yín blew out a breath and reached for the coffee mug on the glass desk. "So. How was your vacation?"

"Um . . . I wouldn't call it a vacation. I told you I was going to Nigeria for a funeral—my father's."

"Right. Sorry. Must have slipped my mind. But wait a minute. Your father?" Yín sipped her coffee. "I thought it was just you and your mom. I thought your dad . . . you know. Left."

Divulging that information was one of Hannah's biggest career regrets. She should have kept it to herself, but in a moment of pure drunkenness at a bar on a Friday night, she had spoken too candidly to her editor.

"Did you reconnect with your dad before he died or something?" Yín placed the mug on the table and folded her arms over the layers of black she wore routinely—come rain or smoldering heat.

"No. I didn't." Frankly, it was none of her business.

"So, how come you went to his funeral?"

"I was invited."

"Oh. And you actually went? Seriously?"

The judgment in Yín's tone was unmistakable; it was bold, blatant, a slap on Hannah's face. She was no longer willing to discuss the matter and feed her editor's curiosity.

"Anyway, I'm back now." Hannah gave a tight smile and changed the subject, hoping Yín would take the hint. "You wanted to see me about the article I wrote. You had comments?"

Yín leaned back in her chair and nodded. It seemed like she

received the hint clearly. "Yes. I have feedback. I read your article and . . ." She pushed her fingers into her chestnut hair and ruffled the pixie cut. "To be honest, your article was trash. We can't publish it."

"What?" Hannah had expected criticism, but not that. She wasn't sure how to react.

"Hannah, you've been writing for *Teddy Girl* for four years, and you've gained a huge following with our audience. Remember your article on women struggling to succeed in the male-dominated tech industry? What about your profile on that body-positive Instagram model from South Korea? Or the article about cultural appropriation through style? Those were incredible. But this . . ." She shrugged. "It isn't great."

Hannah wasn't in total denial. She had rushed the article, too depressed to put much effort into it. She knew it wasn't her best work, but she didn't think it was utter trash.

"Look. I like you, Hannah. You're a talented writer. You're hardworking. You take on more responsibility in this office than you should. And in a few months, when I move to New York, I'm going to recommend you get my position."

"What?" Hannah's heart thumped fast. The air-conditioned office did nothing to cool her heating skin. "Seriously?"

"Yeah. But before that happens, I need a better article. I need a damn good article—something original, fascinating, but also relatable." She took a sip of coffee. "And I need it by the end of the day tomorrow."

THE CAFÉ ACROSS THE STREET FROM HANNAH'S APARTment was a writer's dream—cozy and casual with an array of hot beverages and delicious pastries. She ordered a green tea and a raspberry cheese Danish. Then she settled into an armchair, her laptop on the table and a blank page open before her. She'd spent the entire day at the office staring at a blank page. At seven thirty in the evening, nothing had changed. She had to write something remarkable. If she didn't, Yín would not recommend her for the editor position. And for Hannah, that was a dream job.

She planned to write an article on the lack of women CEOs in the beauty industry, but she was distracted. There was too much going on in her mind. The question Flo had asked her a few days ago was still there, unanswered. She considered it again and triggered a stream of thoughts that came sequentially—one after another like the endless chain of colorful handkerchiefs a clown pulls out of a pocket.

She thought of her childhood. At ten she'd concluded that her father's absence had carved holes in her and made her incomplete. But she had found ways to fill those holes—her mother, her career, her best friend. And when those no longer seemed like enough, she'd found other fillers. Because Hannah had always relied on someone or something to fill her void, but she had never relied on herself.

For years, she had been like a child looking up at something out of reach, waiting for someone bigger to bring it down and place it in her hand. The truth is, she could have stood on her toes. She could have stretched her hands and grabbed it—grabbed the love she needed to feel content in her skin and her existence. It wasn't the kind of love her mother could give her or her best friend or her siblings or her father. It was the type only she could give herself.

She bit into the flaky pastry but could not chew as she processed the answer to Flo's question. Hannah had been depending on her father and her siblings to determine who she was. But more than that, she'd been depending on them to confirm her worth because she didn't love herself quite enough. It was a shocking realization. But it was true.

For a girl neglected by her father, self-love wasn't exactly easy to embrace. It was often overlooked while chasing an external fix. She didn't overlook it now, though. She considered it, slowly realizing the lack of it had unconsciously affected her, even prevented her from growing up.

Hannah was twenty-eight years old, but she still felt like a child—a child waiting by the windowsill, a child dreaming up reconciliations and happy endings, a child looking up at something out of reach. It was time to grow up. It was time to break away from the little girl wearing the prettiest dress in her closet, hoping to impress a father who never fought for her. It was time to rely on herself and to stand on her toes, stretch out her hands, and take hold of that specific brand of love—cling to it, dig her nails into it, sink her teeth into it, allow it to fill those holes inside her. Because nothing else would do the trick. Nothing else ever had. This was the only remedy.

She set down her cup of tea, and her fingers moved on the keyboard, typing thoughts and new realizations. She wasn't sure what she was writing—an article or a journal entry. But it didn't matter. She just needed to get the words out.

And though she didn't feel it yet, that self-love that had eluded her for years, she wasn't bothered. At the moment, acknowledging the lack of it was the only step she needed to take.

More steps would follow later.

FORTY-TWO

LAWRENCE

Every day, for the past two weeks, Lawrence recited the same words like a mantra.

Don't think about her. Don't think about her.

From dawn to dusk, he busied himself. Though even in his office, with so much to do, glimpses of her would sneak into his mind—her eyes, her lips, her curly hair with variations of browns and blonds—gradually assembling until the picture of her was complete.

Hannah.

No matter how much he tried, he always thought of her. That inevitability brought him both pain and pleasure.

On Friday evening—when he should have been in the office, busy with the new responsibilities he'd gained since Chief's death—he stepped into the living room at the Jolade estate. A few weeks ago, she had been in the same room. Now, she wasn't even in the same country.

He missed her. He was angry at her. After everything that had happened between them, why hadn't she believed him? He'd spoken to her about his mother, recalling childhood memories he had never shared with anyone and admitting to difficult emotions he'd learned to keep to himself. She'd been vulnerable with him as well. They'd connected. They'd had those two nights in Akwa Ibom. And he'd realized on the last night, as he held her naked body to his and pressed kisses atop her head, that he was falling in love with her. How could she have thought all that had been a lie? Why, at the first sign of conflict, had she believed the worst of him?

He groaned and sat on the camelback sofa, an elbow propped on the gold-encrusted armrest.

"Well, look who finally came out of his hole," Tiwa said, strolling into the room. Her heels clicked and clacked against the floor before the Persian rug muffled her steps. "Welcome back, Lawrence."

"Your mother asked to see me." He watched her from the corner of his eye and considered leaving the room and the house. "Is she here?"

Since the reading of the will, Lawrence had avoided Tiwa. While he was upset with Hannah for not believing him, he was livid with Tiwa for setting the chaos of that day into motion.

"Lawrence, I've seen you like twice since Dayo read the will. Where have you been? What have you been doing?"

"Working."

"I'm in the same office, and I've barely seen you." She sat beside him and crossed her legs. "I've been to your place several times and—"

"I'm sorry, but I have to go." He stood and strode toward the door. "Tell your mother I'll see her some other time."

"Lawrence, wait." Tiwa paced after him, almost tripping on the long hem of her sapphire sundress. "My mom didn't send you that text. I did. I told you to come over."

He turned to her. "What?" Slowly, his expression morphed from confusion to irritation. "Why the hell did you do that?"

"Because I haven't seen you in weeks. I thought you've just been dealing with things on your own, but Dami and Shola said they had lunch with you on Monday. And Segun said he was at your apartment on Tuesday. Meanwhile, you've been avoiding me. I understand you're upset, but you can't keep shutting me out. I made a mistake."

"One you never should have made." His tone hardened, rippling with his frustration. "You never should have said all that, Tiwa."

"I know. But I didn't mean it. I was just surprised."

"Then you shouldn't have said anything at all—like the rest of us. But you just had to, and now she's gone. And that was the last thing your father wanted." He shook his head, disappointed. "If you had actually listened to what he said in his will, you would have known that."

Tiwa's unblinking eyes turned glossy. "I . . . I . . ." She sucked in air, then expelled it forcefully. "I messed up. I know that. I'm sorry." She sniffed and tears rolled down her cheeks. "I've been trying to make things right. I keep calling her, but she doesn't answer my calls."

"You've been calling her?" The small, childlike voice came from Dami, who stood in the doorway with her twin. "So have I." She stepped into the room, and Shola followed. "She never picks up."

"Can you blame her?" Segun asked, joining his family in the room. He reclined on a sofa and propped his arms behind his recently shaved head. "If you wanna blame anyone, blame Tiwa and her big mouth."

"I've apologized like a hundred times, Segun."

"Then maybe another hundred will do the trick," Shola

snapped. "You know what?" She breathed deeply while clasping and releasing her fists. "It's cool. It's fine. Tiwa, you've already apologized. I'm over it." She flopped on the sofa beside her twin. "But for Hannah, an apology sure as hell won't do it, especially if it's over the phone."

"Exactly," Dami agreed. "We have to do more. We have to talk to her in person—tell her we love her and didn't get to know her because of our inheritance. It certainly wasn't why I got to know her."

"Me either," Shola added.

"It might surprise you all," Segun said, "but I didn't do it for the inheritance either. I actually like Hannah. She's dope."

Everyone turned to Tiwa—the one person who had made the quickest turnaround. One minute, she was smashing cake in Hannah's face, and the next, she was being sisterly.

"Look," she said. "I know that at first, I wasn't the nicest to her."

Segun cleared his throat in a manner that implied something.

"Okay. Fine. I was horrible," Tiwa admitted. "But Hannah showing up here was a lot to process. I had to work through it. And once I did, I wanted to know her. Genuinely." She stared through the window, her eyes on the tennis court. "Because she's my sister. She's family."

"Okay, then." Dami smiled, satisfied with the answer. "Then I guess we're going to San Francisco. Tiwa, ask Uncle Dayo for Hannah's address. I'm sure he has it."

"Urgh. Dayo." Segun pursed his lips and cringed. "Damn, Tiwa. I still can't believe you're dating him. I'm never gonna get used to that shit."

"Well, you should—all of you," Tiwa said. "Because it's happening, and it's likely forever."

"Honestly, there's no time for this bickering." Dami sprung to her feet and started toward the door.

"Where are you going?" Tiwa called out.

"To book the earliest flight to San Francisco."

"Wait." Shola shuffled to her twin. "I'm coming too."

"Yeah." Segun stood. "I'm definitely in."

"Well?" Dami looked at Tiwa and Lawrence; they hadn't made a move to join the mission to San Francisco. "Should I buy five tickets?"

"No," Tiwa said. "Don't do that. We'll take the jet. It'll be faster." She looked at Lawrence. "Are you coming?"

He shook his head.

"Why not?"

"Because she told me she never wants to see me again."

"I'm sure she didn't mean it." Tiwa took a step toward him, her gaze soft and sympathetic. "Once I apologize a hundred times, I'll explain everything to her. I'll tell her you knew nothing about the condition in the will."

"It doesn't matter what you tell her. The point is, she didn't believe me when I told her initially. She didn't trust me, T." He ran a hand over his face and huffed. "She thought I lied to her and used her. I spent more time with her than anyone else, and she didn't trust me." He shrugged. "You guys should go—talk to her, make things right. She's your sister. But she and I aren't what I thought we were."

He pressed his lips in a grim line and walked past Tiwa and then through the front doors. Seconds later, he drove out of the estate, reciting his ineffective mantra.

Don't think about her. Don't think about her.

FORTY-THREE

HANNAH

Hannah pushed a fork through the layers of cheese, tomato sauce, and lasagna noodles. She chewed slowly, savoring the dish she had helped create. Her mother had done most of the work, but Hannah was confident her minor contributions—the dicing of onions and the sprinkling of spices, under her mother's supervision—had been equally significant. In the kitchen, they sat on cushioned counter stools—the only matching set of anything in Hannah's multicolored apartment.

A warm breeze meandered through the open window and filled the apartment with Saturday night air—the urge to dress up and mingle, to explore clubs and lounges, to be kissed and touched without the promise of forever.

Though Hannah wouldn't be going to any clubs or bars, but to the fundraising gala at the Youth Hope Center. She had spent the last week organizing the event, and it had been a welcome distraction that brought some activeness to her life.

"Mom, that was delicious." She dabbed the corners of her mouth with a napkin. "I'm usually too busy to eat at the gala, so this was perfect."

"Glad you enjoyed it. And sorry I can't make it this year."

"It's okay. Seriously. Go to the Guns N' Roses concert with George. Have fun. I like him."

"I like him too. A lot." She smiled and brought a wineglass to her lips. She watched her daughter while sipping the generous serving of cabernet sauvignon. "So are you excited about your new position, editor?"

"I'm not editor yet—not until Yín leaves in a few months." Despite the technicality, Hannah grinned. "But yes, I'm beyond excited."

"You still haven't told me about the article that secured the job. What's it about?"

"You'll find out when it's published, Mom."

"Not even a clue? A little one? An itty-bitty one?"

"Okay. Fine. An itty-bitty one." Hannah pushed the empty plate aside and leaned into the counter, her eyes meeting her mother's. "The article is about me. I wrote about my trip to Nigeria—how going changed me in a way I didn't expect."

It had been one thing for Hannah to write the article—to be utterly transparent with herself. It had been another to send it to Yín, to permit her criticisms. Though, there'd been none of that. Yín had loved the article. She'd called it original, fascinating, and raw. And in a few days, the article would be available to thousands of readers. That would be the hardest part. It felt as though Hannah's diary was being published. It was nerve-racking, but it was necessary. Writing that article forced her to acknowledge her faults and having it published made her acknowledgment irreversible. She couldn't take the words back. She couldn't ignore them. She would have to confront them, tackle them, and work through them. And that was a good thing.

"Well," her mother said. "I can't wait to read it. I'm sure it's brilliant."

"Thanks, Mom." She drank the last of the wine in her glass and shuffled off the stool. "I should get dressed."

"Before you do, I need to tell you something."

Hannah retook her seat. "Okay."

"Your aunt called me a few days ago. She told me what happened—explained the reason your father stayed away. She said you already know."

Hannah nodded.

"She apologized for her part."

"And are you angry?"

Her mother pondered, then shook her head. "No. I'm not. It's painful, but it all happened so long ago. I accepted her apology, and I'm moving on. It's all I can do."

"That's good, Mom."

"Yeah. She wants to speak with you, but she understands that you need some space. I told her you'd call when you're ready." She watched Hannah deeply. "It's been two weeks. Maybe you should reach out to her. And while you're at it, reach out to your siblings. You've been ignoring their phone calls. Maybe one of these days, you could pick up and hear what they have to say?"

"I'd rather not. I just want to move on and focus on myself." It was best that way. Easier too.

"But you must miss them. You must be—"

"I should get ready." Hannah slid off the stool and forced a tight-lipped smile. "Flo will be here soon." She walked to the bathroom door, then paused and turned to her mother. "Thanks for coming over, Mom. And for dinner. This was great."

"Yeah. It was. Have fun tonight, okay?"

Hannah's lips relaxed as a sweeter, more genuine smile appeared. "I'm sure I will."

FORTY-FOUR

HANNAH

While in Nigeria, Hannah had gotten the answers to so many questions—questions about her father she'd asked herself for years. *Why didn't he come? Why doesn't he want me? Why doesn't he love me?* But there was one question she hadn't received the answer to, one question she had, in the past few days, realized only she could answer. *Why aren't I good enough?*

For years, that question had been a repetitive thought. Over the past few days, she'd learned to combat that thought with another. *I am enough.* She said it every day—even on the days when she didn't believe it. They were three simple words, but even with their simplicity, they reaffirmed Hannah's worth. And that affirmation hadn't come from anyone but herself. And there was a certain satisfaction in that, in knowing she hadn't relied on anyone or anything—not her father, not her siblings, not her culture—to confirm her worth or determine who she was.

She thought of what Lawrence had said to her in Akwa Ibom. She thought of it often.

Our culture and our family and the people in our lives can

help shape who we are, but ultimately, I think it's up to us to de-
cide who we want to be—to rely on ourselves and no one else.

She hadn't completely understood what he'd meant back
then. But truthfully, maybe she wasn't ready to embrace what
that statement meant for her, but she did now. And she was thankful he'd said it—that he'd given her something she didn't even
know, at the time, she needed.

Hannah didn't want to admit it, but she missed him. Immensely. She should hate him. She didn't. Something inside
her—something she had no control over—was preserving her
feelings for Lawrence, safeguarding it and fostering it with vivid
images and relentless thoughts. She sighed and looked around
the gymnasium turned banquet hall.

The annual Youth Hope Center fundraiser was in full swing.
The space was energetic, filled with vivacious teenagers and
well-mannered adults. A man slipped through a huddle of laughing teenagers and moved in Hannah's direction.

"Hi." He stood in front of her, one hand in his pocket. "How
are you enjoying your night?"

"My night is going—"

Two teenage girls zipped by and bumped into Hannah, cut-
ting off her speech.

"Andrea and Kenya, slow down," Hannah scolded in a manner that wasn't the least intimidating.

"Sorry," Andrea said. She sipped the drink in her hand and
flipped her braids. "I'm just trying to enjoy my cocktail in peace,
but Kenya won't let me breathe."

"What?" Hannah's eyes expanded. "Cocktail?"

"Relax." Andrea laughed. "Mocktail. I meant mocktail. Seriously, who's gonna give me alcohol? There's a big-ass bow at
the back of my dress." She turned around and presented the
proof.

"Plus," Kenya began, a hand on her hip. "She doesn't even have the boobs to fill in that dress."

"Kenya," Hannah said. "Stop."

"What? I call 'em as I see 'em." She looked at Andrea's chest and snorted. "Or don't see 'em."

They ran off, Andrea pursuing Kenya.

"Sorry about that." Hannah turned to the middle-aged man beside her. "They're just excited tonight."

"Kids being kids." He chuckled. "I get it. I'm guessing you work for the center?"

"I'm a volunteer," she corrected.

"Oh. Beautiful and kind." His eyes moved over her—the gold slip dress that hugged the upper half of her body, then flowed loosely over her hips and onto her knees. "I'm Robert."

"Hannah." She took his extended hand and shook it firmly and business-like—no soft, lingering touch. It was necessary to convey she was not interested in what his ogle implied. "I'm guessing you're a donor?"

"That I am. And since you're a volunteer, I'm guessing your day job either involves acting or modeling?"

"Neither."

"Oh. It's just that you . . ." He slanted his head and watched her from an angle. "You're beautiful and have a very interesting look. If you don't mind, may I ask what your ethnicity is?"

What's your ethnicity? Hannah had heard that question so many times, but she had never answered it without the pressure of trying to answer another question. *Who are you?* But she did so now, knowing that one didn't necessarily answer the other.

"I'm part white and Nigerian."

"Seriously? Nigerian?" Robert frowned and eyed her skeptically. "I never would have guessed."

"Well, she is."

Hannah heard the familiar voice come from behind her. Slowly, she turned around and came face-to-face with Tiwa. Stunned, she tried to voice her confusion but could only produce murmurs.

"Now," Tiwa said to Robert, "if you're done doubting her ethnicity and gawking at her like an idiot, I would like to speak with my sister."

Robert opened his mouth, but no words came out. He grabbed a wineglass off a platter a server held and hurried away.

"Well." Tiwa sighed. "Happy he's gone." She assessed Hannah and smirked. "You look good. Love the dress."

It wasn't exactly what Hannah expected to hear, but she glanced at Tiwa's outfit in return. "You're wearing jeans and a T-shirt. I don't think I've ever seen you in jeans and a T-shirt."

"Well, I didn't really have time to dress for the occasion."

"Right." Hannah twisted the long pearl necklace that dropped to her chest. "What are you doing here, Tiwa?"

"You weren't answering my calls."

"Yeah. Because I don't want to talk to you."

"I know. You must hate me. And I deserve that."

"I don't hate you. I don't hate any of you." Hannah didn't know how to. Even after everything that had happened in Nigeria, she still loved them. It was difficult to just exchange one emotion for another. They weren't a pair of shoes.

"Hannah, I'm so sorry. I meant nothing I said—I swear. I was just shocked. You are part of our family."

"Is this apology another condition you have to fulfill to get your inheritance?"

"What?" Tiwa's expression turned pained. She looked genuinely hurt. "Hannah, listen to me. That condition wasn't the reason we got to know you. We wanted to know you because you're family." Her eyes turned teary. "We love you. And we'll prove it to you—no matter how long it takes."

Hannah considered Tiwa—the strained look on her face, the tears in her eyes, the fact that she was at the fundraiser apologizing. If Tiwa didn't care, she would be in Nigeria, basking in her inheritance and not giving a damn about Hannah. But she was in San Francisco. How could Hannah ignore these facts? Or the fact that it felt good to see her?

"There's something else," Tiwa said. "Lawrence didn't know about the condition in the will. He wasn't even in the room when Dayo told us about it. He was with you."

"What?" Hannah shook her head. "No. If he wasn't in the room, then someone must have told him."

"No one told him. He didn't know a thing. That's the truth."

But she had called him a liar. Why had she done that—discredited him so quickly? For two weeks, she'd thought the worst of him and forced herself to function without him. Now, with the truth out, she permitted herself to need him, to miss him, to feel the full effect of his absence. Tears sprung from her eyes just as Tiwa hugged her. Hannah's arms wound around her sister; she clung to her and found solace in an embrace that had once seemed awkward.

"It's okay, Hannah. It wasn't your fault. It was mine. I messed up. But I'll fix this. I promise." Tiwa's hold tightened. "I should have come to San Francisco earlier. I'm sorry it took me so long."

"How'd you even know I was here?"

"Dayo gave us your mother's phone number. We called her when we arrived. She told us you were here, so we came and split up to look for you."

With everything Tiwa had said, Hannah only fixated on one

word. *We.* She pulled back and wiped her cheeks. "Who else came?"

"They did." Tiwa pointed to Hannah's right, at Dami and Shola, who sprinted toward them.

"Hannah!" They hugged her, throwing their weight on her. "We missed you! We love you!"

"I love you guys too." She held them as tight as she had Tiwa and pressed her eyes closed. "I missed you guys so much." More weight piled on Hannah. She steadied her feet and opened her eyes. "Segun." She ran a hand over his shaved head. "You cut your hair."

"Yeah. I wanted to change it up."

"Well, you look very handsome."

The hug broke apart. Everyone stood separately and regarded each other with wide smiles.

"It's so good to see you, Hannah. And that dress." Dami whistled as her eyebrows danced. "I'm impressed."

"Thank you."

Even with the happiness that provoked both smiles and tears, an unspoken expectancy made Hannah anxious. *Lawrence. Where was he?*

"Um . . . what's going on here?" Flo appeared with a drink in her hand. She looked at the people gathered around Hannah. "Well, I'm gonna take a wild guess and say you're the Jolades. I suppose y'all came to your senses. Mm-hmm." She surveyed everyone again, then arched an eyebrow. "Someone's missing. Where's Lawrence?"

That was what Hannah wanted to know. She searched the crowd for him in a frenzy until she felt a grip on her arm.

"Hannah, Lawrence is not here," Tiwa said gently. "He didn't come. He . . . he's not coming. I'm sorry."

Hannah breathed intensely, sucked in air as if it was something dense, incapable of dissolving inside her. The lightness that had come from seeing her siblings turned into a heaviness that weighed on her heart and made it thump rather than flutter.

Maybe he had not forgiven her for doubting him. Maybe he never would.

She looked at her siblings, who watched her with sympathy.

"It's okay," she told them, nodding fervently, pushing back gathering tears, and forcing an unconvincing smile. "It's fine. You guys are here. It's fine."

But it wasn't.

Without Lawrence, the reunion was only half of what it should have been.

FORTY-FIVE

HANNAH
dubai

The Bentley pulled up to the Cavalli Club at the Fairmont, and Dami clenched Hannah's hand.

"You're nervous."

"Yeah. A little," Dami said, her grip trembling faintly. She looked through the window at the group of girls in tight mini-dresses, ambling on the red carpet that led to the entrance. LED screens on each side of the doors flashed images that gleamed against the night. "It's just . . ." She turned to Hannah and blew out a breath. "I haven't deejayed since Dad passed."

Shola—seated across from Dami and Hannah in the rear-facing seats—extended a hand to her twin. "You'll do great. You always do."

"Yeah." Segun, beside Shola, nodded in agreement. "You've got this."

"And in case you need a little motivation, we got you something." Hannah pulled out the box she'd hidden in the drinks cabinet before they left their Palm Jumeirah villa. "A present."

"Guys, this wasn't necessary. You really didn't have to." Even as Dami said this, she grabbed the black box and flipped the lid.

When she saw the gift—a set of Beats headphones embellished in red, green, black, and white Swarovski crystals—she gasped. She traced a finger along the four colors, which were identical to the ones on the Dubai flag. "Dad used to get me headphones for every city I deejayed in."

"We know," Hannah said. "We'll continue the tradition."

"This is perfect." Dami looked at her siblings, smiling even as tears filled her eyes. "Thank you."

Hannah found it was rare to have moments of complete happiness. Their father's death was always there, hovering over them. Hannah had grown used to it and suspected everyone else had too.

After their reunion at the fundraiser, her siblings stayed in San Francisco. For a week, before heading to Dubai, Hannah got to know her family without the intent of filling some emotional void. It was incredible. They talked and laughed and bonded. Though sometimes, before they got too carried away, they would recall the circumstance that initially brought them together—the death of their father. Even in those moments, the pain had been bearable because they'd had each other just as they did now.

"You still nervous?"

Dami answered Hannah's question by shaking her head.

"Good." Segun squinted while peering through the window. "'Cause I think Tiwa and Uncle Dayo just pulled up." He turned to Dami and jutted his chin out. "You ready to show them what a *Naija* girl can do?"

"Born ready, baby!" She pulled the crystalized headphones around her neck and tapped a knuckle on the window.

The chauffeur opened the door, and they stepped out of the car.

Tiwa and Dayo stood beside the red velvet ropes, their arms wrapped around each other as they kissed.

"Can you guys give it a break?" Segun said when he approached the pair. "This is exactly why no one wanted to ride with you. No one wants to see all that mess."

"What was that?" Dayo demanded, pulling away from Tiwa and sporting a mean mug.

"Not . . . nothing." Segun dropped his eyes, took a step back, and then several hurried steps through the entrance.

"Dayo, would you stop?" Tiwa protested. "Stop intimidating my brother. He's scared of you, and I don't like it."

"Baby, come on." Dayo laughed, then relented to Tiwa's stern gaze. "Okay. Fine." He kissed her, then backed away toward the doors. "I'll try to be nice."

"In his defense," Shola said, once Dayo had disappeared, "Segun talks too much. The boy says whatever comes to his mind."

"If we've learned to deal with it, Dayo must too. He's family now. He's going to be my husband." She grinned and set her eyes on the emerald-cut engagement ring on her finger—the perfect accessory to her silver sequin dress. "I'm getting married."

"Yeah." Dami's tone was as flat as her expression. "I'm happy for you guys and all, but that's literally yesterday's news. Tonight, we're focusing on me, supporting me. Or have you forgotten that detail?"

"Of course not," Shola said. "We're totally here for you. Right, Tiwa?"

"Yeah. Absolutely. We're totally here for you."

"Good." Dami perked up. "That's what I wanna hear. Now, let's go in." She turned away and strutted toward the double doors, Shola trailing behind her.

When Hannah attempted to follow her sisters, Tiwa gripped her arm and waited for the twins to step through the entrance.

"Hannah, there's something I need to tell you." She bit her lip, and her eyes dashed around the outdoor space—at the people laughing and taking pictures and at the series of exotic cars pulling up to the curb. When she looked at Hannah, she expelled a sharp breath. "Lawrence is here."

Hannah's heart skipped, tumbled—did everything but move steadily. It was a familiar feeling. She felt it whenever she thought of him.

Lawrence.

They never said his name. In the few instances Segun and Dami had mentioned him, they had stopped mid-sentence and instantly started speaking on another subject. The weather was usually the best and quickest filler. Hannah appreciated their sensitivity, but it was excessive. Lawrence was part of the family. She had told her siblings that. They couldn't pretend he didn't exist for her sake. She hadn't seen him or spoken to him since leaving Nigeria, but she would eventually—probably at Dayo and Tiwa's wedding. Though Hannah had not expected to see him that night, especially since Tiwa had assured her he wasn't coming.

"Work," she'd said. "He's really busy with work right now."

"Tiwa, you told me he wasn't coming."

"Yeah. That's what I thought too. But he changed his mind at the last minute and caught a flight. He called me in the car and told me he'll be here shortly. He said he'd like to talk to you."

"What?" Hannah shoved her fingers into her curls, freeing the pins she'd used to hold a style in place. "Why? I thought he hates me."

"He doesn't hate you. He was just hurt. I think he needed space to work through everything, you know?"

Hannah nodded. "Yeah. I get it."

"So, would you speak to him?"

She almost agreed, but reconsidered. "Are you sure about this? Are you sure he really wants to talk to me? Because he didn't even take any of my phone calls."

"I wasn't ready at the time. But I am now."

The voice came from behind, and Hannah recognized it, remembered all its unique qualities, like the distinct combination of a Nigerian and an English accent. It was regal, indisputably attractive, and very much Lawrence's voice.

"Well," Tiwa said. "I'll give you two a moment." She offered Hannah a tight-lipped smile that was both apologetic and encouraging. "Talk to him," she whispered before walking through the entrance.

"Hannah." Again, his voice came from behind—closer this time. "I know this is sudden—me just showing up here. But can we talk?"

She reached for the embellished fringes on her strapless midi dress, twiddling them while working through her nerves.

"My car is still here. We could go inside. Talk for a little while—five minutes. Just give me five minutes."

He didn't say please, but she heard it anyway, in the way his voice softened and cracked. That one word, unvoiced but somehow heard, made Hannah turn around.

Their eyes connected. He was so close. She could smell the spicy woody blend of his fragrance, feel the heat emitting from his body, and feel their connection that was still strong even with the time apart.

"Where's the car?" she asked.

He led her to a spot on the curb. A chauffeur standing beside a Jaguar pulled the door open when he saw them approach, then closed it once they were inside.

"Hannah." Lawrence looked at her, looked away, then ran a hand over the trimmed beard that enclosed his lips. "I read your article. Tiwa sent it to me."

"She did?"

"Yeah. I didn't want to read it." He shook his head. "I couldn't read it, not with everything that happened between us. But then I did. Only a few hours ago actually."

And what did he think of it? What did he think of the article she'd titled "Grown but Still Growing: An Unexpected Journey, An Unexpected Love." She had written in detail and with no reservation, about the absence of self-love triggered by the absence of her father. She wrote about how she never questioned it, but lived with it, blinded to the many ways it affected her life. She grew compliant with unhealthy romantic relationships, taking scraps because they were better than nothing. She relied on people, waiting for them to validate her worth and solidify her identity—to tell her she was loved and that she belonged.

Tears pricked Hannah's eyes as she thought of everything she'd written. The truth, her truth, was painful. But the article was the necessary diagnosis before the cure.

"My father let me down," she told Lawrence. "Then men I dated in my past let me down. So when it came to you, I didn't question it. It was easy for me to believe the worst of you because . . ." She paused. "Because no other man had ever shown me otherwise. The worst was all I was ever used to. It was all I ever expected. It was all I ever accepted." Her voice shook, unsteady as she fought back tears.

"Lawrence, I am so sorry for not believing the best of you. We spent so much time together, so when that whole situation happened, I should have given you the benefit of the doubt. I should have known what you were capable of. But I didn't." She edged close to him and took his hand. "I am so sorry."

"Hannah, I owe you an apology too."

"You? Apologize? For what?"

"For not coming to San Francisco with everyone else. I was hurt, but I should have worked through it by talking to you. We should have worked through it together. I'm sorry. I made a mistake." His head hung low. "Can you forgive me?"

"Of course. Absolutely." She held his chin, lifting it so their eyes connected. "I love you, Lawrence." The words instantly unraveled a knot that had been taut in her for weeks.

"Hannah." He squeezed his eyes closed as if soaking in those words, allowing them to sink in and wash over him. When he looked at her, his lips stretched in a smile. "I love you too." The smile grew wider. "So much." He leaned into her, a request in his gaze.

After three weeks apart, Hannah needed to touch him. She flung her arms around his neck and dove into his face, puckered lips first.

There was a keenness in his kiss and his touch, as if he was also trying to satisfy a need that had been neglected for too long. His hand slid between her thighs, and her fingers worked against his belt. When a heavy *rat-a-tat* sounded abruptly, they froze and looked through the tinted window where Tiwa stood, waving.

"Sorry to interrupt your conversation or . . ." She giggled. "Whatever's going on in there. But you guys should probably come inside now. Hannah, Dami keeps signaling for you."

"Yeah. Sure. Sorry," Hannah said. "Give us one minute."

"I'll give you two. Just for good measure. See you guys inside."

"So . . ." Hannah exhaled, once Tiwa had walked away.

"So." Lawrence pressed a kiss to the back of her hand. "I heard what happened with Sade—with the house."

"Yeah. I tried to sign it over to her—give her ownership. But she wouldn't accept it. She refused."

"So, it's yours."

"No." Hannah shook her head. "It's ours. It belongs to all of us."

Lawrence smiled and leaned into her. They shared one last kiss before separating and straightening their clothes.

Inside the club, flashing colored lights cut through the dim space and reflected on the curtains of crystals that hovered above the floor. Aerial dancers dangled from the ceiling, artistically contorting their bodies against silk cloths. Hannah's gaze darted from the go-go dancers onstage to the ones in embellished cages. She sighted Dami in the DJ booth, her Afro puffed out around her headphones. She danced while twisting various nubs on the controller, the Roberto Cavalli logo lit up in purple behind her.

"I think I see them," Lawrence said, guiding Hannah toward the packed dance floor.

Tiwa and Shola lit up the instant they saw the pair approaching hand in hand. Segun released a breath, exaggerating his relief by dropping his shoulders and slouching. Dayo, holding Tiwa's waist and swaying gently to the music, only tipped his head to Lawrence, a silent *well done*.

"Yay!" Shola said. "You guys made up!"

"Finally," Segun groaned. "Now, I can stop biting my tongue every time I accidentally mention his name."

"Or you can make biting your tongue a regular practice," Dayo added before noticing Tiwa's glare. "I mean," he said, dropping a hand on Segun's shoulder. "Express yourself. Wag that tongue as freely as you like."

"Really? And you won't give me that look . . . that threatening look?"

It seemed to take a lot of effort, but Dayo got the words out. "No. I won't."

Segun looked upward, his hands pressed together, and mouthed *thank you* before pumping a fist in the air and shouting, "Yes! Freedom!"

Everyone laughed, and when Hannah's stare shifted to the DJ booth, she saw Dami watching them and laughing even though she was too far away to have heard Segun. Hannah waved at her sister, and Dami nodded before placing her mouth above the microphone.

"This next track is dedicated to my family! Love you guys!"

Afrobeat filled the club, and the crowd's energy amplified. Bottle sparklers emitted flames all around. Shola danced while screaming something inaudible to Dami. Segun, given the liberty to speak freely, expressed that he would never get used to seeing Tiwa and Dayo together. The newly engaged couple, enamored of each other, ignored him.

The moment was chaotic and simply perfect, and as Hannah wrapped her arms around Lawrence, she smiled and mouthed three words slowly as if they were too sweet to let go of.

I love you.

And she did feel it, *love,* in all its many variations—familial, romantic, the self-love that now filled the holes inside her and overflowed. And she found it was the best remedy.

The sweetest remedy.

Acknowledgments

In 2019, I went to Nigeria for the first time in seventeen years. It was an amazing trip that helped me prepare to write this novel. While there, I looked at Nigeria with a foreigner's eyes and also with a sense of familiarity. When I set out to write this book, I wanted to portray a Nigeria people rarely see. People like the Jolades—those who gather resources and talent to build empires and legacies—exist in Nigeria. They aren't fictitious. It was important that I portray this. I also wanted to depict a Nigeria that people are perhaps more familiar with—the world of Lawrence's early childhood. Though, I hoped readers wouldn't only perceive this image with sympathy. Rather, I wanted them to also see Nigerians as ambitious and resilient people. I am so very proud to be a Nigerian. I am so honored to have a platform where I can tell their stories, and I am grateful to all the remarkable Nigerians in my life—my mother, sister, and brother, who support me endlessly. You guys really love me, and I love that you love me. Keep it up.

I am grateful to so many people who make the writing process easier. My oldest friend, Rita Kodida, who is always there whenever I need her to read something or brainstorm. Helen Ojo, who read one of my first novels and kindly offered all the help she could. It was a terrible book, and I had no idea what I was doing, but her support was constant. I will never forget that. And Yasmin Angoe and Louisa Onome, who have listened to me vent and freak out about the often emotional road to publication. I'm thankful to my agent, Kevan Lyon; my editor, Kate Seaver; and my truly incredible team at Berkley. And always, I am thankful to God. I love writing, but it isn't always easy. It can be hard. But God, however, has equipped me with everything I need to tell a story—the ideas, the words, the zeal, and all the right people who love and support me. I feel truly blessed.

THE

sweetest remedy

❧

JANE IGHARO

Discussion Questions

1. There are a lot of strong characters in the Jolade family. Which member do you identify with the most?

2. Hannah learns a lot about Nigeria through the course of the book. Do you think she was surprised by anything she discovered? How did it meet her expectations, and how was it different? What parts of Nigeria were you familiar with? Did you learn anything new about the country as you were reading?

3. Hannah's father had an interesting way of teaching his children about prejudice. For example, he pulled them from the comfort of their country and sent them to a boarding school in England. What do you think of his methods? Would you have done things differently?

4. How did the appreciation of the Nigerian culture or lack of it shape Segun, Shola, and Damilola?

5. Identity is multifaceted. How is that portrayed in this book?

6. In Akwa Ibom, Lawrence said, "You don't have to rely on your father to determine the kind of man you want to be. You

don't have to rely on anyone but yourself." How do you think this quote helped Hannah and even Segun?

7. How do you think Hannah's relationship with her mother changed throughout the novel?

8. Hannah had a pivotal moment in the café when she realized the absence of her father had affected her in many ways. What were some of those ways?

Photo © Borada Photography

JANE ABIEYUWA IGHARO was born in Nigeria and immigrated to Canada at the age of twelve. She has a journalism degree from the University of Toronto and works as a communications specialist in Ontario, Canada. When she isn't writing, she's watching *Homecoming* for the hundredth time and trying to match Beyoncé's vocals to no avail.

CONNECT ONLINE

JaneIgharo.com
AuthorJane.Igharo
VictoriousJane
Jane_Igharo